"*Riot Son* is both encyclopediac and intimate, fictional and factual, love story and riot story. It is a sumptuous urgent read, and L.A. Fields is a master of her material, and better yet a master of what matters."

Keith Banner, *Next to Nothing*

"*Riot Son* by L.A. Fields is a tender and tumultuous May-September romance which ignites during a series of riots in the summer of 2020. Protestors Devon and Garrett explore their sexualities, how much of themselves they're willing to give to the cause, and who they want to become while ducking tear gas canisters in the sultry sun."

Erik Rebain, *Arrested Adolescence*

"Provocative, timely, and insightful. I found myself riveted from the start, eager to see where the summer of 2020 would take Devon, Garrett, and the makeshift family of social warriors they form along the way. With *Riot Son* Fields has given us a masterfully written gem of a novel."

Eugene Cross, *Fires of Our Choosing*

"*Riot Son* encapsulates the warlike atmosphere of both the 2020 Black Lives Matter protests, and the high anxiety, high stakes of fragile, young love."

Jill Mceldowney, *Otherlight*

"Garrett and Devon enter a relationship that is equal parts sexual and paternalistic [...] As documentation of a specific time in history, this succeeds."

*Publishers Weekly*

Published by Lethe Press
lethepressbooks.com



Design & Typesetting: Ryan Vance

# L A Fields

# PART I:
# SEASON
# OF THE SON

# I. SPARK

## 1.

While a worldwide pandemic percolated and another election year began in the United States, on Memorial Day a Black man was murdered by police. In broad daylight, in front of a half-dozen cameras, again.

It had happened the week before, the month before, and the year before:

- In July of 2014, a Black man and bystander: Eric Garner, age forty-three, a father of six whose dying words, "I can't breathe," became a rallying cry for the Black Lives Matter movement.
- In August of 2014 in Ferguson, Missouri, a Black teenager walking in the general vicinity of an alleged convenience store robbery: Michael Brown, age eighteen, who liked video games, getting high, creating rap songs, and spending time with his family.
- In November of 2014 in Cleveland, Ohio, a Black child, playing outside with a toy gun: Tamir Rice, age twelve, who loved soccer, basketball, drawing, and joking around.
- In February of 2015 in Charlotte, North Carolina, a Black woman at home and in need of mental health treatment: Janisha Fonville, age twenty, who had a mood disorder, a history of self-harm, and a girlfriend whose baby she doted upon.
- In July of 2016 in Falcon Heights, Minnesota, a Black man in the passenger seat of his fiancé's car during a traffic stop:

Philando Castille, age thirty-two, known as Phil by the children he fed in the cafeteria at J.J. Hill Montessori Magnet School, and whose death was witnessed by his fiancé's four-year-old daughter.

- In September of 2018 in Dallas, Texas, a Black man sitting at home with a bowl of ice cream: Botham Shem Jean (Bo to his friends), age twenty-six, a joyful preacher, singer, and volunteer.

- In October of 2019 in nearby Fort Worth, Texas, a Black woman at home babysitting her eight-year-old nephew: Atatiana Jefferson, age twenty-eight, who was caring for her unwell mother while saving up to go to medical school.

- In March of 2020 in Louisville, Kentucky, a Black woman woken from sleep by a no-knock raid on her home: Breonna Taylor, age twenty-six, a former paramedic who was defended by her boyfriend, Kenneth Walker, with whom she planned to marry and start a family.

- In May of 2020, in a Minneapolis, Minnesota neighborhood about fifteen minutes away from where Philando Castile was fatally shot, a Black man accused of using a counterfeit $20 bill: George Floyd, age forty-six, described as a gentle giant, rapper, and father of five, who was suffocated for eight minutes and forty-six seconds as he repeated the same plea spoken by Eric Garner, "I can't breathe," and called out for his mother, who'd died two years previously.

In late May of 2020, with summer blooming and unemployment spiking as the regulations surrounding the pandemic shut down jobs, the citizens took to the streets. Self-stylized, hateful militias were ready and raring to go. Conscientious protesters of all ages, from Vietnam to Occupy Wall Street, heeded the call. Suburban moms and dads were also getting energized and ushered into the fold. On-the-ground journalists prepared to suit up once again.

Chicago, Detroit, Portland. Atlanta, Los Angeles, New York. Knoxville, New Port, Pittsburgh. Everywhere was tear-gassed, which is a war crime sometimes, but since crowd control was not technically a war, it was fine to fog the streets of the United States with chemical gas. The press was frequently corralled to show 'em what for, and tear gas devices sometimes sailed directly at their heads. This was a hostile tactic that was not allowed on paper, but still strangely frequent on the streets.

"Incoming!"

A tear gas canister arc'd toward a young man's head. This was Garrett Robertson: redheaded, slight, and seventeen, going on eighteen. Recently emancipated from a religious cult upbringing, Garrett had already finished high school online, and didn't have anything else to do that summer but bear witness to the upheaval. Had the canister hit him as intended, he could have lost an eye, broken a nose, gained a scar, but a tall, bearded white man stepped in front of it first.

The tear gas canister glanced off the shoulder of Devon Amis to ricochet back the way it came. When asked how to pronounce his last name, Devon would tell people it's not "ah, me?" but more like "aim, miss." He was from suburban Dallas, had a deep interest in firearms like the kind that had just wounded him, which could have easily led him to become a soldier. But Devon also had an unbreakable habit of bucking authority, so he became an independent reporter rather than reporting for duty.

"Johnny on the spot, nice one," said a woman wearing kneepads, wrist guards, a helmet, and water bottles strapped across her back like the opposite of ammo. Tula Callis was third-generation Greek, and an untold-generation democracy preserver. She was her grandfather's favorite because he felt she had the best concentration of Old-World pride compared to his other five grandchildren, each seemingly more American than the last.

"Thanks," Garrett said to his new friends.

"Where'd that fucker go, want to get a picture with it?" Devon asked, before holding out his hand to shake. "Are you sure you're old enough for a press badge?"

"I'm not, but my editor is," Garrett said.

Tula let out a "Ha!" through her face mask, and Devon smiled under his. Garrett could see it in his cheeks, his eyes; Devon had a smiley, jovial face that neither his beard nor his mask could hide.

"I actually took a nice selfie with a spent canister earlier. Check it out." On his phone, Garrett scrolled through photos of raised batons, burning eyes, aggressive blockades, and found the one where he looked the cutest: curly red hair with great volume that day, playful eyes over his neck gaiter mask, and an exploded canister held up like someone having a far better day might take a picture with their Starbucks frappe-lappe milkshake.

"Nice," Devon said, zooming in first on Garrett's face, before sliding the focus to the canister. "It busted open so evenly it looks like a steampunk poison flower, don't you think, Tula?"

Tula leaned over to pass her hooded gaze over the image. "I'd accept a bouquet of those from the wasteland warrior of my dreams."

Garrett would later come to realize that the word "warrior" was gender-neutral (like "comrade" and "co-conspirator"), and that Tula's dream warrior would be a Furiosa of her own. However, as it stood on that day, in the quiet afternoon light before the curfews came down and those who didn't disperse were open to brutal assault, these three talked tactics.

Devon and Tula were veterans of melees across the country and world, and wanted to make sure that Garrett, who was at his first rodeo, knew what he was up against. Did Garrett have copies of his IDs on him, a lawyer to contact should he be arrested, the right kind of cell phone with nothing but emergency numbers in it, no valuables on his person, and enough protective gear? Yes to all of the above, and no, he wasn't wearing contact lenses, which could cause poison gas to fuse against one's eyeballs.

"Do you rendezvous with anyone if the shit goes to shit?" Devon asked.

"Want to share our spot?" Tula offered.

"Sure." Garrett had a few friends out on the street already, but they went home when the sun went down, and Garrett stayed every night until the end. Once his new pals each whispered the location to him (to test whether they themselves were in sync), Garrett told them about a neat little trick he had ready to go if he felt the heat was on: save his photos to the data card in his camera, drop the card in a stamped envelope addressed to himself in the nearest post box, and then wipe his camera clean in case he was detained and the cops went snooping.

Tula and Devon looked fondly at one another over Garrett's head and smiled.

"He's got the best of us both, dear," Tula said.

"He really does. I'm so glad we adopted a riot son, darling," Devon replied, setting an avuncular hand on Garrett's slender shoulder for a squeeze.

Garrett wondered just how friendly this new friend would be, but he didn't have time for anything but a flutter of a yearning before the police decided the press punks were too close to something, even though they'd been put there by the cops in the first place. It was time to dance the do-si-do of that old tune, "Get Back, Move Along, Nothing to See Here."

Garrett would be called "riot son" for the rest of that fateful summer.

# 2.

"Again with the milk," grumbled Devon's voice that first night. Already Garrett knew it from the rest, even with his eyes closed and day-temperature milk drooling down his neck. "Are you guys out of water?"

"The cops slashed open the water bottles," said the medic who was pouring milk, the only resource left, over Garrett's face. She'd said her name was Hazel.

"How heroic of them," Devon said, which made Garrett snort some milk up his nose. "Here, I've got a couple of water bottles left, you guys and gals can have them, my night's about done unless I can help."

"We'll take the water," Hazel said, letting up on the milk pour and splashing some water on Garrett's face as a final rinse. "The cops stomped and slashed as many water bottles as they could, slit open our saline bags, threw sutures and bandages into the dirt, threw us onto the pavement."

"Did anyone film it?" Devon asked, just as Garrett opened his eyes and said, "Did they even give you a reason why?"

Hazel blinked at them. "Yes and no. Yes, several people filmed it, one was my friend Lena, she's over there if you want to talk to her about it." Hazel pointed.

Devon clocked Lena, and nodded, but didn't leave. Garrett blinked around to see that Lena was using a headlamp intended for camping to assess a cut on someone's scalp.

Hazel turned to Garrett and checked his pupils with a penlight. "They didn't give us a reason why, they just destroyed over $500 in medical supplies and caused a few more scrapes and bruises on people they knew were only medics. I mean, we're all wearing crosses on our front, back, and sides that say MEDIC in English, Spanish, and Vietnamese — I added that. If any of us tried to ask why, we got shoved." Bitterness was likely keeping her awake better than black coffee.

"Are you alright from the shove?" Devon asked.

"I am, thank you for asking." After snapping off her light, she said to Garrett, "If you're feeling better, I'm going to check on others, okay?"

"I feel much better, thanks," Garrett said.

Hazel nodded. "Any time, stay safe."

When Hazel got up from Garrett's side, Devon sat down. Garrett gave him a hello smile before raising up his mask again.

"Breathing that spoiled-milk goodness off your mask aren't you? Feeling it congeal against your skin? I really wish people didn't insist on bringing milk to a tear gas fight, water works just as well if not better. I mean, if you splash milk in your eye at breakfast you're not like, 'wow, great, refreshing,' you run to the kitchen sink to rinse it out with water."

"Plus there's no cruelty-free way to get cows' milk, really," Garrett said, "but that's a different rant entirely for those thinking about becoming vegan."

Devon laughed, a delightful sound that Garrett would soon find all the more wonderful when he learned about the things that haunted Devon. In this moment, Garrett was merely glad that his joke had landed.

"I live nearby if you want a shower and change before you head home," Devon said. "Or you're welcome to crash for the night if you're just going to come back out here tomorrow."

"That's an awfully trusting offer," Garrett said, again unsure if this was a come-on or just a Samaritan-style offer, or perhaps six of one and half a dozen of the other.

"You haven't seen my place. It's full of knives, guns, and ammo, and I'd have the home-court advantage. See, there's the catch to the offer: it's a dangerous-looking place."

Garrett had seen his share of weapon caches, there'd been a whole walk-in closet's worth in the compound he spent his formative years on. He was not interested in disclosing that information quite so soon, but he was most assuredly not intimidated by a claim of "full of weapons" — one man's "full" was often another person's endless vast of disappointment.

"But it's got hot water?" Garrett asked.

Devon's apartment was empty in a lot of ways. There was no *Fengshui*, no hard divide between kitchen and living and sleeping space, no art on the walls that wasn't practical somehow: a rack of guns, machetes up against magnetic strips, empty liquor bottles on top of a bookshelf that was also populated by sci-fi dystopian novels, political texts, biographies of history's best bastards, and old nut tins that may or may not have still contained nuts. Maybe those tins were full of bullets, or loose change, or thumb tacks, or teeth of former victims ... who could tell without giving them a shake? Garrett didn't plan on snooping.

"I don't have any clean towels, but I can do a quick load of laundry with your stuff if you want, or you can dry off with, let's see ..." Like a magician, Devon pulled out one, two, then three dish towels from a cabinet above his microwave. "Doable?"

"Absolutely," Garrett said, and was he partially talking about Devon when he said it? Yes, but he wasn't entirely sure this was a flirtation quite yet. When one grows up in a cult, one understands that some men just like collecting acolytes.

Garrett brought his bag, pants, and jacket into the bathroom with him, just in case, but let Devon wash his layered shirts (they did smell of spilled milk, after all). Garrett emerged from the shower with his skin pinked by the steam and his hair in drippy ringlets like melting copper coils. He slowly redressed, putting on a shirt that Devon lent him. It featured McGruff the Crime Dog in his Bogart-looking coat over the words "Take a Bite Out of CRIME." Garrett turned out the bathroom light first so he'd be acclimated to the darkness without before opening the door. Again, this was done just in case of sudden ambush.

The caution was unnecessary. Devon was dead-asleep in his bed. A note taped to the bathroom door read: *Dear Son — Zonked, sorry. Your shirt's in the dryer. You're welcome to sleep on the couch and to anything you find to eat/drink in the fridge. If you leave, please lock the door behind you. — Dev.*

Garrett felt too clean to hit the streets again, so he decided to stay. He found a jar of large olives in the fridge, ate three. He found a few unopened hard seltzers in the crisper drawer and selected one, knowing that just a little bit of booze and sugar would put him to sleep like a baby. He unfolded a blanket he found on the armrest of the couch that looked like it was stolen or otherwise obtained from a hospital, and he got comfy. He plugged his phone into an outlet and used it to search for the inspiration of McGruff (not a Bogie character, but instead based on Peter Falk's Columbo, which made sense since Columbo had a hunting hound in the show, a basset).

When he finally felt his eyelids getting droopy, Garrett put his phone down and turned to his side. There was a fiery-red kimono draped over an old recliner, either as a sort of slip-cover or because that's just where Devon last disrobed from it. Garrett watched the fabric's patterns of birds and blossoms appear to swirl in the room's shadows. Under the spell of that kaleidoscope, he fell asleep.

# 3.

Garrett awoke to a brilliant set of staring eyes, a heavy weight on his chest, a moment of panic … until he realized he was being examined by a kitty cat. A large, shrewd tabby, holding him down, checking him out.

"You're awake?" Devon peered out from the kitchen, where he was mixing something in a bowl with a whisk. The smell of bacon sizzling made Garrett's stomach rumble, which prompted the cat to launch from his chest.

"Good morning," Garrett said, then sneezed.

"Oh, shit, are you allergic? I should have asked that before inviting you, dude. I can open a window and I think there's some antihistamine stuff in the medicine cabinet."

"I'm good." Garrett sat up and felt pleasantly dizzy, a combination of the sneezing, the rapid rise from a reclining position, and probably hunger. Breakfast was going to be awesome. "Not allergic, just some dander and dust up the nose or something."

"Phew! Not trying to rescue people from tear gas just to give them anaphylaxis," Devon said, ducking back into the kitchen. "If you're vegan or kosher I've got some food, if you're not, there's bacon."

Garrett checked his phone to clear the cobwebs of sleep: a text from his current landlady, Aunt Lilith, hoping Garrett was still alive since he didn't come home (reply was, *Found shelter, all good*); trash news bulletins about who was arrested and in need of bail money (response was the action of re-tweeting); marketing emails revealing how his movements were tracked all night and all the time (*How about that bank you were herded towards, huh, what about this smoothie chain you hid behind?*). Garrett got out of his sofa bed and did a few toe touches to wake up his blood. Then he went to see about breakfast.

"Hey, so, here's the packaging for the pancake mix, the almond milk, and the margarine, in case you've got dietary restrictions," Devon said, speaking around a piece of bacon like it was a cigar, like Columbo's cigar. Garrett was still feeling surreal in this place, but he finally had an answer for his gracious host.

"Free-gan," he said. "I try to be vegan when I have the choice, but food that would otherwise go to waste should not be wasted, is how I justify eating whatever."

"Justify, cool." Devon gestured to the one good seat, a cafeteria-looking chair, and sat himself on an uneven stool. "This maple syrup is sugar-free, too."

Garrett couldn't help but smirk. He finally had some questions for Devon. "Do you have a lot of friends with dietary restrictions? You're well-practiced."

"My ex-fiancé had Celiac's, and her now-girlfriend has Crohn's, and we were all roommates for a while, so yeah, I guess well-practiced about sums it up," Devon said.

"Hmm." Garrett dipped a piece of bacon into some maple syrup before putting it in his mouth. The salt-and-sweet combo made his mouth water instantly. He had to swallow a lot of saliva before he could open his lips again for a sip of coffee. "Where are you from?"

"Hearing an accent? North Texas mostly, the Dallas 'burbs, plus a couple of really rural summers in Bumfuck, Oklahoma. You?"

"Born near Portland, spent a lot of time growing up in Nowheresville, Alberta, Canada."

"No shit? I love Nowheresville. East of No Man's Land, right?"

Garrett's smile deepened. After hearing that Devon was down to date people on the LGBT spectrum, he was up to 80% sure this was their first of many brunches, if not the day they'd ultimately designate as their true anniversary.

"It's actually west of East No Man's Land," Garrett said. "So confusing I know, I forget sometimes myself."

"No worries." Devon reached down to feed his cat a piece of his toast. "No one can ever remember Bumfuck from Shitsplat, Oklahoma either."

Garrett giggled, couldn't help it. He covered his mouth in a way his father once told him (disparagingly and aggressively) was coquettish. Now Devon was smiling at him dreamily, and Garrett was ready to engage.

"I grew up in a religious compound, actually. I call it a cult, they still don't. My parents think it became a cult somewhere between them joining and them leaving but … it was always a cult. I tried to tell my brother and sisters as much before I was asked to leave the family, maybe some of them heard it, I don't know yet."

"That's a damn shame, I hate it when compounds are sullied by religion," Devon said, shaking his head. "They don't got enough churches, gotta mess up the good name of collective farming and organized anarchy? They were farmers, I assume, not doomsday folks?"

"Bit of both, actually. Like, they figured it would be nice to eat well before the rapture. They weren't great at it, but they were getting there, selling unused solar energy to stock up on staples like rice and beans, growing and canning their own veggies, chickens for eggs, all that jazz."

"Sounds good on paper. Did someone get a messiah complex and start marrying everyone else's wives and daughters?"

Garrett took the last piece of bacon with Devon's nodded approval. "Close, they wanted to start controlling the women more. Like, educate boys and girls separately when that's not how it was pitched. It was supposed to be one big happy family."

"Too many untamed uteruses running around, huh?"

"Like wild mares, so unacceptable."

Now Devon was laughing, and Garrett did love to see it. He checked the time on Devon's microwave then, however, and that burst the breakfast bubble.

Devon saw him do it and said, "That's not the exact right time, but it's close. What are your plans for today?"

Garrett got up to retrieve his phone, and once he was moving, he couldn't sit back down again. Devon stood to watch Garrett get himself together.

"First I've got to get back to my aunt's place, sort my photos and videos, upload the good ones. Then I gotta answer some emails, draft something for my editor, although it would be better to finish something before I head back out tonight."

Phone in his pocket, check; camera still looking just fine all packed away, check; press markers taken off his backpack so he could be a civilian for the journey home, check; shoes ready to go but then, oh, what was this? What about Garrett's shirt and hoodie?

Devon's following eyes knew what was needed. When Garrett looked at him with a questioning face, Devon nodded to a hanger on the front door's knob. One garment was tucked into the other, *a la* Brokeback Mountain.

"Thanks," Garrett said. He stripped off the McGruff the Crime Dog shirt, and watched to see if Devon took notice of his body. Devon did, briefly, but like a gentleman, he didn't ogle.

"You could keep that shirt if you wanted, it looks better on you," Devon said.

"I can't be walking around in something that promotes law enforcement even ironically, not with the kind of cops we've got out there." Garrett put McGruff over the back of his neck like a scarf while he got his own shirt free.

"Paw enforcement," Devon corrected, as he stepped closer to take the McGruff shirt back. This was done to get it out of Garrett's way, presumably, but the way he did it was to grab one end between two fingers and drag it tenderly across Garrett's shoulders and down his chest.

The way the fabric slid across Garrett's skin made him blush, and as a redhead, there was no hiding the flush that erupted on his torso, neck, and face. Garrett scrambled into his clothes in an attempt to hide it. Devon seemed to misinterpret this reaction.

"Aw shit, I shouldn't have touched you like that, not cool. Sorry I made you uncomfortable." Devon retreated back to his kitchen and started cleaning up loudly, probably to let Garrett know for sure where he was in the space: over there, minding his own business.

"You didn't touch me, you touched the shirt." Garrett couldn't say he wasn't made uncomfortable, exactly, because he was quite flustered by such stimulation, but it wasn't necessarily bad. This was just not the time to be so galvanized, he really did have stuff to do today.

Garrett got all suited up to leave and went to say goodbye. "What are your plans today?" he asked Devon.

"Me? Uh, start drinking early so I can sober up before going out later. I've got an appointment to call in for a friend's newscast to tell the people, at least some people, what these protests are like on the ground. I want to research a few other mass movement protests before that happens, and also get online to debunk some bullshit and amplify anyone who needs bail after last night."

"No rest for the righteous," Garrett said, which made Devon turn and face him again. For a moment they looked one another square in the eyes.

"Hey, I hope I see you out there again sometime," Devon said, then went back to washing dishes and other dirty things in his kitchen (a litter scooper, a vacuum cleaner's filter, an ashtray). "If you're ever in a pinch, you're always welcome to crash here. Sometimes it's crowded, I've given that invite to a few folks since I'm so close to the action, but we always make room."

"Thanks." Garrett noticed his breakfast plate was still untouched, and grabbed a dry pancake from it to take on the road. He could eat this flapjack hand-held, like someone normal might do with a bagel or a rice cake.

"*De nada*," Devon said, which Garrett knew was Spanish for something agreeable.

Garrett turned to leave, was debating between "take it easy" or "see ya later" as a nice non-committal goodbye, when he thought of one better.

"Hey, before I go, what's your cat's name?"

"Oh, he's Oskar," Devon said.

"After Wilde?"

"Schindler, the ex-fiancé named him, but he's my little gutter muppet. She just refused to call him Gutter Muppet, so we compromised."

"Well, tell Oskar thanks for keeping me warm last night, would you?"

Devon smiled. "Will do. Hey, if you like Wilde, have you read his essay, 'The Soul of Man Under Socialism'? Fucker was talking about machines replacing jobs and universal basic income way before any of our presidential candidates."

"I have," Garrett said. It had been a while, but he quickly decided he would review it again, and soon. "There was a *Complete Works of Oscar Wilde* on the compound they didn't think would do any harm, but it radicalized me."

"Still corrupting young men from the grave," Devon said with a grin. "I think he'd be proud."

"I hope so," Garrett agreed.

An awkward pause moved in like a fog. For the first time in a long time, Garrett realized it wasn't his lack of functional social skills showing, it was Devon who was struggling, perhaps rusty with flirting. Garrett gave him a bright smile to dispel the tension. Then with a nod and a salute, they parted.

# 4.

## *What's the Deal With Tear Gas?*

### What Is Tear Gas?

Tear gas, aka mace, aka pepper spray is a lachrymator agent, because it irritates the eye, causing tears to flow. For the Humanities majors in the crowd, the word "lachrymose" is often seen describing weepy women in classic literature of the 1800s (when its use positively peaked), and originates from the Latin word for "tear," which is *lacrima*.

### What Is Tear Gas Made of?

These chemicals are not gasses, but rather solids that can be dispersed in pyrotechnic aerosols (aka a great name for a punk band). Common chemicals in tear gas may include:

- **2-Chlorobenzylidenemalononitrile (CS):** This key ingredient was named by its inventors, chemists Ben Corson and Roger Stoughton, in 1928. The United States military adopted CS as an official riot control chemical in 1959, aka "the good old days" of peace and tranquility (just kidding).
- **2-Chloroacetophenone (CN):** A chemical that causes eye, skin, and throat irritation.

- **Chloropicrin (PS)**: This is an agricultural soil fumigant that was used in large quantities for chemical warfare in World War I and stockpiled during World War II.
- **Bromobenzyl cyanide (BBC, like the news)**: An obsolete lachrymatory agent of the Allied Powers of WWI which can cause eye damage and severe skin burns.
- **Dibenzoxazepine (DBO or CR gas or "firegas" colloquially)**: An incapacitating agent developed by the British Ministry of Defence for riot control in the late 1950s.
- **Oleoresin capsicum (OC)**: An oil from plants in the genus *Capsicum*, often present in pepper sprays meant for self-defense. Capsaicin makes chili peppers spicy, while capsicum oil forms the basis for bear spray. Mace Brand mace is one option for personal protective pepper spray, while ground mace spice is a flavoring made from crushed nutmeg coating — it's sort of a cross between cinnamon and pepper, and essentially a spicier version of nutmeg unrelated to hot peppers or CS tear gas. Don't go substituting these different ingredients in your recipes.

Contents vary by oppressor.

### *What Does Tear Gas Do?*

Though classified as a temporary, non-lethal irritant of the eyes and respiratory tract, a lot of tear gas in an unventilated space can kill you. It can also cause:

- Skin rashes, watering, redness, and burning of the eyes, blurred vision, and corneal abrasions due to rubbing/scratching one's eyes
- Burning nose and mouth
- Difficulty breathing and swallowing
- Nausea and vomiting
- Coughing and wheezing

The effects should go away in about twenty minutes, but if you happen to have asthma or chronic obstructive pulmonary disease (COPD), ha, no. If you have the respiratory infection COVID-19, also no (and those coughing jags aren't helping slow the spread either, are they?). Also, if you're a pregnant person, you may not be pregnant soon enough due to miscarriage, as incidents of miscarriage may increase due to tear gas exposure according to the UN (as far back as 1988), the University of Chile (2011), and the Physicians for Human Rights (2012). Weird that there's no pro-life outcry about the use of tear gas, which can drift through the air and leech into the earth and water supplies after a rain. But even though the response to Black Lives Matter is often All Lives Matter, they actually don't, and that's always been the issue at hand.

### *When Is Tear Gas Illegal?*

French troops first fired tear gas into German trenches in August 1914, an interesting workaround to the restrictions imposed by The Hague Conventions of 1899 that prohibited "projectiles filled with poison gas." They reaped what they launched a thousand-fold in April of 1915 when German forces engaged chlorine gas against the French fighting in Belgium. Chlorine gas can drift across the ground and sink into trenches in a heavy yellow-green cloud, an inescapable poison fog. The Germans brought another hammer down in 1917, again in the area near Ypres, Belgium, this time against British and Canadian soldiers: mustard gas, which was invisible, and more lethal than chlorine gas. Mustard gas burned the skin, blinded some soldiers, and killed thousands of others by way of choking suffocation thanks to blistered lungs. After the war, the Geneva Protocol of 1925 banned the use of tear gas and all the rest ("asphyxiating, poisonous or other gases"), and the 1993 International Chemical Weapons Convention in Geneva reaffirmed that ban from use of tear gas in places where military forces are at war. Weapons of war outside of war, however, are just a gas!

*

## *How Many Has Tear Gas Killed? Maimed?*

There are strict guidelines for using tear gas in public, but strict is (sometimes literally) in the eye of the beholder. Tear gas may only be used outdoors, fired from a distance, and like rubber bullets (aka "baton rounds," which vary in size from a large chicken's eggs to Monster energy drink cans) are not supposed to be aimed at human targets, but instead fired at the ground nearby. This is not always the case, however. Being exposed to tear gas even once increases a person's chance of later respiratory illnesses like bronchitis and influenza (not to mention coronavirus) according to a 2014 study on Army recruits at Fort Jackson in South Carolina. Longterm, a 2017 study published in *BMC Public Health* found that 31 studies from 11 countries showed 27% (63/231) of tear gas-related projectile injuries were severe and included major head trauma and vision loss, while of the 5,131 people who suffered injuries overall, two of them died and 58 of them suffered permanent disabilities due to the use of tear gas.

## *Is Tear Gas Flammable?*

And then there's the question of Waco, Texas, and the so-called Mount Carmel compound headed by David Koresh. He and 75 members of his Branch Davidian followers (28 of whom were children and two of whom were pregnant women) died in an engulfing fire in 1993 during a joint ATF and FBI clusterfuck of an operation. Could it have been the tear gas launched into the non-open space of the compound that rendered the air flammable enough to catch fire from a small, possibly accidental spark? The 2018 TV show Waco summed it up nicely:

> *The FBI and the Branch Davidians each claim the other started the fire, and we may never know the truth. So, instead, let's talk about what we do know. Fact: Fresno, California, 1973. A standoff with law enforcement ends when tear gas turns to fire, killing those inside. Fact: Los Angeles, '74. Standoff between the SLA and law enforcement ends when tear gas turns to fire, killing those inside. Fact: '81, West Fork, Arkansas. A standoff, tear*

*gas, fire, death. 1983, Smithfield, Arkansas. 1985, Philadelphia. 1987, Escondido, California. All of them standoff, tear gas, fire, death. The FBI knows this happens, and yet they made no plan to put out a fire if one started.*

The FBI admitted that flammable devices were used during the standoff, just a little bit of domestic war in response to Koresh allegedly violating federal firearms regulations. The child-brides-and-multiple-wives thing at the Mount Carmel compound was a secondary concern at best. In many states, there is no legal minimum age for marriage (though there is a legal minimum age to file for divorce, a real catch-22), so long as the child has parental consent. Only four states as of 2020 (Delaware, Minnesota, New Jersey, and Pennsylvania) ban underage marriage altogether, and in Texas, before 2017, a child of any age could be married to an adult of any age so long as a judge approved it. That's what should have been inflammatory about Waco, but it wasn't.

# 5.

Once Devon was alone again, he kept moving so he wouldn't have time to review what a fool he'd been. All his thirty-odd years on Earth, and he was still so desperate for a new friend it disgusted him. *Come to my apartment, sample my wares, why are you leaving, can't I make it more comfortable for you to stay forever and ever?* His ex, Delilah, had cited this overwhelming neediness when they broke up. "I'm not saying there's anything wrong with you, just that you're wrong for me, you understand? Someday you'll find someone with exactly as much supply as you have demand, and I'll officiate your commitment ceremony, okay?"

It was not okay with Devon, but not at all his choice; Delilah did not want to be with him anymore, and Devon spent about six months not wanting to be himself. He got to keep Oskar, though, which helped him maintain some sort of schedule: give food, give treats, scoop the litter, dangle the feather toy. That was over two years ago, the breakup, and Devon was still thinking about it, talking about it, way too much. Surely Garrett didn't care to hear all about his interesting ex, that was a bad look, but ... there's no undoing what was already done.

Devon cleaned the dishes, vac'd the cat bed, Febreze'd the sheets on his bed, cleaned himself. He brushed his teeth before throwing one shot of Jim Beam onto the back of his tongue, then buckled down to research. By the time he had to get on a video chat, Devon was giving himself goosebumps listening to chants of "Allahu Akbar!" ("God is great!") over the rooftops of Tehran in 2009, one aspect of the protests over the "surprise" "landslide" re-election of Ahmadinejad. That was back when the citizens of Iran thought they could reform within the scaffolding of the republic. It took about a generation, roughly twenty-five years, before people realized the rules of the casino always favored the house. That slow-burning fury helped Devon engage with his buddy about what was happening on American streets in 2020.

"I think a lot of people who otherwise would never have attended a protest are finding out just how brutal cops can be. When they have even the slightest permission to abuse you, they will do so with gusto. On the ground, they take sides with avowed neo-Nazis and Klan members against any peaceful, lawful assembly you can have because they're literally and metaphorically not on the side of the people. At best, they think they're sheepdogs guarding the sheep. Good sheep go home when they're told even though they have a right to stay, good sheep go inside their houses even though they're allowed to stand on their porches on their own property as militarized thugs of the state swarm down the street. Bad sheep assert their rights and are treated like crafty foxes in sheep's clothing, which included not only being detained, arrested, and charged unlawfully, but also humiliated, brutalized, maimed, and sometimes killed."

Devon took a deep breath and smiled at the camera in his computer, the one that Edward Snowden let the people know collected everyone's data for the NSA just in case. In case of needing to thwart bad criminals, is what the good sheep think. Bad sheep realize that's the kind of information that could keep anyone quiet if they start getting too uppity, engaging too large a following, and pulling the wool off too many eyes. That puts a person into the black sheep category, and one only need refer to the fates of Martin and Malcolm to know how dangerous a designation that can be.

"Devon Amis, always great speaking with you, brother," said his friend and host, Wayne David Williams, a reformed former soldier with a delightfully thick hick accent out of North Carolina. "Follow him, donate, subscribe, help keep journalists like Devon on the ground doing what they do best. I'll be heading out there myself in a week or two to report back first-hand, but until then, we need folks like Dev here."

"Thanks, man, see you soon," Devon said, and then it was cover back over the camera and Devon back to the silence of his apartment. Oskar the cat was sitting exactly where Garrett's head had rested on the couch cushion the night before. Devon didn't know if that meant he liked the smell of Garrett or was trying to overwrite it with his own stank glands, but it was a reminder that the boy had been there, and that was a nice thought.

Part of Devon wanted to stay right here with his cat forever and never go outside again. He knew this impulse for what it was, a symptom of post-traumatic stress disorder. Some people wanted to stay in with their cats because they preferred bubble baths and cuddles to raucous nightlife. Devon used to love going out and getting rowdy as a teenager, finding trouble and reveling in it with his friends and firearms, a fabulously good time. And then …

When he was twenty-five, Devon got enough funding to go to Iraq and report from a real-life war zone. It took him two months after returning home to realize that the feeling of being stalked when he was out in the open would never go away.

Delilah told him, as kindly as she could, "Welcome to the club, that's how every woman feels from the age of puberty, if not earlier."

Devon wondered what hurt more: to never know the difference between feeling safe vs. feeling hunted, or to know exactly what it used to feel like and have that belief ripped away, to feel the absence of it. Like, was there a psychological difference between being chronically ill from birth vs. becoming chronically ill later in life? Devon assumed that having religious faith and losing it was worse than having no faith at all, even if you never knew that Super Special Feeling of being God's Best Favorite. They say it's better to have loved and lost, but … that's easier to say than to believe, isn't it?

These were the thoughts plaguing Devon as he barfed out half an article on what he remembered from the night before. He compulsively checked sources and sentence structure so he would not turn to look at the clock. He had an alarm set for when it was time to have some food and switch to coffee, and another for when it was time to pack up and head out, but he could tell by the angle of light in the room when the afternoon was waning, and it made him antsy. He could feel his heart squirming around in his chest (like a mouse in a sock) and he hated it, but the only cure for the fear of going outside was to get out there already.

The waiting was worse than the doing, every time. But at least today, when Devon told Oskar to hold down the fort and willed himself to the other side of his apartment door, he had a reason to endure the dislocation: Garrett could be waiting out there somewhere.

Through the hall, down the steps, onto the sidewalk, and Devon was outside. The distance of the sky felt so much farther than he remembered somehow, with puffy clouds scooting around it that made Devon hyper-aware of the Earth as a very big snow globe floating through infinite space.

Devon's own breathing sounded louder than ever when it was strapped against his face by a mask. It was a sound that made him even more paranoid that his own breath was the breath of someone else, someone approaching who didn't like his leftist reporting and wanted his scalp to brag about on alt-right message boards. Probably Devon could hold his own in a fair fight, as he was a big guy with a lot that could trigger his own latent violence, but fair play wasn't big among white supremacists. It was why the Negro League existed, among so many other separate-but-unequal institutions and practices.

Before he entered the throng again and had to be on the lookout, Devon's last pleasant thought was whether Garrett was named after Pat Garrett, the lawman who killed Billy the Kid. Wouldn't it be funny to be named after a cop only to become one of their natural enemies, the independent reporter?

# 6.

"Kettling" was the practice of confinement by police of protesters or demonstrators in a small area to control the crowd. It was not unlike "kenneling," the act of confining a domesticated animal in a kennel or cage. "Kettle" comes from the Latin word *catinus*, a deep vessel used for keeping, cooking, or serving fish — like a tea kettle, but for animals that are meant to be eaten, or worse (like shooting fish in a barrel).

Devon's city was about to make national news. He was among a group of people roughly 1,000 deep that police led (misled) onto a bridge when the official curfew hour was suddenly updated from 6 PM to Right Damn Now. Presumably, this was an alternate way to the parking structures where many had left their cars, or it was a temporary holding tactic so the police could sort out heavy 5 o'clock traffic and then let the protesters disperse themselves before the real curfew. These were among the theories people had as they did what they were told and moved where the police put them. Parents, children, elderly, protesters, and reporters alike — all were under the impression they were doing what they were supposed to do, until the megaphones of the police informed them otherwise.

"Curfew has begun. Those of you on the bridge will be charged with obstructing a freeway if you do not disperse immediately," said the spokesman of authority.

"What? They told us to get on the bridge!"

"How are we supposed to get out of here? They're standing in the way, they've blocked us in!"

"Did they trap us on purpose? They trapped us on purpose!"

To the best of his ability, Devon informed people to help keep them calm.

"Hey, y'all, you may be detained or arrested on your way out, just let them do it. They'll probably let a lot of us leave after some light hassling, and if they do charge you, most of you will have the charges dropped, but!" Devon raised his voice because this was the important part. "If you've got anything that you don't want the cops to find on you, now's the time to lose it! Drop it, kick it away, kick it off the edge if you can, wipe your prints off it first."

"Oh shit, that's a good idea," someone mumbled, which gave Devon a little fluff to his ego for a second before the first tear gas canister sailed indiscriminately into the crowd, and people started ducking and screaming.

Someone shouted, "Jesus, there are kids out here, what are they doing?" To Devon, it sounded like this was baby's first brush with the business end of the law.

"Try to stay calm and appear docile," Devon suggested as loud as he could before the tear gas reached its tendrils out to him, and it was time to shut his mouth.

Devon's advice went unheeded as people started feeling trapped and terrified (rightfully so), so he instead went hunting for the tear gas canister. He would try and punt it off the side of the bridge so it could gas the rocks and weeds of a dry flood channel below them instead of human lungs.

Devon wished, not for the first time, that he could come to these shindigs with a lacrosse stick so he could scoop up such poisonous trash without touching it. But naturally, a stick of any sort would be considered a weapon by the cops. Cell phones were the most egregious weapon of all, of course — cell phones have cameras and cameras are snitches. Garbage cans were also considered weapons by police, and soup cans, cans of any sort really, plus bottles, bricks, apples, and other foods because it's not a show, right? So no throwing tomatoes if you disapprove of the performance of your city's "finest," nor flowers if you do approve. The flower children of 1967 tried something like that in their March on the Pentagon to protest the war in Vietnam, a week after batons cracked down on those who protested Dow Chemical (proud makers of napalm, another inhumanly brutal chemical weapon). By 1970, four students were shot dead at Kent State for those same sorts of peaceful efforts, so the flowers didn't work but … hey, at least everyone got a great Crosby, Stills, Nash & Young song out of that particular massacre. What was true in 1970 was still true a cool Grant's worth of years later, the only difference was guitars were out and autotune was in.

Devon saw a video of a protester in Hong Kong neutralizing a tear gas canister by shaking it up in a thermos full of mud. He liked the image of it; like if you can shake a good martini you can also stop a chemical weapon from spewing its toxicity into the air. But Devon hadn't been able to verify that viral video yet, and furthermore, he didn't have a tumbler of mud on him at the moment (too early in the evening). So it was a matter of finding the offending cartridge and nudging it soccer-style through the crowd and towards the road's edge.

"Know your rights, hey there, know your rights, here, take a card and know your rights." That was the voice of Michelle Whitney Adrian cutting through the noise, a Black woman and attorney Devon had recommended to others based on Tula's endorsement, since they'd gone to undergrad together. Her contact info was on one side of her glossy business cards, and on the back (in English, Spanish, French, Chinese, Japanese, Tagalog/Filipino, Vietnamese, Korean, Armenian, and Persian): an individual's rights regarding self-incrimination, privacy of personal belongings, and when exactly you have to disclose your name, residence, immigration status, etc. Devon had carried around those cards rather than a photo ID a few times when covering previous protests. Whenever the cops searched him and found nothing but his own rights on him, the contempt it engendered in their faces made Devon hard.

"Hey, Michelle, if you've got extra cards, I'll pass them around for you," he said, once he sent the smoke bomb bowling towards the ledge of the sidewalk. He watched to make sure it would clear the underside of the rails, and then turned to see Michelle smiling wryly at him. She had a scarf-made mask that matched her outfit on over that smirk, but Devon had seen it before and knew it well.

"There's my favorite anarchist, you sure are good for business." Michelle pulled a rubber-banded pack of cards out and handed them over like cash. Her fingernails also matched her mask and outfit, a level of attention to detail that Devon only had when he was futzing around with drug or gun paraphernalia. "That's a pack of twenty-five, you know I trust you with them."

"It's a trust I treasure," Devon told her, slipping the cards into one of the zippered pockets on the straps of his backpack before moving closer to Michelle for a little *sotto voce* sidebar discussion. "How hinky does this feel to you?"

"Oh, they're about to arrest some folks, maybe even us," she said. Usually lawyers and reporters were not arrested, since they had considerably more power than the average bear to strike back later, but the cops hated being observed more than they liked to adhere to the law, so it was always a luck of the draw with which cop you got and how cranky they were that day. "If they'd stop gassing us they could probably get people to line up for it, but, you know."

"Right, why deescalate when you can put baby in a corner and agitate her until you provoke a panic response?"

"Haha," Michelle said with a point of one long nail. "You do have a way with words, don't you?"

"I might have made a good lawyer, if only I didn't disagree with having laws in the first place," he said. "Also if I hadn't spent my brief stint in college completely drunk."

"You think that's a barrier to becoming a lawyer?" Michelle asked. "You haven't seen the way law students drink, honey. Half of them only know the law so well because they want to skirt it better."

Devon laughed; it was funny because it was true. "Hey, speaking of drinks, if we get out of here alive and un-molested, Tula's having a little rooftop get-together at her place, BYOB and socially distance, but it might be nice to unwind and have some normal conversations."

"Sounds good. Can I bring Jarvis?" Jarvis was her husband.

"The more, the merrier," Devon said. "If it gets too crowded, we'll just drink six feet apart in the stairwell all the way down."

"Sounds like a party."

# 7.

The cops at the bridge looked at Devon's press badge and told him, "The show's over, so if we see you hanging around after we let you go from here, you're back to being a civilian, understood?"

"Understood," Devon told them before ducking out of sight, reversing his hat and jacket, putting on a plastic pair of fake glasses, and coming right back out to film the arrest of about thirty people.

He stayed until he caught one hero berating a seven-year-old and his mother in the same breath: "You can stop all this crying, okay? We're out here protecting your right to protest but not the lawless blocking of the bridge, and you really should know better than to bring kids out to subject them to this."

"Subject them to what?" the mother asked. "Subject them to your protection?"

"You keep talking, and your kid goes to CPS while you're processed for impeding traffic *and* child endangerment," the officer told her, finally relaxing his tense lecture posture when her face blanched with panic. "Mmhmm, that's what I thought. Go home and get smarter."

"Get smarter," Devon murmured to his camera and himself. "The fucking gall."

Devon closed up shop then and headed home to shower and change before Tula's get-together. He had a cache of liquor in his apartment that he kept much more hidden than his guns, concealing it from himself as much as from any opportunistic friends who might go rooting around when he was passed out. He kept at least one bottle in the toilet tank most of the time, *Lost Weekend*-style, and a few more on top of the high cabinets in his kitchen. The most accessible place was the broiler drawer under the oven he never used, and his closest stash was a flask-sized bottle zipped between the foam inserts of his most supportive pillow. Devon took an unopened fifth of plain, unoffensive vodka for his contribution to the party and also grabbed two small shoulders, aka naggins (if you're Irish), aka "temporary flasks" of whiskey for himself. With two shots for the road and one 350mL bottle on each hip like a pair of pistols, Devon left his apartment again. Twenty minutes of haunted walking later, he arrived at Tula's.

Buzzed into the building, Devon hiked to her apartment. A handwritten sign on the door read, *Be Quiet = Prevent Cop Calls. Wear Mask When Not Drinking. Use Hand Sanitizer NOW.* Three arrows down pointed to a homemade aloe and alcohol sanitizer mix in a pump bottle. Devon took two squirts, one for his hands, and another to rub all over his face and lips, in case that helped. Then it was three more flights up to reach the roof.

There were roughly thirty people spread out under the night sky, which glowed red with city smog and probably a good helping of sweet, tasty tear gas still. Devon recognized maybe five people, but it was dark, so there could have been more friends in the shadows, he didn't know. He waved hi to Michelle and Jarvis, huddled together, two peas from the same isolation pod. He spotted Tula talking to the friend of that Vietnamese medic: Lena, like Dunham, the one with the footage of cops trashing their supplies. Devon set his contributing bottle of vodka in the storage bin of ice and went meandering towards them, avoiding other potential disease vectors as he went. They bumped elbows in greeting. Devon traded social media handles with Lena so he could ask about her videos later, and then she wandered off to mingle. Tula sighed and stuck a straw under her mask for another sip from her drink.

"I invited the whole medic station hoping only one of them would come," Tula said. "So, of course, she's the one who didn't show."

"What's her name?" Devon asked.

"Hazel," Tula said, her liquored lips fuzzy on the Z.

"I know her! Or I met her," Devon revised. "She was pouring milk on our riot son last night. Do you like her? Is she gay?"

"I don't know; that's why I invited her," Tula said, her gaze tolerantly amused. "I intend to do some hard-hitting investigative work."

Devon snorted. Masks, he was finding out, often served as old-fashioned hankies. If you had to blow your nose, you could just let it rip, and no one could see what a mucus-y mess you were behind the covering.

After a beat, Tula asked, "You like him, don't you, our 'riot son'? You seem pretty smitten-kitten about the kid."

"I can't tell if I want to adopt him, eat him up, or marry him, so yeah, I suppose 'smitten' about covers it." Devon didn't know exactly how this sudden infatuation would work out in the long run. Would consummation consume it? Would it turn avuncular, taking Garrett under his wing as a little brother, a mentee? Would he be told, "Thanks but no thanks regarding the attention, please stop seeking me out?" There were a thousand tentacular ways these feelings could resolve at the moment.

"You'd told me you'd been with guys before, but I assumed there was always a woman involved," Tula said, turning to look at Devon instead of watching the party as they talked. "I pictured some big stud humiliating you and making love to her, just some perversion of masculinity you were working out."

"Alright, who's been talking to you?" Devon asked. "Because all those dudes signed a damn NDA, and I'll sue those fuckers."

"Ha," Tula laughed. "Fuckers, indeed."

Devon popped his mask down to swallow a burning mouthful of whiskey and then put it back on. If only sterilizing his mouth and insides with bourbon helped stop the spread of the virus, but he just couldn't be that lucky.

"It's funny when these right-wing chuds call me a cuck, they don't even know how right they are or how fun cuckolding can be."

"What those assholes don't know fills about every library in the world," Tula said. "But we were talking about the ginger snap. What was his name again?"

"Garrett," Devon said with relish, and didn't notice that a nearby head perked up and turned towards them. The head was hidden under a brown fedora *a la* the fourth Doctor Who, and in the leaning shadows of the rooftop, Devon wouldn't have noticed what color the curls beneath it were anyway.

"Garrett the carrot top, bet that was rough in grade school," Tula said. "Are you going to ask him out? Or ask him to … something, since we can't go out these days? Invite him to a scenic protest?"

Devon sighed. "I mean, I already asked him back to my place to crash last night, so depending on what kind of impression that made, I might have already shot my prospects."

Tula then realized who was edging closer to their conversation, grinned within her mask, and said, "If you could tell him something sweet right now, what would it be?"

Devon took this as a rhetorical challenge and thought, "Ah," for a moment before saying, "Something like, 'You've got the kind of hair and aplomb that could tell Timothée Chalamet to sit the fuck down and learn something.' Or maybe, 'You remind me of myself in all the best ways but none of the shitty ones,' but that's no good, that's more about me, not him."

"That's right, you cis-gendered WASP, you stomp that ego," Tula said.

Devon snapped into a salute and said, "Yes, my liege-woman," and then went on. "Maybe if I could find the right way to sell him my devotion, like … people aren't attention-seekers for nothing, they enjoy it, don't they? I want to beam at him all day, moon at him all night, teach him things, learn from him, and maybe make out a little."

"Or a lot," Tula said.

"Preferably a lot, and viruses be damned," Devon said. "The kind of love that makes you do a few lines of coke, rob a bank, punch a cop, and drive off a cliff together, just normal summer fling shit."

"I mean," said a familiar voice on Devon's periphery. "It's a punch-a-cop kind of summer, isn't it?"

Devon turned to confirm: yep, there was Garrett, standing less than six feet from Devon and close enough to hear everything he'd just said. Tula put up her hands and started backing away, leaving them to it. She'd baited Devon into spewing all that nonsense so that Garrett could hear, and while he should have been embarrassed — truly, deeply, mortifyingly ashamed — Devon and the whiskey within him only thought it was too funny. It wasn't very often that real life served up rom-com/meet-cute moments like this, and he couldn't help but laugh.

Garrett laughed with him.

# II. CLASH

# 8.

Their first kiss happened at Tula's get-together, but far out of sight from anyone who would (rightfully) scold them for swapping spit during a viral plague that literally spread via mouth moisture. It was Garrett who asked for it. He figured Devon had done enough heavy lifting with his little love soliloquy that he could take some chances of his own.

"I'm in for making out, but only if we both agree we really shouldn't," Garrett said, stepping closer to Devon, and hoping they did acts even more egregious than make out, like make love, like maybe tonight actually, since it had been a while since he felt that alive and connected and he missed it.

"Informed consent, you've got it," Devon said, reaching out to touch Garrett, a hand under his elbow. "We should know better, I mean, I was born in the 80s, for fuck's sake, when the one thing that could have halted the spread of HIV was to stop fucking, but, you know ..."

"Right, what's the point of living if you're gonna deny the biological imperative to spread your seed?" Garrett asked, with a shrug that allowed him to slip back his arm until he and Devon were holding hands, just as cute as could be.

"Guess if we were alive back then, we'd be some of those *kamikaze* dicks that just couldn't quit," Devon said.

From the darkness, a voice called out, "It's racist to use *kamikaze* out of context," to which Devon replied, "It sure as shit is, thank you for educating me."

Garrett tipped his head to the side, bemused at his new friend. "Do better, sir," he said.

"I'll try," Devon said, leaning closer so he could speak quieter. "But right now I'm in the process of trying to seduce a teenager, so I think I'm still getting canceled."

"Oh, you think you're seducing me, do you?" Garrett asked. "Don't worry, everyone here is already in trouble for facilitating my underage drinking."

"Hey, speaking of, do you want my other flask?" Devon offered. "Do you like whiskey?"

"*Other* flask," Garrett repeated. "I don't not like whiskey. When you're not allowed to drink, you don't turn down many offers."

"A free-gan for booze, too? Good lad."

Devon looked around for a hidden corner of the roof. Every few yards there was another generator or electricity structure or fan or something, and Devon led them to a vacant one in the darkest, creepiest part of the rooftop. They finally stopped holding hands so they could each uncap their booze bottles and take a swig. Devon's bottle went back into his pocket, and Garrett set his on the ground by his feet. When he stood up again, he rose into Devon's hands, which cupped his face in the exact right position to be kissed.

This was a real kiss, slow and sensuous, with tongue. Garrett could only hope he was doing it right. He tried to abandon his mouth to Devon's purposes, to let him in and to fill the spaces he created. It was strangely invasive but also overwhelmingly hot; Devon was inside of him. It was a different kind of penetration, one they could do outside, in public.

Garrett had kissed only two boys before this man. One of them was his second cousin, a childhood experimentation that neither of them would ever speak about again, and the other was a boy at the weird alternative learning high school they put the cult kids in once his parents returned them to the world. That boy, Casey, was in the alt-school for a lot of behavioral problems, the least of which was inappropriate sexual advances (not that Garrett minded). They had done more than kiss but less than fuck, and they did it a few times before the adults realized Casey was at it again, though not with

Garrett — they caught him with one of the girls and brought down holy hell for that. Garrett got away clean, only to come out on his own like a brave idiot, and get booted from everywhere, too, at fifteen. Everything he was meant to learn from high school, he did through a GED program at his aunt's house, and everything he wanted to know about sex he learned when he was given a smartphone with internet access on his sixteenth birthday. And now he was being tickled by the mustache of some big, cheery Texan. It was already quite a life.

After a few rounds of lip-pressing, Devon began to pull back, and Garrett hung onto his lower lip with a light bite. When he let go, Devon tucked his lip between his teeth and shook his head.

"Where did you come from?" Devon asked.

Garrett shrugged, took his hat off as Devon released his face, and used the brim to fan himself. His face felt blushingly hot. He sat down next to the liquor bottle and leaned against the bricks to take another sip. Devon joined him, and took two bigger sips before broaching conversation again.

"The first girl I kissed, her name was Cindy Jo. It was fifth grade, a game of spin the bottle. The first guy I kissed, his name was Isaac, my college girlfriend's high school boyfriend. She taught him everything he knew. I was the better kisser, but I'm not sure who was the better lay."

"Too intimidated to ask?" Garrett wondered.

"You know it," Devon said. "Not sure if I kissed anyone in between or outside the genders. I've got a tendency to blackout when I'm having my biggest adventures, so even if someone did tell me otherwise, I wouldn't remember."

"I've never kissed any girls, don't think I want to, particularly, but I wouldn't fight a girl off if she asked nicely."

"You're a gentleman," Devon diagnosed.

"I hope so, I didn't learn to tie a bowtie to be some scoundrel."

Devon giggled, a high and clear sound, and turned to look at Garrett, feasting his eyes up and down. There was enough of an exhibitionist inkling in Garrett that he liked the scrutiny, felt it tingle through him like static electricity.

"Can I play with your hair?" Devon asked.

"So long as you don't tug it, go ahead."

Devon started raking Garrett's hair off his forehead and lovingly tucked it behind his ears. It tempted the breeze to Garrett's brow, made him want to nuzzle Devon's hand like a happy kitten, though he resisted the urge.

"So can I ask you if you're gay, then, specifically?" Devon said. "Or do you have any preferred pronouns I should use?"

"Yes, gay, or at least I'm shaped like this and am into dudes. I don't know if I'm trans really, or trans yet. I've thought about it. I do like wearing dresses, and heels, and makeup, so maybe I'm a transvestite, but I don't think that has any honorific attached to it."

"Transvestite Honorific would make a great band name," Devon said.

"I like genderqueer for all of the above I guess, and I don't care about pronouns."

"I like genderqueer, too," Devon said, his fingernails trailing through Garrett's locks, and against his neck.

Garrett nodded, and after a moment of silence said, "I'd like to go home with you again tonight, just so you know."

"I'd like to take you home right now, is now good?"

Now was the only thing in the world. There was only yes, only tonight, do it or die without having done it at all.

"Now or never, right?" was how Garrett said yes. Devon stood immediately, and held out a hand to bring Garrett with him.

# 9.

What a difference a day made, for Garrett's reentry to Devon's armory of an apartment was like a whole new world that night. Garrett was no longer looking around to figure out if he was safe there, only interested in Devon enough to verify that he wasn't dangerous. Instead, he was wondering how much fun he could have here, and was interested in what set of circumstances made someone so strange as Devon.

Devon turned on the overhead bulb in his ceiling, flooding the whole room with light. While Garrett squinted, felt his pupils recalibrate, Devon cleaned up, and narrated everything he did.

"Lemme just get these boots out of the way, all this shit on the ground is a tripping hazard," he said. "I've learned to shuffle in the dark instead of just picking up after myself, but I can't have you taking a header into the dresser, so let's clear a path."

Garrett smiled, and took off his mask. He set his bag on the top of said dresser, wedged off his shoes and tucked them beneath it.

"I'm actually, you know what? I'm going to change the sheets," Devon said as he stripped the bed and degloved the pillows. "I've been passing out in this rat's nest all sweaty and pepper-sprayed by the po-po, and I think we deserve a fresh set."

Devon's fresh set of sheets was solid navy, the pillows accented with a chevron pattern. Garrett texted his aunt to tell her he'd be staying with a friend again tonight, then set his hat on top of a beautiful, sturdy bong shaped like a genie's lamp. He tied up his hair in a band and took off his flannel overshirt.

"Are you too warm?" Devon asked. "Check this out." From under his bed came a fan which he mounted atop his nightstand and turned on. "Great for these summer nights."

Garrett took off his socks by stepping his heels on the toe of the other foot, one after the other. Once they slid off, he had nothing else to do but drum his fingers on the dresser top, waiting, waiting.

Devon finally stopped scurrying around and stood where Garrett could get a really good look at him, top to bottom. Devon slicked back his hair and started dissembling his clothes to match Garrett: socks and shoes said *sayonara*, face mask fell to the floor. He paused, then took off his shirt. He had a few tattoos, and Garrett approached to ask about them.

"How many tats?"

"Four, for now." Devon looked pleased as punch to have Garrett examining him.

Garrett touched one over Devon's heart, a five-point star. "Texas?" he guessed.

"Yep, the Lone Star."

Garrett moved to Devon's left arm, where another design encircled his bicep muscle. This one was linking chains, except one of the links was broken.

"Freedom?" Garrett asked.

"And anarchy," Devon nodded.

Moving around to his back, Garrett found another tattoo between Devon's shoulder blades, a shot glass with a bullet sunk to the bottom.

"Guns and booze, you're a fan," Garrett said.

"My two favorite kinds of shots, yep," Devon confirmed. "Might add a syringe for COVID, and, ya know, drugs."

The fourth tattoo was on the underbelly of Devon's right forearm, and Garrett couldn't tell what it was supposed to be.

"It looks like ... some kind of Greek or Roman column split longways?" Cylindrical, lined, with leaves adorning it, Garrett couldn't make out what it was supposed to be or why it was bisected as if by a lightning strike.

"It's a fasces, an ancient Roman symbol of authority," Devon said. He pointed out the details. "It's a bundle of rods bound together around an axe, surrounded by bay leaves or laurel leaves. Some people will tell you they're olive leaves meant to symbolize peace, but I'd question that because the leaves only went on when the lictors marched in victorious military processions. I chose laurels; that's what they crowned Olympians with back then, laurels for victory. But whatever the leaf, the intent is clear: the axe is force, the rods justice, and only with both of them do you have peace or victory. There are fasces all over our capitol. They're carved into the Lincoln Memorial and have pride of place in the House Chamber, right above the rostrum on either side of the flag."

"And the reason you've got it chopped in half is …?"

"Don't tread on me, that's why," Devon said with a smile.

Garrett nodded and took off his own shirt to reveal his complete lack of tattoos and melanin. He had a cluster of freckles on each shoulder, one innie nipple and one outie, and a few shockingly blue veins that could be seen through his thinner planes of skin. Devon put his hands on Garrett's neck, then skated them over his shoulders, under his arms, and down his sides. If Garrett were a lump of clay being shaped into a vase, this was how he would feel in Devon's hands.

They hugged hard and for way longer than either of them expected. After weeks and months of treating everyone like a leper, an act as simple as a hug, with skin against skin, no more lewd than you might hug another guy at the beach, had them both holding on for dear life.

Garrett had wondered a few times before what kind of wholesome perversions might come out of this worldwide lack of touch. People would emerge from quarantine finding lips more attractive than they ever thought possible. Just blowing a kiss, because it had been so forbidden for so long, would be wildly stimulating. Garrett himself, hardly a season into what looked like a year-long ordeal at least, was intoxicated by the spicy musk of Devon's armpits, the faint yeast of his scalp, and the salt of his skin. He put his tongue out to taste Devon's neck, and heard him moan, felt that moan vibrate through his chest.

"Let's go to bed," Garrett suggested, and they did.

With the ceiling light turned off, a string of LED lights over the bed was turned on. The room was awash in flattering purple. Their pants were shed to the floor and kicked to the corner. They talked only as much as they had to:

"I've got condoms."

"I don't want to go that far tonight."

"What are you into? What can I do? Suck you?"

"Yeah, we can do it to each other, maybe sixty-nine?"

"Ten-four."

They kissed and masturbated themselves and each other until the excitement was ripe, and then Garrett flipped around and settled atop Devon. He circled his finger and thumb around Devon's shaft just under his lips and moved them together because he read that the added pressure made it better. Devon, meanwhile, swallowed Garrett whole, and with every light thrust of Garrett's hips, he yanked Garrett deeper, until the act could be called nothing else but throat-fucking.

Garrett was overwhelmed at first; he had never done anything so goddamn primal before. He dropped Devon from his mouth, gasping. He tapped out, sat back on his heels, and finished himself off over Devon's face and chest because Devon said, "Cum on me, do it," and so Garrett did. For a moment, the release was dizzying, like doing a flip in midair.

When Garrett caught his breath, Devon held out his arms and said, "C'mere."

Garrett came down from the head of the bed with his joints feeling loose, his limbs as shaky as a newborn calf. He nestled against Devon's side until Devon urged him to get on top of him again. There, face to face, they kissed as Devon reached around and jerked himself off against the cleft of Garrett's ass, nothing penetrative, just enjoying the seam of him. The last surprise was when he started to cum, Devon sucked Garrett's tongue into his mouth like it was a piece of raw sashimi. Garrett made a noise because he couldn't articulate "whoa" at that moment. He next felt Devon's fluid erupt against the back of him, felt Devon buck beneath the base of his balls.

They panted together until what was sticky became gluey, and then got up to shower off. Devon entered the water first, Garrett joined him, and then Garrett was given space to himself as Devon went to spruce up the room even further.

Garrett emerged wearing a towel and was offered another shirt to sleep in, this one with some semi-socialist slogan on it. Devon had a bag of pretzels, a bad sci-fi movie, and a bed to share with Garrett for the rest of the night. Garrett once again said yes to all three and fell asleep to a feeling he never would have predicted liking so much, the feel of Devon's breath on his hair as they spooned together under the indulgent eye of Oskar, the cat.

# 10.

"Look at us," Garrett said the next morning. "We're like a subversive Ozzie and Harriet."

After eating breakfast and catching updates on their electronic devices regarding an alt-right pop-up rally coming soon to their area, Devon and Garrett were suiting up for another day in the shit.

"Where do you get all these Boomer references?" Devon asked. "Aren't you a Gen Z baby?"

"I am," Garrett said.

"You ..." Devon began, then shook his head in shame. "You were born after 9/11, weren't you?"

"A couple of years after, actually."

"Ugh, I disgust myself," Devon said, "but I'm not even sorry."

Garrett smirked and kissed his new friend on the cheek. He thought, given enough time, that Devon's self-deprecating schtick would get old, but maybe it would pass, maybe it was new-date jitters.

"We were only allowed to watch pre-approved DVDs in the compound, so I've seen a lot of stuff the elders liked when they were growing up."

"Elders, were they? Buncha Gen X try-hards, I bet," Devon said, as he double-checked that his emergency contacts, cash, and ID were in the right pockets.

"Oh, you've met them, you should have said," Garrett replied, standing at the door, ready to go, watching Devon repeat his pocket-check ritual about three times before he moved from where he was stuck by the dresser. Garrett wondered … was that a little bit of OCD, or was it just incidental brain fog, some hangover of distraction from last night? He wouldn't ask, but he was totting up data, a compulsion of his own that served him well in reporting.

"Ah, before we go, I just wanted to say, or to ask," Devon began, then rolled his eyes at himself and tilted his head to look directly at Garrett. "I'd love it if we met back here again tonight, so what I'm telling you is, you're welcome. To come back here. Tonight, or any night."

"Okay," Garrett said.

Devon waited a beat, then a flicker of disappointment clicked over his face and was gone the next instant. He put on his mask as a last touch and approached the door (and Garrett) saying, "Alright, let's roll out."

"Hold on, that 'okay' didn't mean 'no,' just so you know," Garrett said, stopping Devon with a hand on his chest, just over his star-heart tattoo. "There's just a lot to it. I mean, I'll have to go home sometime, as much as my aunt's den is home, and if it starts getting easier to stay here, it takes about two bags of stuff before I just live here, more than anywhere else at least. If we slip into that, and agree to meet here every night, what if I get here before you or you get arrested and I'm locked out? It's a conversation is all, but we don't have time right now to …"

Devon's eyes took on a steely cast and he pulled out the top drawer of his dresser to access something taped to the back of it: a spare key.

Devon ripped the tape off and handed the key over like a promise. "You won't be locked out," he said.

If Devon could see Garrett's smile under his face-covering, he'd know how apple-cheeked and filled with childish glee it was. Garrett tried not to grin like that very often, as he was already treated like a kid by everyone, and the dimples in his cheeks didn't help discourage those notions. But as he accepted Devon's key and clipped it to his own set (already three spare keys thick), he felt the overwhelming urge to giggle. It was too cute, too much, and made him want to buy a diary covered in hearts and sparkles to deal with it.

Garrett secured the key and tucked it away. Devon put his hand across Garrett to grab the doorknob, as it was time to go. Garrett paused that hand by covering it with his own. He stretched up on his tiptoes to kiss Devon, mask to mask.

"Thank you," he said.

Devon only nodded, but peace pervaded his eyes again, and he let Garrett out the door with exaggerated butler motions. *After you, right this way, sir, quite good.*

From Portland to Kalamazoo to Stone Mountain, something was in the air that week that riled up the alt-right. They came out armed and waving the flags of enemies foreign and domestic, bearing the Nazi spider-like *Schwarze Sonne* or Black Sun symbol, and the good old-fashioned stars-and-bars rebel flag of the traitorous Confederacy. They came with guns, bear mace, shields, batons, and fireworks. They came with plans to lure unsuspecting protesters from the anti-fascist or pro-Black lives side into ambushes for beatdowns.

Two things quickly became apparent to Garrett and Devon when they arrived to watch the edges of opposing sides fray together. The first thing was that most (though not all) of the racists and xenophobes were cowards. Some embraced this fact, dressing theatrically as Uncle Sam or in head-to-toe flag flare, and largely staying out of the shove zones. There were men and women with big mouths and maybe wearing something in the form of military cosplay like camouflage or flak jackets, but they weren't there to throw a punch, just to call every jostle an assault. There were those in bullet-proof vests that didn't fit over their beer guts, and folks draped in ammo Rambo-style who clearly liked guns and had many but somehow still didn't know better than to sweep their own side with their muzzles, fingers on triggers. One loud noise could startle them into a massacre. These were people Garrett and Devon did their best to stay downwind from.

However, for all the clowns simply there to walk in the parade, there were also people who meant to do serious harm. They dressed specifically to appear non-threatening, to start some shit and blame either side until fights broke out. Though many of them posted anonymously online about how great the scalp of a cop would be to start the next great American civil war, they ingratiated themselves with police on the ground. Garrett never ceased to wonder at how officers, of all people, weren't more suspicious of these grinning sociopaths, but since their bosses at the end of the day were politicians, maybe their bullshit detectors were deadened from overuse.

Garrett and Devon had different methods and missions that day. They separated wordlessly when the police told people to keep to opposing sides of the street or else get shut down. Devon could blend with the alt-right crowd pretty well, so he was off to glean info regarding their plans for today's mischief. As a tall white man with a genuine interest in guns, all he had to do was speak admirably about their weapon specifications, and he was immediately one of the boys.

That sort of tactic would never work for Garrett. He looked too precious and sounded (so he'd been told repeatedly and vehemently) like a faggot. He was planning on talking to some of the activists on the ground, and monitoring police behavior on a day when they should have been girded against the right, but instead kept their backs to that side and glared at the anti-fascists. Uniformed thugs seemed to understand that they put the "fa" in Antifa, and everybody hates a critic.

"Hi, my name's Garrett, I'm an independent reporter hoping to get your views on …" This was how Garrett introduced himself when he knew he was around friendlies, but he didn't get to ask anyone about the counterprotest, how they felt about the police presence, or even how they felt about the weather before someone from the BLM side crossed into no-man's-land to retrieve a flag that had blown away.

Probably this protester didn't want to allow the other side to rip the flag up or light it on fire. He stepped forward only halfway, bent down, and reached to tug back a banner featuring two symbols of its own: a black flag for anarchy and a red flag for communism.

Garrett thought, because he knew his Shakespeare relatively well, *Rosemary for remembrance, pansies for thoughts … columbines and rue for you, some for me too.* Garrett's mind was making a scattershot amount of free associations from this. He thought that he himself was a pansy for thoughts in a way, and that Columbines as in mass shootings were handing out rue pretty freely these days. That was when he saw someone put a boot on the shoulder of the guy retrieving his flag, and kick him back into the leftist side of the crowd with such force that he bowled half a dozen people over.

That's when all hell broke loose.

# 11.

## *How to Make an American Fascist in One Week or Less!*

### *What Is a Fascist?*

The word "fascism" comes from our old friend the fasces, that bundled axe which once symbolized Rome's power, and was adopted by Benito Mussolini between World Wars as an emblem for Fascist Italy. Fascism is a far-right ideology, so-called because when the French National Assembly gathered to draft a constitution in the summer of 1789, the revolutionist anti-royals took to the presiding officer's left, while the conservative aristocrats who supported the monarchy staked his right. In general, "left-wing" views seek greater economic and social equality by way of progressive reforms; from moderate social safety net programs to revolutionary society-wide socialism or communism. On the other hand, "right-wing" stances resist such changes, instead favoring conservative strategies to maintain already existing institutions and restore previous conventions; in moderation this may mean incentivizing traditional family unit structures, *in extremis* it can mean xenophobic nationalism, racial supremacy, and theocratic domination. Fascism specifically entails dictatorial rule, ultranationalism, and ultra-violence to enforce a regimentation of society and extermination of "undesirables," which the Nazis defined as your Jews, your Romani and Sinti (Gypsies), your various other racial outsiders, your homosexuals, your Jehovah's Witnesses, your leftists (commies and socialists), your Poles, any captured Soviets, and those termed "useless eaters," i.e. folks with a disability (physical, mental, or emotional) that meant they couldn't sew, soldier, or swing a hammer for their supper. The dubious American vision of the fasces as a strength-through-unity emblem (*e pluribus unum* and all that) is not how Mussolini saw it when he rose to power in 1922, and fascism worldwide still adopts brute force to achieve uniformity. A fascist is a person who thinks that's a great idea.

### *How to Make an American Fascist in One Week or Less (4 Different Methods)*

In the 1960s and 70s, psychological experiments hadn't fully embraced the "first, do no harm" directive. Here are four instances where the question, "How can normal people become fascist/racist/inhumanly brutal?" revealed immediate, stark, and terrifying results.

**The Milgram Experiment, 1961 (1 hour)**
- The experimenter: Stanley Milgram, a twenty-seven-year-old psychologist at Yale University, and son of a Hungarian immigrant father and a Romanian Jewish immigrant mother.
- The participants: A group of 40 men between the ages of twenty and fifty.
- The place: Yale University at New Haven, Connecticut (first) and Bridgeport, Connecticut (second).
- The experiment: According to *Obedience to Authority: An Experimental View* (1974) by Stanley Milgram, each subject (the "teacher") watches another person (the "learner") being strapped into a chair and fitted with electrodes. An experimenter then takes the teacher to another room with "an impressive shock generator," the dominating feature of which is "a horizontal line of thirty switches, ranging from 15 volts to 450 volts" with verbal descriptions escalating from "SLIGHT SHOCK" to "DANGER — SEVERE SHOCK." It's the teacher's

job to administer a series of questions to the learner, and to apply increasing shocks when the answer is wrong. While the learner is an actor who receives no shocks at all, the teacher is "genuinely naive" and thinks he is causing real pain. The learner's responses progress from "grunts" to "complaints" to "increasingly vehement and emotional" responses until the 285-volt mark elicits "an agonized scream." Ultimately the learner will stop responding as if unconscious.

- <u>The results</u>: Not good! In the Yale/New Haven experiment, 65% of learners administered the final 450-volt SEVERE SHOCK. In the Bridgeport experiment, it was 48%, a difference Milgram attributed to the auspicious Yale University as the issuing authority instead of the invented "Research Associates of Bridgeport," an "unimpressive" organization that lacked imposing credentials. These results suggest that the Nazi defense at Nuremberg — "I was just following orders" — might be a defense for an average of 56.5% of humans (or at least men).

## The Third Wave Experiment, 1967 (1-5 Days)

- <u>The experimenter</u>: Ron Jones, a twenty-five-year-old Stanford University graduate with a Master's in education, a first-year Social Studies teacher, and a basketball coach.
- <u>The participants</u>: A 10th-grade classroom of 30 sophomore students generally between ages of fifteen and sixteen.
- <u>The place</u>: Cubberley High School, Palo Alto, California.
- <u>The experiment</u>: According to Ron Jones's self-published report, in an effort to show skeptical high school students how normal people allowed (and then denied) the Nazi atrocities, Jones implemented a one-day mini-fascist state that lasted a week.
    - *Monday*: With "Strength Through Discipline" written on the chalkboard, Jones started with focus drills, strict speaking guidelines, and sitting with attentive postures.
    - *Tuesday*: When students displayed these disciplines on day two, Jones continued, writing "Strength Through Community" on the board, creating a special salute,

and telling his students to greet each other with it outside the classroom (which they did). Their movement was named The Third Wave.

- *Wednesday*: To learn "Strength Through Action," Jones issued exclusive membership cards and told the students to report on fellow classmates who weren't following the rules, guard the classroom from outsiders, and recruit friends they thought would make good insiders. The students created a banner for The Third Wave, which the librarian hung over the library's entrance. The principal stopped by to give Jones The Third Wave salute, and by the end of the day, 200 more students were recruited.
- *Thursday*: The "Strength Through Pride" lesson brought 80 students to the classroom. Jones told them, "The Third Wave is a nationwide program to find students who are willing to fight for political change in this country." Jones then selected three female students who'd questioned The Third Wave principles, and expelled them from the room under the guard of other students who escorted them to the library.
- *Friday*: The final lesson, "Strength Through Understanding," occurred in the auditorium at a rally full of unified chants and salutes. After elevating their expectations, Jones revealed: "There is no such thing as a national youth movement called The Third Wave. You have been used. Manipulated. [...] You are no better or worse than the German Nazis we have been studying." He then showed footage of the Nuremberg Rally.
- <u>The results</u>: He left many students traumatized and in tears. Remember the scene in The Dead Poets' Society where the students are allowed to mill about a courtyard and organically conform to marching in lockstep? It appears getting swept up in fascism could happen just like that, to almost anyone; we're built to conform.

## The Blue Eyes/Brown Eyes Exercise, 1968 (15 Minutes)

- <u>The experimenter</u>: Jane Elliott, a thirty-four-year-old 3rd-grade schoolteacher who pointed out, "I was born the year Adolf Hitler and Franklin Roosevelt came to power, in 1933. I remember what the Nazis did from 1933 until 1945. And I saw that same thing happening in this country where skin color is concerned."
- <u>The participants</u>: An all-white 3rd-grade class, with 28 students generally between the ages of eight and nine.
- <u>The place</u>: Community Elementary School, Riceville, Iowa.
- <u>The experiment</u>: The day after the assassination of Martin Luther King Jr., when her students asked why someone would kill "the King," a man who'd recently been their "Hero of the Month," Elliott divided the class between blue-eyed and brown-eyed children to illustrate how racial prejudice feels. On the first day, children with blue eyes were deemed superior, and brown-eyed children were given special collars to better ID them from afar (similar to the yellow patches mandated for Jewish people not only in Nazi Germany, but many times previously, even before the invention of Christendom). The next day, it was reversed, and brown-eyed children were the superior ones. Superior students got more recess time, more lunch, first choice in everything, became bullies, and gleefully discriminated against their classmates. Inferior students felt hopeless, immediately performed worse on tests, and lashed out when called what they were (blue-eyes or brown-eyes) because who they were had become an insult.
- <u>The results</u>: Elliott said in a 1970 interview, "I watched what had been marvelous, cooperative, wonderful, thoughtful children turn into nasty, vicious, discriminating little third-graders in a space of fifteen minutes." This phenomenon was also found in adults, as the PBS FRONTLINE episode "A Class Divided" (1985) showed the same bullying and lashing-out behaviors in adult employees of the Iowa Department of Corrections (prison guards and parole officers). One of the adults deemed inferior described his feelings about being discriminated against and

was asked, "You were this uncomfortable in an hour and a half?" He replied, "I was amazed at how uncomfortable I was in the first fifteen minutes."

## The Stanford Prison Experiment, 1971 (6 Days)

- <u>The experimenter</u>: Dr. Philip G. Zimbardo, age thirty-eight, a South Bronx son of Sicilian immigrants who was often mistaken for and targeted as Jewish, Black, and Puerto Rican, which led him to an interest in social psychology.
- <u>The participants</u>: A selection of 24 male Stanford University students between the ages of eighteen and twenty-three.
- <u>The place</u>: The basement of Jordan Hall, Stanford University, Stanford, California.
- <u>The experiment</u>: To study the psychological effects of becoming both a prisoner and a prison guard, Zimbardo and his team set up a two-week simulated carceral experiment that lasted only six days. With the aid of Palo Alto police, designated prisoners were arrested, booked, blindfolded, strip-searched, humiliated, reassigned new identities as numbers, chained, and confined in windowless cells. The guards were given uniforms, batons, and mirrored sunglasses to prevent eye contact, but otherwise left to make their own rules. They quickly began punishing and tormenting prisoners with pushups, a tactic also used in Nazi concentration camps. Day two started with a prisoner rebellion that the guards combated by taking away their beds, spraying them with fire extinguishers, isolating their leaders, and ramping up their harassment going forward to prevent another uprising.
- <u>The results</u>: According to a slideshow presentation from Zimbardo, after 35 hours, one of the prisoners began to "act crazy, to scream, to curse, to go into a rage that seemed out of control." The powerlessness of the prisoners made them feel helpless, hopeless, and isolated, while the guards bonded, volunteered for extra guard duty, and pit the prisoners against each other to achieve obedience. After six days, when parents began hiring lawyers to get their sons released from this prison,

Zimbardo concluded, "At this point it became clear that we had to end this experiment. We had to do so because it was no longer an experiment." From Greek hazing on college campuses to concentration camps to Abu Ghraib, it appears the "ultimate aphrodisiac of power" brings out sadism in some and helpless conformity in those around them.

In conclusion: there's more than one way to skin a human and find a fascist.

## Is Anyone Truly Anti-Fascist?

These experiments make one despair. Are most of us just latent fascists and/or cowards? Are there no true heroes, no real good guys? That brings us to the subject of Ron Ridenhours (plural). In British philosopher Jonathan Glover's book *Humanity: A Moral History of the Twentieth Century*, he claimed that a Ron Ridenhour who supposedly refused to give the first shock during a Princeton recreation of Milgram's experiment was the same Ron Ridenhour who exposed the My Lai massacre (the brutal slaughter of over 500 unarmed elderly men, women, children, and babies in Vietnam in 1968). Without the whistle-blowing efforts of 11th Brigade soldier Ron Ridenhour, murderer and former Lieutenant William Calley may have never been convicted of leading that atrocity (he claimed that he was "just following orders" too). Likewise, a hero like Warrant Officer and Army helicopter pilot Hugh Thompson (who landed between soldiers and fleeing villagers and threatened to open fire on his own side if they didn't stop the massacre, then flew dozens of survivors to medical care), might never have received the Soldier's Medal in recognition for his bravery. There may be another experiment worth doing: finding all living Ron Ridenhours to see what percentage of them display such stern moral clarity.

# 12.

Devon's back was turned to the action, so he didn't know he was part of a melee until the crowd shifted and he was in the thick of it. His first actions were to impede people he could reach on the "right" side of the street, possibly blowing his cover to any adversary who noticed, but unconcerned for himself in the moment. When there was work to be done and panic-fuel being dumped into his blood, Devon could move through a crowd like a combine through tall grass: mow through, scythe down, and toss back. He not only wanted to return to his people, he wanted to stand in the gap between his people and the enemy, partly because he knew a portion of these cretins would go for the most vulnerable (targeting women instead of men, the young and the old rather than adults in their prime, anyone already on the ground), but mostly because of what he was there for regarding his job: to gather evidence of viciousness on film so the cowards couldn't hide anymore, so they wouldn't get away clean.

He wasn't the only man in the crowd with such drive, and one of them on the opposing side found Devon before he found them. The man would later be identified as Tyler Travis, a long way from his home in suburban Indiana, who had traveled specifically to join up with a gang (colloquially and erroneously termed a militia) and come into another city's streets to fight a turf war over America. Travis saw Devon running towards a skirmish with his camera extended before him. Travis jumped out with a shield that looked like it was made in someone's garage from plywood and cabinet handles found at Home Depot. Travis brandished an ASP extendable baton in his grip. Out of the crowd came this racist and doughy DIY warrior, and down came his baton on Devon's hand, knocking his camera to the ground, and breaking at least one finger, if not more.

Devon snatched back his hand, and ducked down to retrieve his camera to make sure it was still working. He filmed his bleeding and crooked finger, watching on screen and in real life as it throbbed pain waves up to his brain. Devon was now filming left-handed as he documented all he could of his assailant (face, clothing, tattoos, and other identifiable markings), and got knocked back by his assailant and two more just like him who'd locked their basic shields together, and started advancing on their new target: a smallish man with shriveled legs, sitting in a wheelchair.

One of these chuds screamed, spittle flying against Devon's face, "Move or get maced, bitch!" Devon had been maced by far tougher men than these boys, by cops and terrorists and soldiers, and he didn't move.

Devon held his ground beside the protester in a wheelchair until the police barreled through the crowd like a battering ram (they called it a "bull-rush"), and the wuss-hearted wilted away. The cops started arresting people who couldn't stand fast enough to flee, for who knows what kind of charge, maybe for getting blood on the street without a permit or something. Devon fell back and kept filming until a lull overtook the atmosphere of the street. He then had time to review and post his footage, put out a call for an ID on his attacker, and evaluate just how badly his hand had been smashed.

His right middle finger was most assuredly broken, possibly the index one too, if not badly bruised. The pinkie and ring finger were fine, but the rest of Devon's hand felt traumatized, and he knew he'd have to take a back seat to the rest of the day's action, though he wouldn't call it quits until there was nothing left to witness. He texted a picture of it to Lena the medic asking for general advice on how much damage might have been done, but she only forwarded his message to Hazel saying, *I'm not out there today, working, maybe Hazel can help or knows who's nearby.* Hazel responded a few minutes later.

*I can help you stabilize that temporarily but it's going to need an x-ray*, she sent. *Where are you located?*

Devon begged off for the time being, scheduled to meet her later towards the end of the day, and wincingly wrapped his first two fingers together with gauze he had in his IFAK kit. He kept filming and posting and checking on people and amplifying useful information on where was safe, what the fascists were planning, and what the cops were responding with (a whole lotta "meh"). Only when the crowds dispersed, and someone winced at Devon's hand and said, "Yo, guy, my cousin had broken his finger in football practice and he threw a clot, you gotta go get that checked out," did Devon finally make his way towards the medic's stakeout that day. He spotted Hazel standing off to the side, no one to help at the moment, a thousand-yard stare over her mask, and he waved from several feet off so as not to startle her out of whatever cosmic space she was suspended in.

"Oh, hi, your hand." She closed her eyes for a moment before she could rally to help him. "Let me take a look."

"Are you okay? You looked … a little disturbed just now," Devon said, following her to a table of cleaning solutions and bandage supplies. "I live four blocks from here if you need a break, or a coffee, or a real drink."

"Um, you know what?" Hazel paused for another out-of-this-world moment and said, "Yes, thank you please." She grabbed a few things they would need for Devon's hand, told her crew she would be back, and joined Devon for four blocks of silence.

Devon expected his place to be empty and calm, but Garrett was there filling jugs with water from the sink, and ingeniously using a dust pan handle as a funnel. Devon felt his cock stir just to see him, but that surge of blood pressure only made his fingers throb and flare with pain. Worth it, though.

"Hi there," Garrett said to him. "Stealing your water for the cause, figured you wouldn't mind. Oh, and you," he said when he saw Hazel come in behind Devon. He slipped his mask back up for her sake and told her, "I like you, I mean I think we all do, having medics out there. You're a real port in the storm. Is it Holly?"

She sat down at the kitchen table and said, "Hazel," then gestured at Devon's hand. "Look at what happened to this one."

Garrett sucked in a hiss through his teeth. "Is it broken?"

"Oh, yeah," Devon said, and Hazel nodded affirmatively. She tested the bend-ability of his other fingers, then measured a tongue depressor against the other hand's index, before scoring it with a pen and snapping off the excess against the table.

"I'll tape this up with a brace for now, just so you don't keep injuring it, but you need an x-ray to make sure there aren't any slivers of bone in there and to make sure it's set straight before it heals. Sooner is better than later. You understand?"

"Got it," Devon said, and bit down on his good hand as she straightened out the busted one.

"Get your dirty hand out of your mouth," Garrett said. "There's still a pandemic, you know. Should I make an ice baggy? Do you have ice cubes?"

Hazel and Devon both responded "yes" at the same time. Garrett started cracking cubes out of an ice tray and tying them into a dish towel.

Devon was still concerned that Hazel needed more help than he did.

"Did something happen to you today?" he asked her. "Want that drink I offered? Want to talk about it?"

"I can pour drinks, I've got ice," Garrett said.

"No, I'm allergic to alcohol," Hazel said.

That was the worst thing Devon had heard all day, but he didn't express that emotion. "Coffee? Cold glass of water?"

"Water, please, yes," she said.

Garrett popped out ice for her as well, filled a glass with water, refilled the ice tray, then sat down with them both to assist. The glass of ice water made a faint tinkling sound like a wind chime. When Hazel finished taping up Devon's fingers, she set the bag of ice on top of them, and took several gulps of her drink before setting it down again. She used the condensation to cool her neck and forehead, then spoke.

"I went to help someone today, her face was bleeding." Hazel touched just above her own eyebrow, illustrating. "She wouldn't let me near her, said she didn't want to catch the China Flu."

"Jesus fuck," Devon said.

Hazel shrugged and swallowed another sip. "It happens all the time, with patients, with lots of people. I don't know why, today it just hurt more. I keep worrying about my parents going to the store and my grandmother walking her dog. These people are everywhere."

"Yeah, they are," Garrett said with a sigh.

"It's not much," Devon offered, "but if you feel unsafe out there and you see me, you can get behind me. I'll get in their way."

Hazel's eyes darted up at him, and Devon didn't know if he'd caused offense or if she maybe didn't believe him, but before he could start throwing out caveats and *mea culpas*, Garrett seconded him.

"He means that, it's how I met him, he body-blocked a tear gas grenade from hitting me in the face," Garrett said. "It bruised his back."

"It did?" Devon asked. He hadn't seen his bare back recently, but Garrett had.

Garrett's eyes hooded a bit like that look Bogie taught Bacall to do. "Yeah, it did."

Hazel finished her glass of water and said, "Thanks." Whether it was for the water, the offer of protection, or for having a little room to speak, Devon did not know.

# 13.

When Hazel and Garrett returned to the action, Devon was left with nothing but silence, an aching hand, and his own screaming, careening thoughts, which irritated him on a regular basis. It was time to refocus his intentions for the day.

No more street action. That was a done deal, what with his hand distracting him and making him vulnerable. He hit the internet to find a walk-in place where he could get an x-ray, and also a rapid STD test (Chlamydia, Gonorrhea, Syphilis, Hepatitis B, and HIV results within the hour) just because ... wouldn't it be nice to show Garrett? *Hey, no pressure, but I want your trust and I'm here to earn it.* Devon knew he was contagion free (at least below his belt), but he would never expect Garrett to take his word for it, and would in fact berate him if he did. *It's not insulting to stand up for yourself,* he'd say. *Please have enough self-respect to protect yourself from everything, including me.*

Maybe especially Devon, because he wasn't exactly FDA-approved, certified organic. But for everyone and anyone: the asymptomatic walk among the rest of the population. Should a person trust someone who doesn't know that he or she or ze shouldn't trust themselves, two people could be sorry, and it all could have been avoided with the bonding experience of a couple's STD panel.

Devon did not necessarily take his own good advice, of course, because if Garrett was bad for him, he didn't want to know. Still, there had been something erotic in going to get full STD panels done with Delilah, then waiting 10-14 days to fuck raw, like ... talk about edging, that was some seriously delayed gratification, and it prompted a wonderfully carnal honeymoon period.

But getting horny wasn't helping Devon, and naturally it was his preferred jack-off hand that was injured, so he threw himself into other practicalities: answering emails with hunt-and-peck replies, taking out the garbage, straightening up the old sty. He spent all day waiting for Garrett, straight-up Jay Gatsby-ass pining for Garrett. He did several dozen things he never usually set aside time to do, like clip his toenails while they were soft after a shower, wipe pink mildew off all of his faucets (kitchen sink, bathroom sink, bathtub spigot, and shower head), search for what that mold actually was (*Serratia marcescens*, gross), and then ordered some groceries to be dropped no-contact style outside of his door, so he could at least feed Garrett if the kid came back at all that night.

Devon took some kratom in the afternoon for the pain in his hand and to get a second wind for his attention span. Two hours later, he added some whiskey on top. An hour after that he boiled some pasta to help sober himself up, ate it with a little tahini and soy sauce and crumbled tofu, then took a food nap. When he woke up it was dark, and time was meaningless until he found a clock, and it was still early enough that Garrett might come home any minute, or not. There were no messages from the boy on Devon's phone. He was weighing how much more alcohol would put him back to sleep vs. how much would the nurses or whoever smell on him the next day when he heard a key grind into his lock, and nearly swooned.

"Jesus Hieronymus Bosch Christ on a cracker," Garrett said when he came in and spotted Devon upright in bed, waving his busted hand hello. "What a day."

"Tell me about it," Devon said, watching his riot son disassemble everything he was wearing, totally at home in the place already, probably because he was one of the nation's many unhoused LGBTQ+ youths, and used to adapting to new crash pads. "Or don't, talk to me about anything except the day you had, dealer's choice."

"Let me rinse off first," Garrett said. "I'm starving also, what smells good in here? Can I have some? I'm not trying to be a diva and boss you around, I'm just, like, totally tapped out."

"Sometimes I like being bossed around." Devon was an anarchist in the streets and a slave in the sheets, and he had no problem embracing both of those identities. Life was too short to be demure.

Devon made another bowl of tahini noodles, and the smell of it mixed with the soapy-sweet steam coming out of the bathroom created a pleasant miasma, like a springtime swamp. It made Devon reminiscent of the week he spent in New Orleans after he dropped out of college — great memories. Devon put on his kimono, set up Garrett's dinner in the living room area, and only responded with "yeah?" and "wow" for the next hour as Garrett ate and expounded on all his accumulated drama.

"I got plenty of footage of cops straight-up conspiring with these militia dipshits, not that it'll matter. It's like when the teachers side with the bullies in class so long as they keep the peace, never mind that people are being tormented, they just don't want to be bothered." Garrett dropped his fork, like a dinner bell in his empty bowl for Oskar, who arrived promptly to lick up the salty sauce residue.

"I mean, there's a reason police and mafias work hand-in-hand," Devon said, leaning forward to pet Oskar. "They're the same types of guys, and in a lot of ways on the same damn side. The law isn't the dividing line, the separation is between who has power and who doesn't, and they don't answer to the powerless."

Garrett rolled his eyes. "Even though that's supposedly the whole goddamn point of police."

"Well, policing in America actually started as slave patrols," Devon said, picking up Garrett's dish just before Oskar licked it off the edge of the footlocker he used as a coffee table. "Notice how closely 'overseer' sounds to 'officer' and you've pretty much cracked the code."

"Ah, fuck," Garrett said, slumping back.

Devon delivered Garrett's dinner bowl to the kitchen sink, and Oskar hopped up to follow it. When Devon returned to sit across from Garrett again, a quiet fell over them like a collapsed blanket fort. Garrett took a good, long look at Devon, and talked to him rather than at him for the first time since he'd arrived back.

"I don't own a lot of stuff, I've told you that," he said. "And if I keep staying here every night, I'll pretty much be moving in. I know we're both out most of the time with these protests but … eventually the protests are going to dry up but my toothbrush will still be here. Is that what you meant to do, with giving me a key?"

"Yes," Devon said, crossing his legs knee-over-knee and kicking his heel as he leaned back to reflect Garrett's posture. "My friends say lesbians do this all the time, U-hauling they call it. Meet, make out, move in together within a month."

"It's been three days, though," Garrett said. "Barely."

Devon shrugged. "We live in apocalyptic times."

Garrett smiled, then yawned. Devon stood, offered him a hand, and led him to bed, killing the lights as he went. As soon as they were under the covers, Garrett fell asleep in Devon's arms, and all the thoughts that were so loud in Devon's mind during the lonesome daylight hours were blissfully stifled and silent.

# 14.

By the time Devon returned with a splint around his fingers and a clean bill of sexual health, Garrett had moved in and moved a few things around. He had two suitcases under the bed he said he'd be using like drawers. Half of the bathroom sink was suddenly full of hair ties and sunscreen lotions and toothpaste for sensitive teeth. He'd added a fancy chest to the kitchen that looked like a great stash box but actually contained perfectly legal, non-psychedelic herbal tea.

Garrett's aunt had driven his suitcases over. "She didn't like the guns but I told her they all had trigger locks and you were a gun safety instructor and were going to teach me how to shoot like an expert."

"I would love to teach you to shoot," Devon said as they prepared different parts of the same dinner, waltzing around each other in the kitchen with enchanting ease. Devon dropped his spatula into the sink and turned off the heat on a pan of caramelized onions meant to top some stuffed portobello mushrooms in the oven. He wrapped his arms around Garrett from behind and started moving him into a firing stance. "Feet shoulder-width apart for stability, both hands on the weapon for control," he said, putting his leg between Garrett's, running his hands over Garrett's arms.

Garrett leaned his head back against Devon's chest, and being about a head shorter, looked up at him. "I've fired a gun before."

"No virgin then," Devon said. "I can't wait to study your form."

But it turned out Garrett was a virgin, in the patriarchal sense that he'd not been penetrated in every orifice by a penis yet. He had, however, no blushing apprehension about it.

"I've put the handle of a hairbrush up there, the handle of a hammer, a glass perfume bottle," he said when they retired to the bed.

"I've got toys, if you'd prefer to play with those," Devon offered, halfway to the shoebox under his bed where he kept fuzzy handcuffs, dildos, lubricants, and various vibrating devices, but Garrett shook his head.

"I saw them when I was unpacking," Garrett said, getting naked and sliding in between Devon's sheets. "I've been trying to get laid for years, you think I want to keep waiting?"

Devon's first ride out of the gate had been laughably short. His high school girlfriend Izzy was truly shocked by just how insignificant it was. He did better when he tried again an hour after, but what little magic there had been was long gone. One of the best perks of having been slutty throughout his twenties was that, these days, Devon knew what the hell he was doing. He could do it from the top, the bottom, while standing, blindfolded, and with his hands tied behind his back. All good for Garrett.

They started out kissing, fondling. Devon was practically twice the size of Garrett, and took care not to land on him or lean on him. He arranged Garrett's long locks to one side so they weren't in danger of being pinned by elbows. He felt big and rough in comparison to his slim, young companion, but in a way that made him feel male, powerful, and alluringly feral.

Devon took the lead with fingering, opening. He wasn't squeamish about getting his hands dirty, wasn't shy about smells, and he was happy to find filthy delight in Garrett with every new trick he tried. For example, the same move that could work to stimulate a G-spot felt similarly good when applied to a prostate. When that sensation caused Garrett's toes to curl, Devon reached down to tickle his feet in case he, like many folks, got a sexual thrill from having their feet caressed. There was a reason for that, a crisscross in the brain's ley-line map of the body; basically, the brain thought everything below the waist was in the exact same place, so a ticklish fingernail along the arch of the foot was not unlike the stroke of a cock, apparently.

"Too much," Garrett said, when adding his foot into the mix made his body seize like he'd been shocked. Devon left the boy's feet alone, and started grinding their pelvises together, all floppy and frankly silly-looking if one were watching it instead of doing it. The act was deadly serious to those engaged in it, though.

"I love you so much already," Devon said, watching Garrett watch their members undulate against one another, neither circumcised. The L word took Garrett out of that hypnotic focus for a moment. When their eyes met, Devon kissed him. "That doesn't have to mean anything, it's just how I feel, thought you'd like to hear it."

"Thanks," Garrett said, and might have smiled if it wasn't so hard to laugh when you were consumed with lust.

"No problem." Another kiss, and then Devon went to work fucking his new friend and lover, tender until he could be tough, generous until he could be greedy. They didn't have anything else to say until Garrett started to buck, close to orgasm, which was always the hottest thing to Devon, when he could feel someone cum from the inside, their whole body in a paroxysm of pleasure around him. He had to ask, "Can I cum inside you?" and though Garrett was speechless, he nodded and made noises beginning with, "Yuh, yuh," and so permission was granted.

Devon kissed Garrett over the crest of his climax, and sucked his tongue into his mouth as hard as he could, completing a circuit between them that Devon wished would never be broken.

# III. RIOT

# 15.

"Oh fuck. I forgot," were the sweet nothings that woke Garrett up the next day. He opened his eyes to see Devon staring at his blank ceiling as if it were some overwhelming calculation with one wrong decimal point somewhere within. "I promised I'd host my friend Wayne David for a week or two, we've been planning this for months." He turned to look at Garrett. "This really changes the whole dynamic."

Garrett closed his eyes again and smiled. "Just tell me when to clear out, I have places I can go."

"I don't want to do that, fuck that," Devon said, rolling on top of Garrett and kissing his face, his neck, his armpits, his nipples. "Call me old fashioned," kiss kiss, "but when I shack up with someone," kiss sniff, "I'm very traditional about it. You've got a key, it's as much your place as mine."

"You promised your friend first," Garrett said, eyes fluttering open again to watch Devon's head descend beneath the bedsheet for some fresh morning fellatio. "It's fine."

Honestly, Garrett had enough to keep him busy and out and about, they both did. Long days of sorting material and researching the news, long nights of hurry-up-and-wait on gassed streets full of shadows that could be friendlies or foes. Plus, amidst all of these unusual events, they still had to shower, grocery shop, sleep, pay bills, cancel or continue subscriptions, do laundry, brush teeth, return texts, stay fit, and enjoy some entertainment here and there — a TV show or a new sex partner, something that made life worth living beyond the daily grind.

"Ah, shit," Garrett gasped as he reached climax. He gripped the edges of Devon's mattress, and almost went mad when he felt the peristalsis of Devon's throat contracting to swallow down Garrett's emission. "Whoo," he exhaled.

"Whoo," Devon replied, returning to kiss Garrett's mouth, a little gross, but more sexy than gross, so Garrett allowed it. "Good morning."

"It is a good morning," Garrett agreed. They were on the same page there.

As they engaged with the business of the day, however, it became unclear whether they were going to have a good night. The police of multiple cities were releasing statements that started with noise about "we respect the rights of law-abiding citizens to have their voices heard," but ended with unequivocal threats that showed how they really felt: "Looting and destruction will not be tolerated. If you choose to defy curfew, you will be held responsible for the actions of the mob."

Garrett and Devon both knew what that meant. If you were on the street when they said you shouldn't be, you were on the hook for anything that happened, regardless of whether or not you were the one who did it. It's like how the get-away driver in a robbery is also guilty of murder, if that's what the inside crew does during the criminal act. But in this case, it was a fundamental American right to protest. There were undercover cops out there breaking windows and setting fires so that when they put their uniforms back on, they had further justification to rough people up.

"Remember the other day when Buffalo cops took a knee with protesters in front of their City Hall?" Devon asked. He was at his desk under the window, in front of two large computer monitors full of research and responses from friends, colleagues, and news outlets.

"Yeah, and the next day they cracked an old man's skull on the pavement and stepped over his bleeding body." Garrett was still nested in bed with his laptop and a few notebooks, updating his diary record of the previous day and looking for where he'd need to be later that afternoon to see the most action.

"Well, since the two officers who shoved the old guy were suspended pending an investigation," Devon said, "fifty-seven other Buffalo officers resigned in protest."

"Fifty-seven?" Garrett asked.

"That's what the reports say."

"Resigned to protest the benching of those cops, not the abuse of a seventy-five-year-old peacenik?"

"That's right," Devon said, a tone in his voice like he was almost impressed with such tremendous bastardry.

Garrett scoffed, disgusted but unsurprised. "Boy, when cops protest, they sure do have their priorities in order, don't they?"

"Yes, indeed. When we protest it's against police brutality, but when cops protest, they take the pro-brutality position," Devon said with a sigh before clicking to the next story. "So it goes."

Just as a police protest was a Bizarro photo-negative inversion of how normal people protested, a police riot was a horse of a different color from a civilian riot. Garrett and Devon were about to witness the difference firsthand.

A riot instigated, escalated, and exacerbated by the police doesn't dissipate naturally. It has no goals to accomplish other than to continue to rage, like a wildfire that's only aim is to be, and get bigger until it can consume all there is to destroy.

The afternoon began seemingly normal enough, but when the cops started getting cagey at the approach of dusk, Garrett felt jumpier, and he trusted that feeling. It was less than two weeks after the daytime murder of George Floyd, and already the cops were itchy, tired of even attempting restraint. When their patience snapped in Garrett's city, when bicycle cops linked their frames together and started shoving, when police shields started getting used as assault weapons, and when people started getting maced without warning, Garrett knew what he was looking at. The cops were annoyed, and they wanted to take back the streets.

When a cop hits you, you can't hit back. When they fire less-lethal projectiles at your throat, your eyes, and your junk, they'll say they didn't mean to, and you have to agree with them. When a cop grabs a woman's hair and drags her away from the safety of the crowd, and five more officers surround them to fight off any citizens who try to rescue her from a beatdown, you have to let them, or you'll be the one charged with felony riot, and ID'd as a gang member. If anyone was getting named and blamed and fired for such an act, it would be you and not them.

When a cop got close enough to Garrett to see the whites of his eyes, Garrett let his instincts take over. Though he and Devon arrived together, Garrett didn't look for his new boyfriend when he made a split-second decision on what to do. Devon could take care of himself, and so could Garrett, a fact that still surprised him sometimes and which he always welcomed with gratitude like a new revelation. He wouldn't have guessed that being kicked out of his house was something he could deal with, but he'd dealt with it. He thought getting a GED and a job in the same year would be impossible, but he'd done it. He had worried that he wouldn't know what to do when the winds of a riot finally turned against him, but he did. When Garrett felt the abyss look back at him, before it could heave forward and drag him down, Garrett leapt back and ran.

# 16.

"You did the right thing," Tula assured Garrett later that night, pouring him a drink and setting it on her kitchen counter so he could come to retrieve it while staying socially distant. "When I was young and spry, I'd take off running from trouble. But let me tell you, young punk, when you're pushing thirty-five, you can twist your ankle doing anything."

"And tweak your back doing nothing," Hazel said. She was having an elaborate cup of tea that Tula had made for her first. Garrett didn't know if they were ever destined to be involved romantically, but at least Tula was finally getting some time with a new friend tonight. It turned out Hazel had skipped Tula's rooftop shindig because she didn't drink alcohol and therefore didn't frequent boozy gatherings, but they were past that now.

"I've had plantar fasciitis in both feet for about two years," Devon said. In an aside to Garrett he added, "In case you see me limping in the morning, that's why."

"And plantar fasciitis is ...?" Garrett asked.

"Inflammation of the plantar fascia ligament," Hazel said, lifting up one of her socked feet and demonstrating the location. "It attaches the heel to the toes."

"And it really hobbles a motherfucker, not because I have some kind of bone spur —"

"Unlike our fearful leader," Tula interjected. "I hear you can dodge the draft on that very serious condition."

"— but because my calf muscles are too tight, and I don't do enough yoga or something."

"Nobody does enough yoga," Hazel said with a sigh, stone serious. When the rest of them realized she wasn't joking, they laughed, and Hazel laughed with them. It was a relief. None of them had laughed enough all year.

Tula's apartment was small, cozy, and crowded with plants. Herbs in the kitchen, sturdy potted monstrosities in the living room, succulents and air plants by the windows dominating the sill and hanging on knitted ropes like curtains. Garrett was able to pick out confirming evidence of the few things he knew about Tula quickly (the Greek flag on a fridge magnet, plant art in the vaginal style of Georgia O'Keeffe, stickers on a guitar case that had intertwined female symbols), but there was more to be seen and gleaned. There were pictures of Tula holding babies (probably nieces and nephews if Garrett had to guess), a lot of used mugs left in strange places (no food plates, nothing rotting or smelly, but tea cups everywhere), and twinkly lights around certain bookcases and plant shelves that could all be snapped on with one power strip and clearly took a lot of effort to festoon together just so. The outlier in what was otherwise a lot of handmade crafts and fair trade bric-a-brac was a glossy poster of a hyper-marketed K-pop girl group that was either pinned up ironically or had a backstory Garrett hoped to one day hear.

Tula sat on a bar stool just outside her kitchen. Hazel had the big chair in the center of the living room, a comfy high-armed throne surrounded by stacks of books, your classic reading chair. Devon and Garrett sat on a futon couch against a wall that was covered with a crocheted throw. There was just enough room for the holy ghost between them, which was the amount of space Garrett was told to leave between his date to the teen dance back on the compound, lest their lusts be ignited.

Garrett had recounted his adventures, how he had run through the streets dodging left and right around random corners until he found a smaller gathering of protesters on a corner that was as yet un-fucked-with by the police. He slowed so he wouldn't be gasping when he informed everyone that the cops were on the move in a phalanx-style formation. For reporters like Tula, who'd been making her way through this corner cluster, it meant getting closer to the action. For those who wanted to protest only as legally as possible, it meant going home. And for those who were there for the ruckus, it meant running towards what Garrett had just fled.

He and Tula teamed up then to find a safer observation point, which ultimately meant climbing up on a hefty lidded dumpster in an open alley across the street from the hand-to-hand stuff. From their vantage point, they could record the events, and were they spotted, they hoped they could retreat the way they came. If they happened to be boxed in by goons "slicing the pie" as they called it — angling down the alleys before corralling stragglers towards the fracas — that would have just been their bad luck that day. But it had been a good-luck day, perhaps because the glow of Garrett's good morning had protected them.

When a few arrests were made and the tear gas deployed to break up the clot of people before sundown, Tula invited Garrett back to hers. Garrett messaged Devon to say that was where he'd be next, and Devon had a treat for Tula: he'd struck a rapport with Hazel and could get her to Tula's as well, in a friendly accidentally-on-purpose way that very evening. That was how they all ended up in Tula's suburban forest, eating mixed nuts and drinking tea for the day's debriefing.

"I wasn't close enough to the action today, I guess," Hazel said. "It's like that when we're at the station sometimes, you know there's action somewhere, but your truck isn't the one called up. Some days you're slammed, other days, it's like hitting only green lights. All your calls are canceled, and the other rig gets every mess in a row and can't even nap in between."

"I rode with the medical truck while reporting around Syria," Devon said. "It was just like that there, too; one minute playing cards and having a smoke, the next minute screams and blood and the ground's shaking. Sometimes it was days of downtime, and weirdly the medics were calmer when the emergencies came regularly than when the quiet lasted too long."

"Maybe they feel like it's only a matter of time until something bad happens again, and they just want to get it over with already," Garrett said.

Hazel nodded. "It's very easy to believe that the longer things are okay, the more bad is building up somewhere else, and when it hits you, it'll hit you all at once."

"Like there's an electrical charge in the universe that will be balanced eventually," Tula said.

"Just like that, like a law of energy," Hazel agreed. "What is up must come down, and what is calm will be disturbed because it's the calm that is temporary and the chaos that is eternal."

Garrett and Devon looked at one another and smiled. They'd successfully gotten Riot Mother the one gift she wanted for the Strawberry Moon: an intimate conversation with this healer.

"Uh, Devon, how was your day out there?" Tula asked after a beat.

"Oh, and how is your finger, did you get that x-ray like I told you?" Hazel asked.

"I did. The finger's okay. It hurts like a bitch, but whatever, life is pain," Devon said. He smiled when he said this, but Tula's gaze sharpened, and she glanced at Garrett, perhaps to see if he, too, found such fatalism disturbing. Garrett didn't know what to think. He was only on day four of knowing Devon, and he didn't have enough data to know when he was joking and when he was pretending to joke through the pain. "I got crushed in with a few people but managed to hold my space, and, I'm proud to say, I snapped this off one of the cop's bikes."

Devon pulled out what looked like a little flashlight that could be mounted on a bicycle's handlebars.

"Is it their flashing lights?" Garrett asked. "Because that could be a useful decoy. Turn it on and toss it back at the police sometime to distract them when you need to make an escape." He reached out to touch it, but Devon held it back.

"Careful," Devon said. "It's got a light on this button, but it's actually a siren, so don't turn it on in here, it'll split our ears."

After this warning, Garrett was allowed to hold Devon's prize, a little thing about the size of a 35mm film canister, and probably expensive for no reason, just because precincts had money to burn and liked their toys.

"That would still make a good decoy," Tula said, "but really do be careful because if any of you set that off and my neighbors start complaining about me, I'll make sure you're sorry about it."

Garrett could understand her concern. Though there was supposedly an eviction moratorium, there were always ways around such things, and with all the intertwined decor in Tula's place, it would be an extra hassle to get evicted during the pandemic. Where would the plants go?

# 17.

Before the night ended, and while Devon was in the bathroom, Tula took Garrett aside and told him something that would haunt him for the better part of the next week.

"Hey, while Devon's draining the snake or pissing up the porcelain or whatever weird way he announced it," Tula began.

"He said he had to shake the dew off the lily," Garrett says. "He takes such delight in naughty words and dirty jokes, like a little boy."

"Yeah, it's cute at first, isn't it?" Tula asked. When Garrett raised his eyebrows, Tula clarified. "Don't get me wrong, he's one of the best guys I know, but he's *such* a guy and it can get exhausting. Your mileage may vary, but that's not what I want to talk to you about. Do you know how Devon and I became friends?"

"No," Garrett said. He knew a handful of intimate things about Devon by then, knew that he was a compulsive chewer (pencils, ice, but not gum). He knew that Devon had a younger sister he called Fi-fi to much annoyance because her name was Fiona (she was in college but still living at home). He knew Devon didn't want to talk about his father but didn't know why (was he dead? deadbeat? dead to Devon and Fi-fi regardless?). He knew that Devon dropped out of college because it wasn't challenging enough, a waste of time (Garrett told him Walt Whitman would have trusted him more as a dropout, and Devon said Whitman was great beard and loafing goals). But Garrett didn't know anything about how Devon met Tula.

"I was a psych major in college, it didn't take," Tula said. "But they let grad students offer free counseling for practice to the general public. I wasn't a grad student but they had undergrads doing the scheduling and reception and shit for work-study credit. Devon came in after his first trip to a war zone, I think it was Iraq, and we struck up a conversation while he was waiting for the counselor. Five minutes later and he decided he didn't want to talk to a trainee therapist, he wanted to have a drink with me."

"Nice brag," Garrett said.

Tula shrugged an eyebrow. "I would have made an excellent therapist," she said. "He eventually did talk out some of his issues with me, just some garden-variety PTSD, some panic attacks and intrusive thoughts and nightmares. I'm telling you all this because, first of all, as an amateur I'm not bound by confidentiality."

Garrett snorted. Tula smiled at him like he was her favorite nephew.

"And second of all," she continued, "because there's no way these protests aren't triggering his PTSD. To be clear, I'd trust that shitkicker with my life, but I also wouldn't want to sleep next to him in a room full of guns this summer. I'm not trying to scare you away from him but, you know, I would feel negligent if I didn't say something."

"Like Schrödinger's cat, both alive and not alive at the same time," Garrett said. "Devon's both trustworthy and potentially dangerous, just as you are telling me but also not telling me to worry about him. Is that your meaning?"

"Exactly," Tula said. "I knew you'd be our top student."

As much as Garrett didn't want this information to influence him, it did. There was an old movie with Humphrey Bogart and Gloria Grahame where this sort of thing happened. There they were, two people falling in adorable, easy, once-in-a-lifetime love, but a cloud hung over them because Bogart was the suspect in a murder. She wanted to believe that he wasn't the killer but kept doubting herself. He needed to know she believed in him regardless of what others thought, but he couldn't trust her until she agreed to marry him before the investigation was complete. Saying yes after his name was cleared wouldn't mean anything, but saying anything else before the detectives closed the case meant they were over. It wasn't fair, and in a lucky life they'd never have to know where exactly their trust ended, but that was life in *film noir*: the picture was black-and-white, but the difference between right and wrong was in a gray area.

Garrett didn't sleep soundly after Tula's warning, though he still loved being wrapped in Devon's big, hairy arms. Instead of losing himself in his work and feeling perfectly at home, Garrett walked on eggshells sometimes, and watched Devon when he was unaware to see if there weren't indications of panic and stress. He was ashamed to find he was relieved when Devon's friend came to town and Garrett was free to stay elsewhere for a week or two without having to make the decision himself. It felt a little cowardly, but it was only a matter of time until he'd be back, and he and Devon could return to normal. Distance leant clarity, absence made the heart grow fonder, and all of that.

Garrett bumped elbows with Wayne David Williams when he arrived as a greeting, a man who wore a military haircut and sounded just like Gomer Pyle from The Andy Griffith Show under his mask with a sneering Hulk mouth on it. He'd driven himself across the country, was ready to crash on the couch and get comfy, but first he got an eyeful of Devon and Garrett's *adieu*.

"I'm not saying you should text me nudes after you get to Tula's," Devon said, for indeed it was Tula who said he could crash with her, in the hopes that Garrett might house-sit for her next month while she tended to some family thing. "But I am saying I would appreciate them."

"I know you're joking," Garrett said, slightly surprised that Devon was sliding his hands up under Garrett's shirt in front of his friend, but willing to roll with it. He didn't do this in front of his female friends, was all, but maybe that was some form of modern chivalry that Wayne David did not warrant. "I can't go sending nudes through the satellites and clouds, what if I want to run for president someday?"

"Oh, you don't want to do that, it's a terrible job," Wayne David said, scrolling through his phone but still aware of them out of the corner of his eye.

"Send nudes now, save yourself from being a war criminal later," Devon said, kissing Garrett's cheek and neck.

Garrett reached behind himself for the doorknob, ready for this performance to end. He wondered if this amorousness wasn't a form of the hyper-arousal some people had as part of post-traumatic stress, Devon's form of restlessness and risk-taking. But then Garrett disliked himself for questioning the attention. After all, Devon was in love; he'd said so himself.

Garrett returned a few kisses once they were on the other side of the door, since there were no on-lookers in Devon's hallway.

"I am kidding about nudes, you know all our messages are being accumulated by the feds, and they don't deserve the thrill," Devon said, smiling and adjusting Garrett's backpack straps like he was about to send his only riot son off to school.

"And I was kidding about wanting to be president, I'm not a monster."

Devon giggled, and they shared a real kiss farewell — the kind that took a minute, and had you holding your breath, and would leave you dizzy with the lingering taste of someone else.

"I'll do my best to be a terrible roommate," Devon said as Garrett descended the stairs to leave. "If it's up to me, I'll run Wayne David off in less than a week."

"I can hear you out there, sir," Wayne David said from within the apartment. "Don't count your chickens yet, I'm very competitive."

"It's all good," Garrett said, pausing to reach up and lace his fingers with Devon. "I'll have fun with Tula, and I'm sure we'll have a playdate or two in the meantime."

"I'll hold you to that," Devon said, though he did have to let go when Garrett took the next step and moved away from him. Garrett thought a little space would do them good, simmer their new passion a bit so it didn't fizzle out. He didn't know at the time just how scorchingly their flame would burn.

# 18.

## *PTSD and Thee: The History, Causes, and Symptoms of Post-Traumatic Stress Disorder*

### *What Is PTSD?*

The Mayo Clinic defines post-traumatic stress disorder, commonly referred to as PTSD, thusly: "PTSD is a mental health condition that's triggered by a terrifying event — either experiencing it or witnessing it. Symptoms may include flashbacks, nightmares, and severe anxiety, as well as uncontrollable thoughts about the event. Most people who go through traumatic events may have temporary difficulty adjusting and coping, but with time and good self-care, they usually get better." The most upsetting word there, of course, is "usually," because sustained PTSD alters the brain permanently. Among other changes, the overabundance of stress and fear hormones may cause the memory center of the mind (the hippocampus) to shrink.

### *What Is the History of PTSD?*

PTSD was first recognized by the American Psychiatric Association (AMA) in the 1980s, but it was called by several other names long before that. Arguably the first recorded case of PTSD can be found in the *Epic of Gilgamesh*, which is itself the oldest surviving substantial work of literature (circa 2100 BC). When Gilgamesh witnesses his friend Enkidu's death, he is plagued by nightmares and intrusive recurring recollections of the event. There are examples in the Bible, and in the works of the ancient Greeks who called it "divine madness," and yet it was still difficult to pin down as a Thing for a while there. PTSD was "nostalgia" according to 17th-century Swiss physician Johannes Hofer. Philadelphia doctor Jacob Mendes Da Costa thought the well-documented symptoms of insomnia, depression, flashbacks, panic attacks, and suicide ideation of the U.S. Civil War veterans were associated with a cardiac condition, and so he called it "soldier's heart." For survivors of traumatic railway disasters, it was called "railroad spine" or "railroad brain" under the assumption that the stress resulted from some physical malady, perhaps lesions on the brain or spine. Cambridge psychologist Captain Charles Myers called it "shell shock" during World War I, and many doctors tried electroshock to cure it. After World War II, psychiatrist Abram Kardiner suggested psychiatric treatment for "traumatic neurosis," aka "combat stress reaction" or "battle fatigue" or any combination of words that described how badly human beings handled copious amounts of horror. By 1952, just in time for Vietnam, PTSD was included in the Diagnostic and Statistical Manual of Mental Disorders (DSM). However, it was removed in the second edition (DSM-2) in 1968, and had to be reinstated in 1980's DSM-3 because it hadn't gone anywhere.

### *What Causes PTSD?*

What terrifies you? What rips the veil off, reveals the matrix, and reminds you that — despite the happy delusion most humans function within — you are not now and have never been truly safe? Though war is a real show-stealer, any one of the following events can cause PTSD: deaths, rapes, accidents, disasters near or far, political and/or economic upheavals, military conflicts, illnesses, non-sexual assaults, and even particularly dehumanizing jobs. This is not an exhaustive list, just an exhausting one.

## *What Are the Symptoms of PTSD?*

The DSM-5 has a super convenient checklist of PTSD symptoms. Test yourself! Instructions: Below is a list of problems that people sometimes have in response to a very stressful experience. Please read each problem carefully and then circle one of the numbers (0-Not at all, 1-A little bit, 2-Moderately, 3-Quite a bit, 4-Extremely) to the right to indicate how much you have been bothered by that problem in the past month.

1. Repeated, disturbing, and unwanted memories of the stressful experience?    0 1 2 3 4

2. Repeated, disturbing dreams of the stressful experience?    0 1 2 3 4

3. Suddenly feeling or acting as if the stressful experience were actually happening again (as if you were actually back there reliving it)?    0 1 2 3 4

4. Feeling very upset when something reminded you of the stressful experience?    0 1 2 3 4

5. Having strong physical reactions when something reminded you of the stressful experience (for example, heart pounding, trouble breathing, sweating)?    0 1 2 3 4

6. Avoiding memories, thoughts, or feelings related to the stressful experience?    0 1 2 3 4

7. Avoiding external reminders of the stressful experience (for example, people, places, conversations, activities, objects, or situations)?    0 1 2 3 4

8. Trouble remembering important parts of the stressful experience?    0 1 2 3 4

9. Having strong negative beliefs about yourself,    0 1 2 3 4
other people, or the world (for example,
having thoughts such as: I am bad, there is
something seriously wrong with me, no one can
be trusted, the world is completely dangerous)?

10. Blaming yourself or someone else for the    0 1 2 3 4
stressful experience or what happened after it?

11. Having strong negative feelings such as fear,    0 1 2 3 4
horror, anger, guilt, or shame?

12. Loss of interest in activities that    0 1 2 3 4
you used to enjoy?

13. Feeling distant or cut off from other people?    0 1 2 3 4

14. Trouble experiencing positive feelings (for    0 1 2 3 4
example, being unable to feel happiness or
have loving feelings for people close to you)?

15. Irritable behavior, angry outbursts,    0 1 2 3 4
or acting aggressively?

16. Taking too many risks or doing things    0 1 2 3 4
that could cause you harm?

17. Being "superalert" or watchful or on guard?    0 1 2 3 4

18. Feeling jumpy or easily startled?    0 1 2 3 4

19. Having difficulty concentrating?    0 1 2 3 4

20. Trouble falling or staying asleep?    0 1 2 3 4

Sum all 20 numbers (the range will fall between 0-80) and use a cut-point score of 31-33 to give yourself an indication of whether you are disordered by post-traumatic stress. If left un-dealt-with, you may find yourself thinking of self-harm or suicide, so if you get a score of 30, maybe err on the side of caution and get some help.

### *How Can You Treat PTSD? Can It Be Cured?*

Bad news: kind of like having cancer or an addiction, once you've got PTSD, you're not so much cured as in recovery. How to get into a state of recovery? Take your pick:

- Use DIY coping mechanisms, aka the "self-care" tactics of avoiding known stressors, or self-calming to get through the stress you can't skip.
- Get psychotherapy for professional insight on how to recognize harmful behavioral patterns, safely confront triggering memories or places, and/or learn eye movement desensitization and reprocessing (EMDR) techniques.
- Take medications like antidepressants or anti-anxiety pharmaceuticals, or better drugs like cannabis, psilocybin, or lysergic acid diethylamide (LSD).

LSD may also help with cluster headaches and migraines, not that medical professionals are allowed to study the effects too much in this here land of the free, because President Nixon once said so.

### *Why Can't You Just Get Over It?*

Some Civil War doctors believed "nostalgia" only affected soldiers with "feeble will." This is not an uncommon assumption, perhaps because some people can experience trauma without experiencing much emotional fallout. The reason for this? Well, we're all special, unique snowflakes, that's why. Those who already have a history of depression, panic disorder, or OCD are more susceptible to being overwhelmed by trauma. Those who might have avoided PTSD if they had a supportive family or friend group, may experience it without those connections. Compounding traumas can wear you down as well, like seeing death once and then having to see it again because it's part of your job, or surviving a rape only to get doxxed, mocked, and threatened during the investigation or trial. That smaller hippocampus mentioned at the top of this topic may not be caused by PTSD, but instead could be a pre-existing factor that makes one more susceptible to improper trauma processing. Factors that make PTSD less likely to manifest are known as "resilience factors" (a strong support network, a bevy of well-oiled coping mechanisms, or moral confidence in the choices you made during the traumatic event), which then makes it sound as if PTSD is the result of a lack of resilience, i.e. weakness. "That's not true," they'll say, "PTSD is common, it's natural, it's understandable." But it's not all that normal, is it? And it doesn't happen to everyone, does it? Additionally, even if you have health insurance, mental health is subjective as hell, and they'll do their best not to cover your treatment because, funnily enough, the insurance you buy specifically to cover your care employs people whose sole job is to find a way to deny your care. Problematically, in America a gun is cheaper than a therapist and easier to get, so good luck out there!

# 19.

The reason Wayne David and Devon were friends was because they'd met under extenuating circumstances. Specifically, while Devon was arriving in Iraq, Wayne David was on his way out, getting drunk and literally turning cartwheels until he was too intoxicated to do anything but fall down. That was a euphoric mania in response to his own trauma, a flood of pleasure hormones on being free to return home that would quickly crash him into a depression when he was back in his stepmom's basement with no job prospects and no direction.

People saw Wayne David so rudderless and often wondered why he didn't sign up for another tour, because a job was a job, right? The fury Wayne David felt at having civilians judge him for refusing to return to a place that would snap their psyches in half was … quite a doozy. It took him six months to even get out of the basement, but ultimately he did, for a position on a lawn maintenance crew called Patriot Pruning that only hired veterans.

He started to dislike his coworkers quickly, however. They complained more than elderly people in line at the post office about not getting the recognition they deserved as heroes. While Wayne David could consider himself a hero, technically, he also knew that he was still the same slob as before, and no more special than anyone else. So Wayne David was a man without a country for a spell, until he went back to the basement and started making opinion videos and posting them online, and now he was doing that full-time. His taxes said he was a Freelance Content Creator, a Self-Employed Sole

Proprietor, both of which were fancy terms for what he actually called himself on introduction: a YouTube Puke.

Wayne David and Devon stayed in contact and remained friends for several reasons. One, Devon met Wayne David when he was at his best, and Wayne David was charming as hell in a good mood. Two, when Wayne David found himself an outsider everywhere he went, the only guy he could think of who'd understand that was Devon. As far as W.D. knew, Devon was a guy who'd never found true cohesion with any group, and he seemed alright, confident and fun-loving and sharp, so it was okay to be a guy just like him. Three, they went camping when Devon got back from Iraq, and they got so stupendously high on acid and mushrooms (a combo known as "hippie flipping") that they were forever bonded on a soul-level that went deeper than blood or country. Wayne David hadn't known his soul brother was into dudes though.

"So you've got a boyfriend?" he asked when Devon returned from the PDA that went down in the hallway.

"He's my riot son," Devon said.

"I see that. And what happened to old what's-her-name … Delia?"

"Delilah," Devon said. "She broke my heart so badly I've turned from women entirely." Devon laughed at his own joke as he retrieved and opened two beers, one for each of them. "No, I've always been pansexual, and Delilah and I were polyamorous." Devon took a long sip. "That's how she met her new fiancé, Calista."

"Oh my." Wayne David grinned because it sounded at once awful and hilarious. "So what I'm hearing is you're the kind of man who takes all cummers, is that it?"

"That's it in a nutshell," Devon said, kicking up his feet in his recliner. "In fact, I want you to make sure they write that on my grave if I die first, can you do that for me?"

"They may not lemme spell it the way we mean, but I'll do my best."

Another laugh, and just like that it was like no time had passed at all since they'd last sat shooting the shit. It was only when Wayne David's stomach rumbled that Devon remembered his hosting duties.

"Oh man, you're hungry." Devon opened up a food-ordering app on his phone and handed it over. "Pick out some lunch and then we'll make our plans."

The discussion they entered into over their tacos and nachos segued into a podcast when Wayne David decided their chatter regarding cop-on-cop crime was too good to deny to the denizens of the internet. They wiped their mouths and paused their munching so people wouldn't complain about the sound of chewing ("I read an article that said people who can't stand the sound of chewing are brain damaged," Devon said, and Wayne David responded with, "Excuse me, we prefer the term 'dain bramaged,' thank you."). They re-donned their masks, got a foot or two closer, and hit record.

"People get upset when they hear 'all cops are bastards' but —"

"ACAB, baby," Devon interjected.

"— there's a ton of evidence that good cops and soldiers and guards all quit, and it's only the bastards who remain."

"The bastards win and flourish and get shiny metals for their service," Devon said. "Let's give the folks some examples, Wayne David."

"That's right, let's tell some true stories. Now, a lot of people know the story of Serpico because they're Al Pacino fans," Wayne David said. "Are you a Pacino fan, Devon?"

"Yeah, but if we're talking about favorite roles, I'll take Cruising over Serpico for cops, and Dog Day Afternoon over Scarface for criminals," Devon said.

"Oh, we got a connoisseur over here, okay then. In the presence of greatness."

Devon laughed and Wayne David started pulling up facts.

"The real Frank Serpico didn't want to be a dirty cop in the 1970s, refused to be on the take to ignore corruption, and for his efforts he was likely set up to be shot in the face. He was for sure left for dead by his brothers in blue."

Devon chimed in with, "Serpico likes to think of himself as a 'lamp lighter' more than a 'whistleblower,' a light-bringer a la Paul Revere. And while Paul's reputation is overinflated, it's a pretty idea."

"Better than the other light-bringer Lucifer, maybe, as far as branding?" Wayne David asked.

"Maybe. I'd go with Prometheus myself, stealing fire from the gods to give to the mortals, because like ... Robin Hood eat your heart out, you know?"

Wayne David laughed. "Okay, so there's one example of a good apple in the bunch, you can't unspoil the rest, that's not how it works."

"Not at all, literally the phrase 'one bad apple spoils the bunch' is about the ethylene gas given off by overripe and rotting fruit, it putrefies the rest just by being near them. You can't unrot the spoiled."

"Oowhee, you should embroider that on a sampler," Wayne David said, and got another laugh out of Devon, one of those delightfully sweet giggles simply too cute to come out of a bearded barbarian, and yet it did. "But it is true that if you're not corrupt like your cohort, they will frag you out."

"Frag," Devon said, Googling definitions as he spoke. "Such a fun word. Comes from the fragmentation grenade. 'To frag' is to kill or wound a fellow soldier intentionally."

"Yeah, probably because he's some snitch. You got any profiles in discourage you want to highlight?"

"Alright, yeah, in more recent memory, let's go to Standing Rock," Devon said, bringing up his own notes. "You may remember: the Dakota Access Pipeline, fondly known as DAPL."

"Dapple like the light through trees in a forest."

"Indeed, we're talking bad apples at DAPL," Devon said. "Quick memory refresh: big dirty oil pipeline going through the Standing Rock Reservation of native land and through integral clean waterways. The people say, hey, fuck you, get off our land, and the government of course said …"

"This land is your land? No, this land is our land," Wayne David said, referencing the song.

"From California to New York island, correct. In come the feds, in come privately hired goons, off fuck Obama and the Democrats, and the abuse against citizens was tremendous. You may have seen uniformed psychos macing people standing in frigid water with glee on their socio faces, you may have seen video of cops spraying people with water hoses in freezing nighttime temperatures."

"You gotta love that," Wayne David said, disgust creeping into his voice even as they struggled to keep this amusing. "You want water? We'll give you water, upside your head."

"Icy jets of water, tear gas of course, and concussion grenades that blew the flesh off the arm of a protester aka water protector. She nearly lost that arm and it's forever maimed, courtesy of her own government. Six months of protest, over 750 arrests, and in the end that pipeline was built anyway and has been operating since June of 2017."

"Goddammit," was all Wayne David had to say about that.

"Well, the reason I bring it up is because I'd heard two cops quit in solidarity with the water protectors, and people were saying, 'See? Good cops either become bad or they quit,' and I was trying to pull up research on that, and guess what? Fake news."

"Shit," was all Wayne David could muster that time.

"My friend Tula was out at Standing Rock, and it was brutal. It actually says more that none of those thugs quit, they were fine with what they were doing. You know you can't unpoison water and soil, everyone, just like you can't un-rot cop apples. When we say they're all bastards, we're right eventually, and you know it."

Devon took another swig of beer, found the bottom of his bottle and didn't like it. Wayne David would have handed over his own, if it weren't for the damn global plague.

"I've got one more for the road for our listeners. Marines, as you know, are merely cops of another stripe, right? In the case of one former special operations chief, you had a whole group of his fellow Marines turn Serpico on him, right?"

"Elite commando Serpicos," Devon said. "The goodest of the supposed good guys."

"Right. While the pipeline's getting laid in the States in 2017, this select specimen is over in Iraq and going full psycho. Members of Alpha Platoon's Seal Team 7 said he stabbed a bound captive teenager to death unprovoked, and made his troops pose for pictures with the body."

"A real no-no since Abu Ghraib embarrassed us so." Devon's festive mood was flagging as well.

"They said he shot civilians dead for sport, including an old man and a schoolgirl, which is, what's the word for doing that again?"

"Murder?"

"That's it," Wayne David said. "This dude's fellow soldiers were told it would tank their careers if they didn't stop talking, but they kept on talking because with comrades like that, who needs enemies, you feel me?"

"His nickname was Blade," Devon said, searching for more facts as Wayne David talked.

"Ain't that charming? They finally just demoted his rank for the charge of posing with that one person's body, which is something he did more often than once, sending emails of selfies and whatnot with decapitated heads, bragging."

"So not in trouble for the killing, just for the snapshot, cool," Devon said.

Reaching peak sarcasm, Wayne David said, "And that's not even the best part. You want to tell everyone the ending of that story?"

"President Dipshit granted him clemency! Said he was a 'great fighter' and invited him to have some bad shrimp and worse conversation at Mar-a-Lago."

"God bless this mess called America."

# 20.

"Is it weird that I'm kind of excited for something to go sideways?" Wayne David asked as he and Devon left the apartment the next morning, masked against gas and dressed to transgress.

"I mean, like any NASCAR fan, you don't wish for a crash *per se*, but you can't deny you would be thrilled to see one," Devon said, leading Wayne David into a train station and swiping his pass twice to let each of them through the turnstile. They had a ways to go for that day's action, taking place at the plaza in front of City Hall.

"You've made a deep cut there, sir," Wayne David said.

"Nah, but really," Devon said as he squirted them both with some hand sanitizer, "you've been inside for what, three months straight?"

"Longer, I was doing social isolating for weeks before it was cool," Wayne David said.

"You're probably just starved for interaction of any sort, my man, good or bad."

Devon was diagnosing himself as well, in part. One night without Garrett and he was jonesing for him as hard as he'd ever missed any drug, and Devon had mourned many substances. He'd jerked off in the shower over Garrett, fantasized about him until he fell asleep, and dreamed about him in confusing disconnected contexts all night.

Devon should have been embarrassed, but he wasn't. Sure, it was pretty immature to be this prostrate over some kid, some fling hardly a fortnight old, but there was no denying how he felt. He loved the little girly fleece sleep socks Garrett wore, the unflappable control he had over his facial expressions, his crooked goddamn teeth whenever he finally smiled, and his thoughts so organized and mature beyond his years (and Devon's years and so many others). Maybe Devon had just been lonely too long, after Delilah and after the lockdowns, but maybe he also knew that he'd found a rare gem on the street covered in multiple layers of fabric and behind a chemical haze. Could be either reason, or could be a combo of both. Whichever way, Devon still couldn't believe his luck, and he never wanted to lose his new treasure.

Wayne David wanted to talk to everyone at the protest, but he wanted to start with the cops. Usually, this was not abided from most of Devon's friends and colleagues, but Wayne David wore a members-only style jacket with one small generic patch that marked him as a veteran ("I would never wear this back home, too much Walmart patriotism, a gift from my uncle's new girlfriend, who I hate, so if I have to burn this to avoid detection, no need to twist my arm."), and of course, old W.D. had that southern charm that could make anyone get the vapors, even thugs of the state.

All Wayne David had to do was ask, "Excuse me, officers, may I get some of your thoughts for the folks back home?" and boom, he was in, and Devon got scarce. He'd given Wayne David his transit card because Devon knew a lot more hidey holes in this city than he'd ever even admit to, and Wayne David might need the safe haven of the subway at a moment's notice, so if they lost track of each other, each of them had the means to squirrel away. He thought they'd spend the day apart, doing their own things, but Devon wasn't out there for two hours of milling, marching, and "mmhmm"-ing to chants before Wayne David found him again, his eyes wide and alarmed.

"Those pricks are about to bull-rush," Wayne David said. "They told me now was a good time to get inside because they are clearing the courtyard today."

"They've decided we've had enough free speech, haven't they?" Devon asked.

"It's Flag Day," Wayne David said. "They like their symbolism and think all this protesting is disrespecting them."

"They fucking would, what did you hear? Any details?"

"I think they're waiting for vehicles with their shields and then they're going to start busting through to secure this area for themselves."

"Bet they're planning on putting up barricades," Devon said. "Bet they've got fencing in those vehicles, too."

"Do we go? Stay? Do you have a tactic for this?"

"I stay, I'm here for this," Devon said. "If you want to go, I'll point you to the nearest subway. If you want to stay and don't want to get arrested, I suggest keeping towards the center of groups, not the frontlines. And stretch your legs; stay loose in case you gotta run, duck, or even climb some shit trying not to get grabbed. And take this just in case." Devon handed over one of Michelle's business cards. "She's a lawyer and a friend of mine if you do get snatched up."

"Where are you gonna be?" Wayne David asked as he disappeared the card into a pocket. He was no runner — it was the aspect of Wayne David that made him a suitable soldier and a better friend.

"I can get a little bit closer because I'm press, but I'm not a participant, officially. I'll stay off to the sides as much as possible and try to get a good view."

"Wither thou goest, my dude," Wayne David said, and Devon would have smiled if he hadn't heard the crackle of a bullhorn, which put him on alert.

"City property is now closed to the public," boomed a voice across the charming trees and sunshine and bustling humanity in the plaza. A round of boos, hisses, and scoffs followed.

"The public has to get off public property, really?" asked a person in the crowd.

The booming voice continued. "You have ten minutes to clear the area before you are subject to arrest for trespassing."

"There's no way to get everyone out of here in ten minutes!" said a far more panicked person among the citizenry.

"Trespassers will be prosecuted to the fullest extent of the law."

Devon checked his watch as he moved into position, Wayne David following in his wake. Ten minutes was more like seven and a skosh, a smidge, some change. As soon as the boys and broads in blue had their gear, they began roughing the crowd back, and consuming anyone who didn't lay back nice and orderly like wheat under a tractor.

Those who were captured were cuffed and made to kneel in a line against the building. The initial line of them soon grew two and then three people deep.

Devon stayed on until he got a bit of footage of those bound detainees getting tear gassed for no earthly reason but assholery on the part of the police. Then he tapped Wayne David so they could move out together, and take their chances with the rest of the fray.

# 21.

As footage and news of the plaza push circulated throughout that afternoon, a new plan was formulated in shadowy quarters of the internet to take back the territory later that night. Devon detected the rumblings of it as he was home during the high noon hours, recharging for the next leg of the day and trying not to text Garrett 400 times, as that would seem needy, suffocating, uncool. He did have a picture of Garrett on his phone, just one picture of him sitting yogi-style on the bed with a spring of hair falling over his forehead, noting something down with a purple gel pen. One day deprived of the kid and it was like Garrett was never here at all, or would never be back again. It annoyed Devon that he was fighting so much seventh-grade emotional drama, but he also kind of liked it, that he could feel so young and foolish again. Kind of nice to know he was still capable of such silly sentiment, it was invigorating, if aggravating.

Wayne David felt similarly about the events of the day, stressful though it was to be in a scrum of panicking people trying to escape an enclosed space. W.D. particularly liked the idea that people wanted to take the building back, occupy that space.

"Are we going to show up for that? I'm game to show up for that," Wayne David said.

Devon smirked at him and said, "What do you think?"

Soon enough it was time to dress in nondescript clothing, cover all identifying marks, and set some safety rules.

"I'm not saying you shouldn't do anything illegal, and I'm not saying I won't," Devon told his buddy as they went back out that evening, stars already glinting in the dusky sky. "But for fuck's sake don't film yourself doing it, and try not to let anyone else film you doing it either."

"Right," Wayne David said. "Don't break anything, don't take anything, don't make the morning news."

Devon snorted. "You got it, dude."

This night was the first egregious fight Devon had witnessed personally. The people who came out at night were not the same sort of people who came out for the cause in the daytime. Allies went home. The people who believed in police reform more than police abolishment, they turned in for the evenings. Those who came out at night were angrier, often had scores to settle against the police or the powers that be in general. People who lost their homes during the housing bubble crash? Would love to occupy public property for a while. People who've paid more on their student loans than the cost of their education with no relief, no release? Happy to throw a brick or two, take back a few cents here or there in repair costs. Anyone who'd ever been personally harassed or humiliated by the police? Eager to chuck their tear gas canisters back in their faces.

Just after 10 PM, the temporary barriers and fences that had gone up that morning, and been decorated with flowers and banners that held the names of the cop-slain dead in the afternoon, were breached. Some citizens had come with power tools, with bolt cutters, and when they opened enough holes for people to enter the courtyard *en masse*, the police attempted to stand their ground.

But the cops were in the building, not the courtyard. When the citizenry flooded in, they used the police barriers to keep the officers in there, barred the doors, blocked the windows. When tear gas canisters were launched at the public, they were quickly scooped up and dumped back inside City Hall, just giving the cops a taste of their own medicine. Moreover, some of the punks in the crowd had fireworks from home, and they launched those in through the windows, presumably to discourage egress. The fire glittered cheerily on the shards with each lighting. Devon found himself mesmerized for a moment by the sparkling, until Wayne David grasped him by the back of the neck in excitement.

"I'm going in," he said. "I haven't felt this alive in years."

"Don't get shot," Devon said, like it was a choice. He watched Wayne David climb through the fencing, his neck gaiter of a mask stretched up and secured under his ball cap, his eyes dazzling with excitement.

Devon hadn't felt like this in years either. When was his last *grand mal* panic attack? Four years ago, five? It had been a while since the last big one, but he knew the symptoms every time. His heart felt odd, like it was floating in water, and his breathing got fast, shallow. The people looking at him could tell something was going down. "Sir, are you okay? Do you have seizures or something, you don't look right." He waved off concern. Devon felt light-headed, even faint, and when his vision started blotting out, Devon knew it was time to go. He wasn't safe here if he was about to pass out.

Devon abruptly left the heat of the crowd, the boom of fireworks. It was too close to nights in Iraq, in Syria, too much like bombs, warring factions, no place to hide. Devon was back home in the U.S.A. though, and he had to remind himself: *you can leave, you can hide, you can rest.*

He did not want to rest alone, however. Being by himself, in this agitated state, would be maddening. He set his path towards Tula's place, on foot because Wayne David still had his transit card, and because the trains weren't running after dark anyway with the city locked down under a curfew. His feet were hurting, his scalp was itchy with the salt in his sweat, and his ears rang long after he was in quiet streets again, a tinnitus hangover from the noise of the crowd. It took him over an hour to get where folks would know his name.

Devon would have come to Tula regardless of Garrett tonight, because she was always his touchstone when he was having a bad spell of the old PTSD. He used to worry he was taking advantage of her — free emotional labor and all that — until he made sure he gave as good as he got, and paid back her effort so he wasn't just leeching off her brain. He ushered her into the dubious world of being an independent reporter, and she seemed to have no regrets about that so far.

Actually, Devon would have preferred that Garrett not see him like this: semi-crazed, jittery, jibbering. But Tula was his sponsor for this problem, basically, and he still wouldn't mind seeing the boy, even if it had to be under subpar circumstances.

As luck would have it, when Devon arrived at Tula's place and knocked, it was Garrett alone who opened the door. Beleaguered and out-of-sorts such as Devon was, Garrett nevertheless smiled wide at the sight of him, and opened his arms wider for a hug.

# IV. INSURRECTION

# 22.

The day of the City Hall Insurrection, as it would soon be known, was quite a bit calmer for Garrett. He made plans with Tula to talk to her college pal, a lawyer who'd been attending the protests and would be the exact right person to answer a few questions Garrett had about the law side of law enforcement. Not for nothing, Michelle was also Black, and how comfortably she sat astride the fence between two sides that shouldn't be (but often were) pitted against one another, was another area of interest for Garrett. Perhaps he might broach the topic after he extracted some legalese about the rights of protesters, and took down her advice on what kind of lawyer he'd need to find for the rest of his questions.

Michelle was a junior civil rights attorney, had a background mostly in housing discrimination, but still felt compelled to advise people when she could, and refer them to more specialized members of the bar depending on their circumstances. Could she help bail folks out of jail? Yes. Could she see them through a full criminal prosecution? No, but she knew the people who knew the people who would. That's why she handed out her card during the day, though she went home each night as soon as the cops said so.

"I do my good deeds on the back end," Michelle said, "but I don't want to get gassed or assaulted or arrested if I can avoid it. I have asthma, I have important advocacy work to do that does not get done without me, and as I tell people: any little bit of help is still help."

Garrett and Tula were standing at the door of Michelle's office, watching her sort through her desk on her lunch break, both the physical and electronic inboxes. She offered them to partake of the instant coffee packets and individually wrapped tea sachets that topped the hot-and-cold water cooler at the door, but begged their tolerance in asking them to stay on the far side of the room instead of come in and sit. The office hardly had room to maintain a couple of stiff chairs and shelves full of law books, let alone six feet of slow-the-spread distance. Michelle said she was hoping her husband might come in and install some higher shelves to create just a little more breathing room — there was wasted space up near the ceiling that could store quite a few dusty old tomes — but since this office like so many she'd had before was only temporary, and since there wasn't any budget for more shelves when there already were shelves that she simply didn't prefer, and the world being what it was … etc. Tula and Garrett agreed to hug the wall. Tula sipped some water through a coffee straw that could slide under her mask without issue.

"Yeah, not everyone has the resources to hit the streets," Garrett agreed, always careful himself to avoid guilting people who didn't walk the talk of revolution. Maybe they were fair-weather frauds who didn't really want the changes they virtue-signaled about, as Garrett often suspected, or maybe they were neurotic shut-ins who would be a liability in the scrum instead of an asset. Garrett only knew that he would dislike himself if he wasn't out participating during this most momentous summer, and he tried to concentrate his energy on what he could do personally, instead of expending it on what others should do if they really wanted to change the world.

"Plus, there are always people who are born for the frontlines, who want to be there," Tula said. "People like Devon, they're champing at the bit to go out and cause a ruckus, sometimes the best thing to do is to rally support for the warriors and let them fight."

"Oh, you know Devon, too?" Garrett asked Michelle.

"As well as he knows me," Michelle said, a sly smile in her eyes as she gave one of those lawyerly answers that neither confirmed, nor denied, nor provided any new information whatsoever.

"Devon really gets around," Tula said, and again that didn't give Garrett any facts, but it did create an impression. It gave Garrett a twinge of … jealousy? He had forgotten for a moment that Devon wasn't his exclusive friend, he was friends with other people — people who knew Devon far longer and in many strange lands and circumstances that Garrett would never know.

"One good thing about men, they've got that recklessness that really comes in handy sometimes," Michelle said, setting aside a folder and opening up a lunch bag as intricate as a tackle box. "Jump in a hole to see how far down it goes, break something to find out what's inside, start a fight just to see who can win." She shrugged. "Sometimes that's the wild gamble you need to win the pot, though I myself disapprove of gambling and don't tolerate it."

"It's men like Devon that go a long way in vouching for the rest of the gender, otherwise I'd be interested in a world without men, without that kind of gambling," Tula said, before turning to Garrett to add, "No offense meant, just a nice thought I have quite often."

"I'm not saying we're worth the trouble," Garrett said with a grin, always happy to be included in girl-talk, despite his lack of qualifying attributes. "But what about procreation?"

"Dolly," Michelle said, taking her first bite of salad and pointing her fork towards Tula, like they'd done this routine before, and could hand the baton back and forth.

"Parton?" Garrett asked.

"Dolly the sheep," Tula said. "Though she was named after Dolly Parton. So you know how we all have to have at least one X chromosome to survive?" Garrett started to nod, but this was a rhetorical exercise he need not participate in. "Okay, so here's the long and short of it: regular human chromosomes are 23 pairs, 46 chromosomes in total. You get some from mom and some from dad, including the sex chromosomes X and Y. Normally, mom has two X chromosomes, making her female, and making her fetus and all fetuses female at first."

"Isn't that fun?" Michelle said. "That Eve being made from Adam's rib stuff is patriarchy nonsense; man comes from woman, every time."

"That's right, there is no man without woman," Tula continues, "and if you've seen a Y chromosome, the one that gives dad his normal XY male genes? It's stunted, weak. Y chromosomes have less information in them, which is why matrilineal conditions like the hemophilia that ravaged the royal families of Europe for a while killed the men, but only dwelt within the women. How, you ask?"

Garrett laughed. He hadn't asked, but he was absolutely curious.

"Because if your body had one hemophilia X and a non-disordered X chromosome to choose from, it would take the better blueprints. To be clear, it's not impossible for women to deal with hemophilia, it's just far more unlikely because it would take two grandmothers giving the defective gene to each parent, and both parents unluckily passing them to their daughter. However, with men, if you get mom's bad X and dad's good Y, the Y chromosome still doesn't have enough information for an override. We all rely on the X for basic human schematics."

"The X has legs," Michelle chimed in, illustrating with her hands. One hand up doing the V for victory and peace, the other giving a downward V like an A or tipi tent. Joined together, they made an X that could walk around and wave.

"The Y may be strong on top, but ..." Tula held out a pinky finger and curled it a couple of times like a wriggling little shrimp. "It's insufficient down below."

"Aha," Michelle laughed, moving next to some sort of sandwich in a pita pocket.

Michelle was getting lunch and a show today, while Garrett was getting hungry and revved up for the women's war, the fem-olution, or the up-sheval, perhaps.

"Which leads us to the topic at hand," Tula resumed a satisfied arched brow over her mask. "Men are the weaker sex, genetically, and they are the expendable ones when it comes to procreation. It's why you can shoot male deer whenever you like, but only the females when you mean to thin the herd. You need a uterus for the next generation, and no one's invented an artificial one of those yet."

"Too busy with boner pills," Michelle said.

"It's going to be quite a fight if they ever do," Tula resumed. "An artificial womb would throw gasoline on the abortion debate. If you could transfer an embryo, no woman would be forced to carry a pregnancy to term for the sake of an unborn life, but then you have to decide if all life really is precious, because we may run into overpopulation, and miscarriages are the body's natural veto abortion. Without that, who wants to support every nonviable fetus in the world? Certainly not men."

"Certainly not," Garrett agreed.

"Glad you concur, comrade," Tula said. "Where was I? Oh, right, so: if you don't have exactly 46 chromosomes, you probably have some sort of disorder. Down's syndrome and Edwards' syndrome are due to having an extra copy of certain chromosomes, I forget which ones. And some people have XYY or XXY or triple X chromosomes."

"Probably they're the superhumans of the future," Garrett suggested.

"May they have mercy on us all," Michelle said, with a mock-solemn nod.

Tula raised her hands in praise. "Some women can even survive, *and reproduce*, with just a single X chromosome."

"XO, like a kiss and hug on your love letters," Michelle said with a smooch sound.

Garrett yelped another little laugh, and thought they should hit the stage with this routine.

Tula went on. "But a YO is a KO, a knock-out, a no-go. So my theory is, if a woman can survive with just an X and a goose egg, nothing else needed and no man required, then we're halfway there. And that's where Dolly comes in. The answer is not in a goose egg, but a sheep's egg."

There went Garrett's free association with Mother Goose. Mother Sheep was the answer apparently, or rather Mother Dolly.

Tula brought it home. "You may not remember because it happened in the 90s and you were an unfertilized egg yourself back then, but Dolly the sheep was 'cloned' by taking a cell from the mammary gland of one sheep and combining it with the egg of another, the surrogate, and it worked. Dolly was a white-face Dorset sheep born to a Scottish Blackface mother, and it was the first time a mammal was cloned from an adult cell, and if that isn't the future of human reproduction in New Lesbos — my ideal all-woman utopian future — then I just don't know what is."

"Men will be vestigial," Michelle said with a tolerant smile for her friend.

Tula looked Garrett dead in the eyes to deliver the sobering news. "Men will not be necessary."

Garrett started clapping. Suddenly his questions about being Black in the legal profession during the infuriating summer of 2020 didn't seem to matter so much. Not when there was a far brighter future possibility out there.

# 23.

On leaving Michelle's office, Garrett had a choice to make. While it was clear that there were more protests to cover, that day just like every day for nearly three weeks, there were also human matters to consider, and Tula was prioritizing those.

"I've got to get to my PO Box, and find an ATM, and go grocery shopping," she said. "If you need anything, let me know and I can pick it up for you. After that I'm sliding into a long, hot bath and then into my pajamas for the rest of the day. You want in on that? Make it a dedicated self-care day?"

"I …" Garrett began, but then halted. On one hand, he saw the rumblings of the City Hall demonstration that morning and felt obligated to go, but he also didn't disagree with Michelle that not all fights were fought in the trenches, and even those that were needed outside support. Didn't he deserve a day of rest? It was Sunday, after all, and even God rested on the seventh day. Besides, time with Tula could prove to be just as valuable as time with Michelle, not just for what she could teach him about surviving on the boom-and-bust of freelance work, but also for all she knew about Devon.

It was the rumblings of another sort that finally made the decision, the rumblings of Garrett's stomach. He was still irrationally hungry for lunch.

"If you could pick me up some ramen if they have it, and any dried fruit or trail mix, I'll get us a hot lunch and meet you back at yours in an hour?"

It was agreed. Tula requested Vietnamese takeout, which Garrett had almost formulated a dirty joke in response to, but Tula beat him to it. "Yes, because I want to eat out a Vietnamese box. Don't pop a gasket trying to talk more trash than me, you can't do it, home school."

Garrett went away laughing to gather their food, enchanted by Tula in ways he never expected, and hoping they would stay friends forever. He'd never had a big sister, and so had no reservations in wanting one.

Garrett arrived back at Tula's laden with spring rolls, pad Thai, vegetarian pho, and a veggie stir fry in sweet chili sauce. There was shrimp in the spring rolls, but otherwise Garrett had secured meat-free dishes full of tofu and greens. He didn't know Tula's preferences, but pork was the one meat Garrett tried his best to avoid, on a theory that they're considered the most unclean animal for a reason, namely that they're so close to human beings, aka "long pigs." Maybe he'd read an article about it once, or maybe it was a holdover from biblical teachings of kosher kitchen maintenance, but … somehow shellfish got under Garrett's wire yet pigs did not. It was illogical, and yet still true.

The pajamas Tula was wearing when she welcomed him into her home again were adorable. A matching set with complementary socks full of pastel colors and images of happy little tea characters: cups, saucers, tea bags, tea spoons — all holding hands and frolicking. Garrett said, "Aww!" the moment he noticed them, and Tula smirked. She was still wearing a mask indoors out of an abundance of precaution, but it too had the proper accent colors to match her outfit, as did the towel turban on her head that surely wasn't necessary with hair as short as hers, and yet, there it was again: illogical yet true.

Twenty minutes later, Garrett was also showered, lotioned, and jealously watching Tula use chopsticks while he had to eat his food with both a fork and a spoon if he wanted any of it to reach his mouth. Apparently Tula learned how to use chopsticks when she spent two years in the Peace Corps in the Philippines.

"Ugh, everyone else has already done so much, I feel like I'm behind," Garrett said, chewing on a particularly firm mushroom like a piece of gum.

"You're a baby, you're what, nineteen? Already out here doing more than most people do in a lifetime."

"I'm eighteen," Garrett said, "as of next week."

"And you still think you're behind?" Tula snorted. "You haven't even started yet. Legally, you're nobody, just someone's tall fetus out here waiting to vote. Trust me, you'll get way more experience than you'd ever want soon enough. Life has a real consent problem when it fucks you."

"Good to know," Garrett said.

"Don't mean to offend you, swearing so much, although I do find my cussing grows exponentially when I'm around the innocent, the goody-goody, the religious," she said. "Devon said you were raised pretty devout, is that accurate?"

Tula finished clearing one paper carton and poured herself more tea from yet another precious-looking teapot. Garrett took a palate-cleansing sip of an iced coffee he ordered alongside the food, then spoke.

"My parents and their group consider themselves neo-Anabaptists, a cousin sect to Mennonites and Amish and such, but a little more 'of the world.' The crux of it all though is that you have to choose to be baptized, it doesn't count the same if it's done to you as an infant or a child, and that non-choice can be overridden later. If you choose not to be baptized, at least in my family, you pretty much demote yourself to any other heathen in the world."

Tula nodded. "Is that why you had to leave home, you didn't get baptized?"

"I was willing, but something else came up first," Garrett said.

"Was it your dick?"

Garrett let out a short laugh. "Yeah, that's pretty much the long and short of it."

"The length and girth of it, you mean," Tula said with a playful leer.

"You are a dirty talker," Garrett said, feeling his cheeks flare hot.

"Aw, blushing babe. I'll stop, I'll reign it back. So no baptism, then. Did you want one?"

"I don't think it matters much either way. I mean, if there is a God, who more than He would understand why some people aren't, can't be, or won't be baptized? Why would he hold something like that against their soul for all eternity? I am of the impression that the

Kingdom of Heaven wants its pilgrims to return home in the end, you know? And if that's so, you have to give people a practical path that leads them there."

"Oh, like DACA kids," Tula said, noticing her fingernails and pulling out a caddy of polishes. "We want Dreamers in the Promised Land, but we also want them to earn it, otherwise how to be sure they appreciate it enough?"

Garrett nodded. "Yeah, the Government of Heaven isn't all about equal treatment either, some people get a greased chute to paradise, some a spiked ladder, but it's theoretically possible for everyone to get in."

"Is that something you believe in, an afterlife? You said 'if' there's a God, is that an 'if' on the afterlife, too?"

"For now, yes," Garrett said. "I've always liked the term 'agnostic' ever since I found it in the dictionary. I think we're all agnostic. There's not really a choice in the matter — we literally can't know until we die forever. But the theory you like best in this life can help form a purpose and a philosophy on Earth, and I want one of those. A purpose or a philosophy, or both."

"On paper, I'm Greek Orthodox, but in reality, I love me some Buddhism," Tula said. "I haven't taken too much time to explore the nuances, too busy getting all that life experience, but I like it better than all the thou-shalt-not religions. It's more of a live-your-best-life instruction."

"I've heard good things. About Buddhism, I mean."

"Well, here," Tula said, getting up to grab a book off her shelf that claimed to hold the *Basics of Buddhism*. "Bone up on it. I don't need that book anymore so consider it a gift, and when you're done, pay it forward."

"Will do."

# 24.

By the time Devon arrived, Tula and Garrett had gotten deep into the self-care forest. Fingernails were painted, toenails also, face masks were applied, yummy-scented incense was lit, and for a couple of hours neither one of them looked at their phones or tracked the news. It was maybe not the best moment to be unplugged. But much like having children, it was never the right time, and yet if you wanted it done, you had to just knuckle down and insist on it. Thus, while Tula was in the bathroom and Garrett looking at the rest of her books to see if he could detect a theme, Devon's knock on the door was the first intrusion of the outside world on their peaceful evening.

Devon looked a sweaty mess. He was panting, his eyes were twitchy, and he had the stink of panic and tear gas about him, which some people said was like vinegar, or gun powder, or less of a smell and more of a sensation like a violently spicy pepper. Devon was dirty, as if he'd fallen down or been shoved against a wall or two, and even though Garrett was squeaky clean and looking forward to staying that way for the rest of the night, he nevertheless opened his arms to Devon without a word, without hesitation. Devon needed a hug more than Garrett needed to stay pristine, and Garrett wanted to be the one to provide that hug more than he wanted to do anything else in that moment.

Devon stepped forward and Garrett was swept up in his embrace. He was a hell of a hugger, Devon, should have gone pro. Garrett let himself hug back with more gusto than he meant to employ, which was when he finally clued into how much he'd been missing Devon all day.

"Oh, it's you," Tula said, coming out of the bathroom, suspicions lifted. "I thought I heard a knock but then silence. But you're not the cuddle bandit, so it's all good."

When the hugging didn't stop, and Garrett looked at Tula wondering if their guy was broken or what, she changed to a serious tone.

"Is it all good, Devon?"

At last Devon let go, and sighed, and touched Garrett's hair, tugging gently on some curls. "It's getting better now that I'm here. You two look so cozy," he said, but he wasn't looking at Tula. "Can I sit down somewhere?"

"If you're okay with sitting on a towel, sure," Tula said, bringing the towel and setting it down on the couch next to Garrett's spot.

Devon kicked off his shoes and took a seat, started breathing deeply and deliberately, like it was a tactic he'd been taught to calm down. Garrett went to sit next to him, while Tula leaned over the back of the couch and stared down into Devon's eyes.

"I'm okay," he told her. "Just a couple of little panic attacks, weaklings, nothing."

"Hmm." Tula ran her index finger down Devon's forehead and the bridge of his nose, then back up again. "Want some spa treatment? We've got all the gear ready to go."

"Sure," said Devon, and that became the plan.

Devon took a shower, barely fit into one of Tula's robes, accepted some facial goo from her assemblage of unguents, and ministrations to his feet from Garrett. Tula supplied a soaking tub and some foot-scraping tools for them, and retired to her room with a final departing note to Devon.

"You two behave," she said with a yawn. "Devon, you know my rules."

Devon threw up the V for peace, and the boys were left alone.

"What are her rules?" Garrett murmured.

"If we do any hanky-panky, she better not hear it, see it, or smell it."

Garrett raised his eyebrows and tried to suppress a silly smile. Dirty words still made him giggle, and the idea of stinky sex hit the same funny bone.

Devon was smiling down at him, green flecks of some avocado-and-charcoal slime still stuck in bits of his beard. Garrett was sitting on the floor, having already taken a Microplane file to Devon's thickest calluses while they were dry, and was now about to scrub and buff the water-softened skin. After that, it would be toes, and after toes, a lotion massage. There was a reason Garrett was so good at this, and Devon finally asked him about it.

"Have you done this before, this pedicure thing? And if yes, is it because of some biblical foot-washing commandment your cult adopted?"

"Yes, and it's called Maundy, or Pedelavium. Jesus washed the feet of his disciples, and then told them that they must love one another as he had loved them, and so the washing of the feet is part of that."

"Maundy Mondays? Sounds like a party."

"Maundy Thursday, actually," Garrett said. "The Thursday before Easter, and we only did it once a year for Holy Week."

"Yeah, well, twice a year or more would be too much, because then it's a sex thing, isn't it?"

Garrett shrugged. "For us, it was part of the Lovefeast: feet-washing before the Agape meal, and then communion after."

"And yet," Devon said, drying one foot on the towel beneath the water tub, and then slouching down in his seat so the underside of his foot could reach Garrett's crotch. "It's making you hard."

"You're making me hard," Garrett countered. "It's less about your feet and more about the whole package, which I can see from this angle, by the way. That robe doesn't cover much."

"Huh," Devon said, smirking but doing nothing to cover himself.

"Feet-washing is a sign of respect, care, and humbleness, also pretty good for your circulation. A couple of the members had diabetes, and the health of their feet was of great concern."

"Do you miss it, your old church life?" Devon asked.

"Why should I? I didn't leave it, it left me," Garrett replied, and that was pretty much all he felt about it, and all he had to say about it. "How was your night?"

"Oh, did I not mention that part? We've got an insurrection on our hands."

"Wait … what?"

# 25.

## *Wet, Hot, American Insurrections, Occupations, and Rebellions!*

### *Insurrection vs. Occupation vs. Rebellion: Definitions*

An insurrection is any act or instance of revolt against an established government or civil authority. This means a rebellion against a government is an insurrection, sedition (speech or conduct that incites rebellion against a government) is part of it, and non-sanctioned occupation of territory to resist a government (aka conquest, takeover, annexation, invasion, or seizure) is also insurrection.

### *The Insurrection Act Through the Ages*

The text of the U.S. Insurrection Act of 1807 states, in part:

> *Whenever the President considers that unlawful obstructions, combinations, or assemblages, or rebellion against the authority of the United States, make it impracticable to enforce the laws of the United States in any State by the ordinary course of judicial proceedings, he may call into Federal service such of the militia of any State, and use such of the armed forces, as he considers necessary to enforce those laws or to suppress the rebellion. The*

*President, by using the militia or the armed forces, or both, or by any other means, shall take such measures as he considers necessary to suppress, in a State, any insurrection, domestic violence, unlawful combination, or conspiracy [...]*

The Insurrection Act was signed by Thomas Jefferson to frustrate the plans of Aaron Burr (lawyer, Revolutionary War officer, senator from New York, former Vice President to Jefferson, and killer of Alexander Hamilton) to claim land in the Southwest of today's United States (land at the time owned by Mexico or newly claimed in the Louisiana Purchase of 1803). Burr wanted to raise an army and establish his own personal rule after the 1804 duel that killed Hamilton ruined his political ambitions. Jefferson wasn't having it. Since 1807, the Insurrection Act has been amended and used to:

- Wage the Civil War under President Abraham Lincoln
- Enforce the 14th Amendment (which granted citizenship to all persons born or naturalized in the U.S., including formerly enslaved persons) during post-Confederacy Southern Reconstruction under President Andrew Johnson
- Enforce desegregation under Presidents Dwight D. Eisenhower and John F. Kennedy
- Quell riots in the aftermath of the assassination of Martin Luther King Jr. under President Lyndon B. Johnson
- Quell riots after the LAPD assault of Rodney King under George H.W. Bush

You may be sensing a racial (racist) theme there, but the act was also used to expand power after the September 11 attacks of 2001 to even higher heights of federal rule, so after that it became everybody's problem.

### *Mini American Rebellions — A Brief History*

With the United States being a country born of rebellion (the American Revolution, largely done over gripes about taxation), it may not be surprising that there have been many attempts at internal overthrow.

Here are a few highlights:

- **Shays' Rebellion (1786-7, Massachusetts):** A series of attacks against courthouses and other government holdings done by former Revolutionary war soldiers-turned-farmers, partially led by Daniel Shays, and regarding property foreclosures and economic rules regulating trade/credit/tax agreements that kept poor people poor. When peaceful redress was ignored, farmers became soldiers again, halting court proceedings, arresting and injuring folks, and raiding a federal arsenal for more weapons. This rebellion tested the U.S.'s fledgling Articles of Confederation, and prompted the Constitutional Convention that began to organize a federal government greater than any one state (plus elected the first president to lead it). Shays himself was pardoned for his participation and lived out the rest of his life in New York with pleasant notoriety. Only two rebels were executed for burglary.

- **Dorr's Rebellion (1841-2, Rhode Island):** A fight over Rhode Island's government waged between those who wanted a new democratic constitution, and those who wanted to operate under their old British royal charter even after the American Revolution, a charter which disenfranchised those who didn't (and practically couldn't) own land. Conflicting governors were elected in 1842, Thomas Dorr on the constitutional side, and Samuel Ward King on the charter side. Dorr decided to arm his supporters, and raided the city's arsenal to do it, an insurrection that failed when the cannons were found to be non-operational. There were no battles waged, and the only death was the mistaken shooting of an innocent civilian. While Dorr was sentenced to life in prison, the *cause célèbre* surrounding "the People's Governor" led to his release after 20 months served. The plaque which marks his grave today still calls him "Governor."

- **John Brown's Raid on Harper's Ferry (1859, Virginia):** An abolitionist attempt to take over a federal armory in what is now West Virginia's Harpers Ferry with intent to start a slave revolt. After a pro-slavery raid on an abolitionist town in Kansas in 1856, white man John Brown and his five sons exacted personal revenge by hacking five other men to death with broad swords on May 25 of that same year. Brown lost one of his sons in that attack, and spent the next three years using guerrilla warfare tactics and assembling a small army of Black and white men to take the arsenal at Harper's Ferry on October 16, 1859. On October 19, a company of U.S. Marines led by Robert E. Lee took it back, tried Brown for treason and murder, and hanged him on December 2 of that same year.

- **The Veterans of WWI's Bonus March (1932, Washington D.C.):** A revolt against the government by World War I veterans who were given "Bonus Certificates" for their service good for $1,000, but not redeemable until 1945 (during which we'd be ending WWII, though folks adorably didn't know that at the time). When these "Bonus Army" vets asked Congress to redeem their payment early to help them through the Great Depression (1929-1933), they did so by hitching, train-hopping, and hiking to Washington, D.C. where they built a shantytown across the Potomac River from Capitol Hill. When their demands were rejected in June of 1932, several thousand people remained where they squatted because they had nowhere else to go, and kept a vigil. They were removed by army forces led by Douglas MacArthur (future WWII General) with tear gas, bayonets, sabers, infantry, cavalry, and tanks. After the veterans and their families fled, their shanty structures were burned.

- **The Malheur Wildlife Refuge Occupation (2016, Oregon):** It began in Nevada in 2014 with an armed standoff between the Bureau of Land Management (the other BLM) and a ranching family regarding cattle grazing fees on public land. BLM said the ranchers were trespassing on federal land and owed back fees for the privilege of cattle grazing, and the ranchers said the land where their cattle grazed was either their land or state land that the federal government had no authority over.

When BLM officials came to capture and impound the cattle in April of 2014, militia members from across the U.S. arrived in support of the ranchers to interrupt the capture and block a highway, and BLM attempted to de-escalate by releasing the cattle. However, the back fees were still unresolved in 2016, when Papa Rancher and his sons led a takeover of the Malheur National Wildlife Refuge in Oregon to support another set of father-and-son ranchers protesting the federal management of land. This other family of Oregon-based ranchers started fires in the early 2000s to halt invasive plants near their property (they said), or to disguise poaching (prosecutors said). After an appeals court overturned the Oregonian ranchers' sentences on arson convictions from 2012, they were resentenced with more time and sent back to prison in 2015. Outrage at that decision prompted the Nevada ranching family and other sympathizers to spend 41 days in an armed occupation of a federal National Wildlife building, a standoff that resulted in one protester being shot dead. The Nevadan ranchers were ultimately acquitted for their 2014 charges of assault, obstruction, threats against the government, and firearms offenses, as well as for their 2016 charges of conspiracy, theft, and weapons offenses.

- **The Standing Rock Protests Against the Dakota Access Pipeline (2016-7, North Dakota):** Another land dispute with the feds, this one involving the Standing Rock Sioux and Cheyenne River Sioux Tribes who filed a suit to stop the Texas oil company Energy Transfer Partners from building an oil pipeline against their tribal lands and under Lake Oahe, the source of their drinking water. In April of 2016, Indigenous and allied protesters formed the "Oceti Sakowin" Camp (which translates as "Seven Council Fires" and is the proper name for the people commonly referred to as Sioux) near the disputed area. In July, the U.S. Army Corps of Engineers approved the pipeline being built under the Lake Oahe reservoir and Missouri River. In August, the Standing Rock Sioux Tribe filed a lawsuit saying they were not properly consulted on this construction.

In September, the lawsuit was denied, and the North Dakota National Guard was deployed to police the Oceti Sakowin Camp, which meant dog attacks, rubber bullets, water cannons, tear gas, and flash-bang aka concussion grenades (which intend to harm via the force of their blast rather than the explosion of shrapnel). The pipeline construction continued throughout the fall, and the crackdown from police escalated during the Thanksgiving holiday. In January of 2017, the Army Corps of Engineers promised a full environmental impact study before continuing construction, but a week later, the newly elected 45th president expedited the pipeline's approval. In February, the drilling at Lake Oahe began and the Oceti Sakowin Camp was cleared out, ending the protest. According to the Water Protector Legal Collective, of over 800 criminal cases created over the DAPL protests, over 390 were dismissed, over 40 were acquitted at trial, over 140 were settled with plea agreements, and 26 resulted in convictions (some with prison time, federal supervision, and potential disenfranchisement from voting for felony convictions). All of those who faced federal charges were Indigenous people.

You may have detected another theme here, a discrepancy between the treatment of white, landed men vs. other sorts when it comes to who can claim what and go where without severe consequence in the United States. But shhh: one time a half-Black guy was elected president, so everything must be A-OK in the U.S.A.

## *Insurrection in Conclusion*

If you're wondering whether insurrection will work for you, first check the color of your skin, the color of those you're fighting for, and the net worth of your holdings, and that will help determine your chances of survival and subsequent freedom after you inevitably fail. You see, the House always wins, because when you defy the government and say you're willing to fight, the next question is, "You and what army?" Americans don't have an army, the American government does.

# 26.

Devon woke up on the floor. Under the couch. Holding Garrett's hand. He'd come to on worse floors, that was for damn sure. Face down in a puddle of puke more than once, with bruises he didn't remember earning, rolling around on rocks that jabbed him in all the wrong places, *ad infinitum* and *ad nauseam.* Most of those were party consequences, post-party-um depressions his friends back home called them, but some were gnarly. Memories of being lost while camping, unsafe in a war zone, kicked out and told not to come back to places he was staying because he was such a bad influence on his buddies according to their mothers, girlfriends, landlords, whatever. But today Devon was allowed, even welcome in the place where he woke, and the couch right above him made him feel safe and hidden, and Garrett's strong hand with its beautifully clear nails was laced with his, hung over the side of the couch where he lay.

"Is this clear polish?" Devon asked, unable to know for sure if Garrett was awake yet, but willing to bet.

"It is," Garrett said from above. "Good morning. How'd you get under there?"

"Instinct," Devon said, before commencing the struggle to get out from under the couch. After that it was a question of where to kiss Garrett that wouldn't inflict morning breath on the kid, and where he'd last left his phone.

Devon's phone, it turned out, was brimming with urgent messages where it sat charging on Tula's desk chair. It was like the device was telling him, *Hey there, old pally old buddy of mine! Just a quick reminder that you abandoned your friend Wayne David in the dark of a foreign city and didn't think to wonder about him until right now, when you notice that Michelle has been texting you to go get your guy out of police custody. It's sunny today!*

"Oh shit," Devon said, already feeling the wrench of leaving again. "I gotta go."

The messages from Michelle were to inform Devon that she was Wayne David's one phone call from downtown's Third Precinct. The cops had rounded up folks leaving City Hall to gain intel on who was still in there, they'd taken everyone's phones (illegal search and seizure much?), and the only number Wayne David had to call after that was the one printed on the card Devon had given him, which was Michelle's.

Walking out of Tula's, Devon called that number himself. "Michelle? Devon. Any updates on Wayne David? How can I help?"

"Last I heard they were just holding him for questioning, which could turn into an arrest at any moment, and if it does he may need bail, or his own lawyer. You wanna help, go down to that precinct and find your boy, find out what they're doing with him, then call me back if I can help."

"You're a queen among men, Michelle," he told her.

"You're welcome, Devon. You know I met your new beau yesterday, he's awfully cute, and he better be legal."

"If he's not, you know you'll be my first call from the clink," Devon said, boosted for a moment knowing everyone could tell his son was special.

"I can't even with you," Michelle said. "Text me when you know about your friend."

Call over. Next up, it was time to order a dangerous (pandemic-wise) rideshare downtown in yesterday's funky clothes. He could have stopped home first, but having been retained by goons before himself, he knew every minute was a motherfucking eternity, so he wasn't going to delay any further, the consequences be damned.

On the bittersweet side, Devon's driver didn't believe in the pandemic anyway. "It's just the flu. The Chinese want everyone to think there's a virus so they can sell us the cure, and then boom, we're all microchipped."

Devon used at least two microchips to pay the man and got out wondering if they didn't need more pandemics to burn some chaff out of humanity, but he quickly rejected the thought. One step down that path and he'd end up at eugenics just like the Nazis, and though Devon thought those Hugo Boss uniforms looked delightful (put one on and play spank games with a riding crop why don'tcha?), white supremacists were terrible company and there was simply no good music without Black people, full stop.

Devon shook his head to shake the thoughts away as he approached the police building. The way one talked to cops was the way one should deal with certain animals: be demure of body, even-toned of voice, and never, ever run. If you ran from even a bunch of neighborhood dogs, they might give chase and rip you down, but if you were confronted by a wild bear? Never forget that it could move faster, climb higher, and fight better than you. It didn't matter what the creature was — eagle, ape, snake, gator, shark — they were all keener than domesticated human beings, sitting soft in offices all day, afraid of the fights that many police officers were thirsty and aching for. Every cop had animal potential, and could be coiled and crouched and ready to strike. Knowing that had kept Devon from ever being arrested so far. He'd been stopped, questioned, hassled for sport, he'd had guns pointed in his face more than once as far back as when he was a teenager, but he had never been arrested, not yet.

Devon hoped today wouldn't be the day that broke his streak, and his wish was granted. For as he approached the police precinct, who should pop out disheveled and blinking at the sun like a newborn fawn, but Wayne David.

"Beautiful timing, Wayne David," Devon called out as he approached. "Walk with me, let's get out of here."

Wayne David fell in step behind Devon as he strolled past the police station like he'd never had any business there at all. After a block or two, when the heat felt off, Wayne David caught up to him, and Devon put a hand on his shoulder.

"How'd that go? Are you okay? What happened?"

"I'm okay, they just questioned me about shit I don't know, and with this accent, they're happy to believe I'm as stupid as the day is long, so that's a win for me," Wayne David said. "I'm a little paranoid they mighta did something to my phone while they had it, but I'm always paranoid about my phone listening to me."

Devon grinned. "That's because it absolutely is. I'm pretty sure William S. Burroughs or somebody like him said paranoia just means being in full possession of all the facts. Hungry?"

"Starving."

"Alrighty, let's eat, text Michelle a pair of 'thank you's, then go back to mine and nap so we can refuel and head out again tonight," Devon said. "If you're up for it?"

"Up for it, down for it, left and right for it," Wayne David said.

Devon laughed so hard he snorted.

# 27.

Some of the folks arrested at the City Hall Insurrection were not as lucky as Wayne David. Reports showed that a few people were being charged with the heaviest consequences possible, felony theft for picking up anything that was city property and moving it around, destruction of property because someone started a fire and even more people busted through windows and into offices. Punishments could include jail time and massive life-squandering fines. At least one person was being charged just for filming it all. Wayne David got his fill of the excitement way faster than he would have predicted, and did Devon a real favor by going home early. That meant Garrett could come back, and Devon wanted to celebrate the occasion somehow. His idea was drugs.

"You do drugs?" Garrett asked, perhaps suddenly, at such a late date, worried about what kind of undesirable he'd gotten himself involved with.

"I've done drugs," Devon said, "and so have you, right? Alcohol and caffeine are drugs."

"They're no meth though." Garrett's face was lit up by the screen of his phone as they lay in bed, winding down until the evening really commenced. They'd already agreed to stay inside tonight, as the curfews were stricter and the cops jumpier after they lost ground to the citizens. Plus, they were tired from producing content all day, for Devon an article describing what he saw at City Hall on the night in question, for Garrett clipping out footage for a video montage of violence against protesters, and for both licensing follow-up and payment accounting. Garrett would need to write up some on-screen copy for his video also, but this was the night of their reuniting, so they stopped when the evening light started seeping in. After the better half of a week apart, Devon was just happy to be spending quantity time wrapped up in bed with his dear son.

"Don't you have a birthday coming up?"

"Tula told you, huh? June twentieth." Garrett dropped his phone on his chest and rubbed his eyes, a bit of the old screen fatigue.

"And today's the seventeenth so … what do you say I take you on a trip for your birthday?"

"When you say 'trip' you mean …" Garrett put up his fingers to make a set of air quotes.

"Yeah, if you're willing, and if you don't have a history of schizophrenia in your family."

"And if I did?"

"They say the right hallucinogen can trigger it," Devon said.

Garrett raised his eyebrows. "That's quite a trigger warning. I think I'm in the clear."

"I don't know how true that is, but I'm a drug user, not a gambler."

"Very noble," Garrett said with a smile. He hadn't said yes quite yet, but Devon was nothing if not patient when it came to talking people into bad behavior. He lifted up on his elbow and drew shapes on the kid's chest with his fingernail, lightly over his T-shirt. He was drawing images of smoke and pills and kaleidoscopic shapes, in case subliminal influencing helped. "Isn't my brain still developing until age twenty-five?"

"That's what I hear," Devon said. "And yet the only thing you can't do until twenty-five is rent a car without some extra paperwork. You need a co-signer or you gotta fork over an extra fee for that. But you can drink at twenty-one, you can smoke and join the army at eighteen, and marry even younger. It ain't right but it's true."

"*That's* what I was going to do this Saturday, thanks for reminding me," Garrett said, reaching up to tug on Devon's beard, a fair enough exchange since Devon had his fingers in Garrett's curls whenever possible. He was more kitty cat than Oskar with wanting to bitty-bat at those curls. "Turn eighteen, buy a pack of smokes, and marry the army."

"I can get you much better stuff to smoke than tobacco," Devon said. "Believe that while you consider my offer."

"Will do," Garrett said, a phrase he had picked up from Devon.

Whatever was going to be said next between them was lost, however, as the sounds of blasts and a bullhorn came from outside, and caused them both to stiffen, alert with fear.

Out of an abundance of caution, Devon and his riot son slithered out of bed and onto the floor, then army-crawled to the window. Garrett put his phone over the ledge first to start recording, while Devon got one of his heavy-duty cameras out from storage. They didn't know what was going on at first, but they knew it was some sort of bullshit.

"Get back inside! Inside! Now!" screamed a man's voice through the bullhorn. Whoever he was had the snotty tone of a schoolyard bully who wanted you to believe he would hit you before he had to actually do it. When he finally got a look at what was going on outside, Devon knew why.

"Oh, they've called in the National Guard!" As surely as the weekend warrior on the loudspeaker couldn't help sounding bratty, Devon couldn't help defaulting to sarcasm when he was otherwise filled with disgust. Not only were there uniforms marching down the street and ordering people off their own stoops, porches, and balconies, their presence was also accompanied by a desert-camouflaged armored security vehicle. It was squat, wide, and almost ridiculous enough on a quiet urban street to be funny. The vehicle was there to help intimidate everyone into following the rules they were already following by being off the public streets.

"The city's new curfew has begun, get back inside your dwelling or risk arrest," said a new voice, a little calmer, which meant Mr. Agitated was wandering free somewhere, yelling at law-abiding citizens person to person.

"My porch is part of my dwelling," someone shouted from the sidelines. "Just like their balcony is part of their abode."

"Get inside your homes, this is an official order," said the loudspeaker, bickering the day away in full combat gear.

Another citizen had their own bullhorn and replied, "You have no authority inside our homes, Third and Fourth Amendments, have you heard of them? Here, let me remind you. The Third Amendment to the U.S. Constitution states, 'No Soldier shall, in time of peace be quartered in any house, without the consent of the Owner, nor in time of war, but in a manner to be prescribed by law.' The Fourth Amendment reads, 'The right of the people to be secure in their persons, houses, papers, and effects, against unreasonable searches and seizures, shall not be violated, and no Warrants shall issue, but upon probable cause, supported by Oath or affirmation, and particularly describing the place to be searched, and the persons or things to be seized.' You have no right to order us around our property unless you've got some paperwork proving otherwise."

Hearing that the law was on their side, an optimistic murmur rippled through the street. That's when the soldiers got really peeved, and after one person said within earshot of Devon (and hopefully his camera's microphone), "We tried to warn them, now light 'em up." Out came beanbag rounds and rubber bullets.

"Okay, then." Garrett retracted his head from over the window sill but left his phone up like the good reporter he already was. Garrett flared his eyes at Devon, his pupils contracted unnaturally small due to fear or anger or whatever combination of the two he was feeling (it made his irises really shine, not that Devon had time to notice, of course). "This is not a drill," Garrett told Devon.

Garrett must have actually been drilled on what could happen if the government came to overrun his cult compound. That was just part of what one did in cults and compounds of all sorts, but until today, in the supposedly free U.S. of A., he'd never actually seen it happen before.

"This is not a drill," Devon confirmed. "And it's no parade either, this is more like a war zone."

Devon had never wanted to see this sort of behavior in his own country either, but he wasn't surprised. These incidents had happened before, but not so widespread, coordinated, and blatant, and hardly ever to white people. Now they were doing it right out in front of everyone's fancy new cameraphones because they weren't afraid of citizen reprisal, and that was the scary part. If anyone was going to be scared it was governments that should be afraid of their citizens, not the other way around.

# 28.

On the back burner, Devon reached out to his friends who either were or knew drug connections to see if anyone had anything to sell in these bad old times when surely demand for getting high was higher than ever. Cooking up front was an idea he thought could marry his and the kid's deadlines together: a question-and-answer podcast on the subject of Juneteenth.

"What is Juneteenth, you ask?" Devon said to his microphone, sitting across his kitchen table from Garrett. "Why it's today, June the nineteenth, the anniversary of the day slavery actually ended in the United States. Did you ever hear about this uniquely American day of remembrance growing up, Garrett? Garrett, by the way, is a young ruffian reporter I met on the street who turns eighteen tomorrow, so watch out for this one."

"I did not hear about Juneteenth even once before you said it yesterday," Garrett said. They had light smiles on their faces, just a symptom of the silliness of performing for a theoretical future audience with one another; it felt like a dress rehearsal, but this was actually opening night. "Although to be fair, I was homeschooled by culty types in Canada."

"By *American* culty types in Canada, isn't that so? What are the chances they know what Juneteenth is?"

"Probably nil. Also, aren't we supposed to not say America when we only mean the U.S. though? Canada is also North America but this isn't about them, right?"

"Great point," Devon said, "but being the sons of imperialists such as we are, we change our name for no one. What are we if not Americans, Ewe-Essians? That's not happening. No, no, we change other countries' names and tell them to like it. The Reino de España is Spain, and Deutschland is Germany, and I'm still not sure how we came up with that one. Regardless, I'll have you know that the way to refer to the United States in Japan — conquering supremes of the East — is America. So that's how it is."

"What does Japan call itself?" Garrett wondered.

"I do not know."

Garrett quickly typed up a search for it. "The internet says Nippon-koku."

"Adorable. Anyway, I was never taught about Juneteenth either, which is particularly egregious because I was educated in public school in the great state of Texas, which is where the occasion originated."

"Were you though? Educated in public school or in Texas, I mean?" Garrett asked, smirking as if he couldn't believe he dared.

"Oho, the sarcasm is strong with this one! Well, the answer I have today is, pretty much no, I wasn't."

"Right, because what is Juneteenth?" Garrett segued them beautifully back on track.

"I'm so glad you asked," Devon said, and then looked down to read briefly from a prepared script. "Juneteenth is the anniversary of the day in 1865 when slavery actually ended. On paper it was over when Lincoln signed the Emancipation Proclamation on January first of 1863, but wouldn't you know it, it took two and a half years to tell everybody about it, particularly newly freed slaves who were forbidden to learn to read lest they, ya know, see a newspaper and get a bunch of big ideas and start spreading the word."

"Hmm, that doesn't seem very fair," Garrett said.

"Yeah, I don't think it was. It was June nineteenth when Union soldiers finally got all the way to Galveston, Texas, which for you Yankees is located south of Houston, on the coast of Texas, right in that taint area before the balls drop into Corpus Christi and Mexico."

"I hear about Galveston when hurricanes smack it around," Garrett parried. Devon was so proud to hear him talking trash with the sweet, youthful voice of a babe.

"Some like to say the news never reached that far south because the messenger who carried it was murdered on his way," Devon said.

"An honest mistake, I'm sure."

"Of course, why wouldn't it be? Unless the slavers wanted to hold the line until they could reap one last cotton harvest on the backs of Black people."

"Oh yeah," Garrett said. "That, maybe it was that."

"Who can tell? History is so touchy below the Mason-Dixon Line," Devon said, then went back to reading. "Juneteenth is also known as Freedom Day, Liberation Day, Emancipation Day, and my personal favorite, Jubilee Day, which is how it started."

"That one sounds so pretty."

"Right? It reminds me of the Rolling Jubilee the Occupy Wall Streeters did to wipe out student loan debt themselves via mutual aid and collective action."

"Collective action for the win," Garrett said.

"Amen. They wiped out about $4 million in debt for a little over $100,000 bucks, and if that doesn't make you turgid, I just don't know what will. But that's not today's chub, today is Juneteenth 2020, which still isn't a national holiday because congress is still choked with racists. Texas was the first state to make it an official holiday, in 1979. So like between the end of the Civil War and the end of disco."

"The end of it," Garrett echoed. "They were a little slow on the draw there."

"Look at you, with your gun phrases," Devon said. "Yeah, the end of disco, when hetero white people were horning in on it. Anyway, in the late 1800s, Black folks would pool their money to buy land on which to celebrate Juneteenth, land that is now spots like Emancipation Park in Houston and Booker T. Washington Park east of Waco, which was first purchased by the Limestone County Nineteenth of June Organization."

"Sounds like it was right under your nose the whole time," Garrett said. "Weird they never mentioned it in Texas schools."

"Yeah, about as weird as the people of Oklahoma and the rest of white America being largely unaware of the massacre of Tulsa's Black Wall Street until it was in a comic book show last year. For anyone who saw the beginning of Watchmen and thought it was fiction that the U.S. ever bombed one of its own cities, nope! If that city is predominantly made up of non-white people, the U.S. government says, 'What city?' Loot it and raze it and we'll pretend it never happened so hard our grandchildren will find the thought of it cartoonish."

"Good lord," Garrett said. "Bombs dropped?"

"Yessiree, and that was in 1921. The Roaring Twenties, the Jazz Age, the Harlem Renaissance, Prohibition Era Chicago, all that shimmering shit kicking off, and also this mid-week, home-grown slaughter you might have never heard of. It almost makes you think history is rigged."

"They say history is written by the victors," Garrett said.

"It used to be, now history is written by memes." Garrett laughed, and Devon laughed with him for a second before continuing, "No, but literally, they've tried to pin down that quote, and while most people think Winston Churchill said it because of memes, it sounds closer to something Hermann Göring said at the Nuremberg trials. Translated from German it's something like, 'The victor will always be the judge, and the vanquished forever the accused.'"

"Aww, was he okay?" Garrett asked. "Sounds like hurt feelings."

"Yeah, that loss must have really stung, although were the Nazis really vanquished? The U.S. soldiers who fought in World War II now have neo-Nazi grandsons crawling all over our military, our law enforcement, and half of both the political parties in America, so who really won that war?"

"Uh, maybe Israel?"

"Maybe," Devon said, "but certainly not Palestine."

The kid sighed. "History is miserable."

"We all agree that history is misery," Devon sing-songed. "Anyway, happy Juneteenth to everybody listening."

"Yes, merry Jubilee, I guess," Garrett added.

Devon signed off by saying, "To those still fighting for freedoms earned long ago, we salute you."

# PART II:
# FALL OF
# THE FATHER

# V. CRACKDOWN

## 29.

June 20, in addition to being Garrett's sweet eighteenth, was also the day of the summer solstice in 2020, i.e. the longest day of the year. When Devon secured some magic mushrooms from a friend of a friend of a guy who knew the woman that grew them from the cowshit of her dairy farm in Montana, he wanted to take his son out of the gritty city and into beautiful nature to touch grass. Devon had a tent, he knew a spot, he had a veteran drug user's knowledge of what to bring in a knapsack, and he made sure Tula knew their location in case they went missing (that's where the search party would start).

Devon rented a friendly little civilian Jeep they could sleep inside of if the ground got wet, and he let the boy choose all the music they listened to as they drove two hours out of civilization for an adventure.

"Let me see your music," Garrett said, scrolling through Devon's phone to see the depth and breadth of it. "Pretty eclectic in here."

"You need a hat for every mood and occasion," Devon said. "For big-energy hype days I'll take a symbols-clashing symphony, rap or punk music for hitting the streets to protest, of course, R&B for romance, pop music when you want to be efficient, piano for rain, violins for crying or dancing depending on how you fiddle it, harmonicas for introspection."

"Rock for remembrance?" Garrett asked. "What's good for doing hallucinogenic mushrooms among the wild mushrooms?" Whenever he said something he knew or at least suspected was clever, a precious look of precociousness came over Garrett's face. His brows perked up (Devon wondered suddenly, fleetingly, whether Garrett could arch one or both of them), his cheeks tensed like a ripened peach about to fall from its tree, his lips pursed like he had a kiss in the chamber and was just waiting for permission to fire it off.

Devon saw this at a glance as they slowed near the highway offramp, nearer than ever to a little bit of leftover wilderness. He ruffled his little poet's hair to acknowledge his witticism and said, "I recommend ambient electronic stuff for this trip, twenty-minute-long house music with no lyrics but a lot of noise patterns for your brain to play with. One time I heard a Deadmau5 song on 'shrooms that actually, I could argue, contains the progression of all human history past and future when you listen to it with the doors of perception left open."

"What did it say about the future?" Garrett asked.

"Space whales," Devon said. "That was my interpretation at least."

Devon was already warning himself not to overwhelm the kid too much, not to be too needy, not to be some bad Riot Dad who wants to download himself into his son but also suck all the youthful wonder out of him at the same time. Devon had already gone over the top a little asking Garrett for reassurance that he wasn't pressuring him to do drugs, just trying to encourage him to not be afraid of them, that if he ever wanted to have an experience like this, he might be looking at the only chance that was ever going to come along. That was Devon's own thinking — he was always grabbing at every opportunity, terrified of being left out of something he could have been there to see, probably some leftover from being sick during the one field trip everyone talked about for the rest of the school year. That fear of missing out (FOMO, as the youths called it) was what made him get up and go to any news event he could feasibly travel to. But it also made him come on perhaps too strong when begging Garrett to let him proselytize about the wonders of drugs.

They arrived at their campsite and admired how green and lush the trees were, how loud the sounds of the bugs and breeze. They ate lunch first, then set up the outside tent, then smoked a little pot on Devon's recommendation that it helped with the nausea some people felt when eating 'shrooms.

"If they give weed to cancer patients for nausea, it must be good enough for us, too," Garrett agreed, and then they consumed the magical caps and stems Devon divvied up.

Devon ran the show because he had done this a half-dozen times before, and Garrett followed every instruction like the A+ student he must have been back in cult class. One of Devon's last bits of sober wisdom was to recommend swallowing the mushrooms whole rather than chew them, as they weren't exactly sautéed to taste good. Staying hydrated was also important, so they chugged down the fungi with big gulps of water. His final suggestion was to stay busy while waiting for the effects, because a watched pot never seemed to boil.

"What should we do instead?" Garrett asked, sitting on the Jeep's bumper. Devon leaned over to kiss him, because that was his big idea, to fool around. Garrett kissed him back in a way he hadn't done in their early days of courtship, nary three weeks ago. There was an assertiveness in him now, some pushback, a thrilling resistance. Maybe he learned it from Devon, or maybe he was learning it by standing up for himself in the streets, but either way Devon's young son was getting more comfortable with his body, his sexuality. There was a boldness developing in him that Devon could taste on his tongue like metal. He loved its flavor.

"Only one thing on your mind, huh?" Garrett said before kissing Devon back and back and back until he was lying flat in the vehicle they'd just so neatly emptied out. "This was all an elaborate ruse to get me alone out here, wasn't it?"

"You caught me," Devon said, delighted to be pinned down by someone so much smaller than him. "No, but really, it's not a horny drug at all, so if we want to have this kind of fun it's now or never, we'll soon be too busy to …"

"Shh," Garrett said, kissing him again. "You're talking past the sale."

Devon got halfway through a laugh — where did the kid pick up that phrase? — before Garrett covered his mouth with one hand, and Devon remembered that line from Annie Hall about sex being the most fun one can have without laughing.

When the magic happened, they talked about it until words didn't work or matter anymore.

First, Garrett started pressing his eyes and blinking around. He wondered, "Am I seeing colors?"

Devon told him, "Yeah, which ones?"

It was green like rubbing your eyes too hard, and purple like the kind that followed if you stared at a neon sign too long, then turned away and blinked only to still see the shape of it.

Garrett picked up his feet out of the leaves. "I know they're not, but they look like they're crawling."

Devon told him, "Ever see one of those seeing-eye posters? Like it looks like a bunch of TV static, but if you stare at it long enough you'll see 3-D things in there? Try to look past the wiggling and you might see the movements turn into patterns."

Garrett stared too hard trying to focus, saying, "What kinds of patterns?"

Devon waved his hand across Garrett's field of vision to try and dissipate that stare and told him, "Whatever patterns your brain makes. I see revolving gears like clockworks, but other people see words or flowers or stars cartwheeling calmly around."

It took a few hours, but eventually what Garrett saw were whales — whales that were possibly swimming through futurespace.

Ultimately, it started to rain just a tiny bit.

Garrett asked, "Can we dance in it?"

Devon said, "Not well, but we can twirl around in it. Try to take off your shoes, slowly, because it might be harder than you think right now. I will make the dance floor safe."

The dance floor was the forest floor, but Devon put down a big blanket and ran his hands over every inch of it searching for rocks. When he found one, he removed it to without the blanket space. When he was done, he presented this safe space to Garrett and told the kid to spin around on his own so Devon could watch him.

"Dance with the world," was how Devon put it, and when Garrett spun down and curled up in a ball, Devon cozied up to his side to provide him some stability.

"The world is spinning," Garrett whispered with reverence. Everyone knew that in theory, that the planet turned on an axis, but sometimes it really hit you and almost blew your mind.

"Hold onto it," Devon whispered back, and that was the last they had to say for a while as the sky spit gently down upon them. Garrett held the Earth, and Devon held onto Garrett, and watched his curls morph into turning cogs like the workings of his exquisitely beautiful brain.

# 30.

The next day, Sunday, was Father's Day. Devon and Garrett spent the morning having the best hangovers ever, still seeing a strange reality and enjoying heightened synesthesia. Devon could swear the bees in the trees were as synced as the atoms around a nucleus, or the planets around the sun, and Garrett found a Bob Dylan song about a moonshiner that had a harmonica "so sweet I can feel it in my teeth." Devon knew that feeling.

On the sober drive back to the city in the afternoon, Garrett asked some relevant questions.

"Since it's Riot Father's Day, can I ask about your family?"

"You can ask me anything, anytime, my son," Devon said. He'd asked enough questions about Garrett's upbringing, mostly because it was so unique, and he'd offered so few details of his own origin story precisely because it was so average and boring. But if the boy was old enough to ask, he was old enough to know, which was something Devon's father used to say when his kids wondered about what dirty words meant.

Garrett asked, "So what were they, your parents? Jobs, religion, country of origin? What were their first names? Mine were Marian and Paul."

Devon said, "Mine were Robin and John. I'm so happy they didn't name me John Junior, it's such a generic name that it's what they call male corpses and shit. Devon is a county in England, not that it's why they chose it, just an Anglo-Saxon fact. A Devon is also a red beef cattle breed."

"It suits you," Garrett said.

"Any story behind your name? I've wondered about it."

"My parents chose G as the letter for naming all their children. We go Garrett, Gregory, Guinevere, Gracelena, and Gabriella."

"Your sisters really won the pot there," Devon said.

"Yeah, they all got ballerina names, we got Gare and Greg, which sounds like a mechanic's shop, a rusty one, but it could have been worse," Garrett said. "The only mockery I got growing up was Garrett the Ferret, that's nothing."

"Like water off a ferret's back," Devon said with a smirk. They could see tall buildings in the distance now, and knew they were driving back into a teeming hive of upheaval. Two hours in one direction it was crickets and green grass perfuming the air, two hours back it was all gunmetal and grim.

"So your parents though?" Garrett reminded Devon.

"Oh, right. Mom was a substitute teacher sometimes, then cashier at the outlet mall, and now she does some ride-share driving for extra cash, last I heard. My dad was the manager at a hardware store when me and my sister Fi were kids, which was good while it lasted, until they closed that store and his choice was no job or take a similar job in Oklahoma. He took the gig in Oklahoma, but left mom and us in the house in Dallas because Oklahoma, as I've said before, is shit. So all during those years when I could have used a man in the house, I had a man in another state. We spent a few summers at his bleak apartment, just a couple weeks in a couple of summers really, and he would come home for big events at first, Christmas and birthdays, but not their wedding anniversary. My parents' marriage disappeared pretty fast. Mom said she felt like an army wife without the praise. I think they're still legally married because of joint property, and because neither one wanted to marry anyone else particularly." Devon shrugged. "That's pretty much the long and short of it. My sister's cool, but kind of a dummy at life so far. She takes a few community college classes, but doesn't think beyond the end of the week, the end of the month. She's going to wake up at thirty-five or forty someday and be horrified, is my bet. Don't know what she'll do after that."

"I think we'll all wake up horrified by something someday," Garrett said. "The real adventure is finding out what will do it to us."

"Ah, young sage," Devon said, reaching to pick up Garrett's hand, bring it to his mouth, and kiss its knuckles. "So wise."

Devon had a few substitute father figures in his early years. First, men of history who'd gotten rich or powerful by sheer force of will or tremendous luck: L. Ron Hubbard bamboozling people so well with pulp science fiction that he'd founded a church and captained a treasure-hunting ship for years; James Brooke and his family who took and ran their own little colonial kingdom on the northwest coast of Borneo as White Rajahs (they're buried in Devon, England, that's how Devon Amis found them). A transition figure was Lawrence of Arabia, whose conquests and curiosities (masochistic and sexual in nature) steered Devon away from imperial scum towards more impressive irregulars: Oskar Schindler who was well known for resisting the Nazis by employing hundreds of Jewish workers in his factory explicitly to keep them from being killed (a clear example of a white man using his power and privilege for good); Raoul Wallenberg, a Swedish architect who also quietly and bureaucratically frustrated the Nazis, saving thousands of Jewish people ("saving a nation," as he phrased it) from being shipped to death camps from Hungary by providing them with forged documents. Each of those Nazi resisters was deemed as Righteous Among the Nations by the State of Israel, an honorable title for non-Jews who risked their lives to save Jews during the Holocaust when it would have been so much easier to fall in line. Delilah pointed out that Lilly Wust was also on that list, a German housewife who had a lesbian affair with a Jewish woman, Felice Schragenheim, and hid other Jewish women from the Nazis after Felice was ripped from her apartment and slowly killed on a march from Auschwitz. Oskar and Lilly had movies made about them; Raoul's legacy still needed more press.

In real life, Devon's healthy male role models were limited. He had a couple of good teachers in middle and high school, friendly and/or kind men who would have been more to him perhaps if they weren't terrified of being too chummy with any student, boy or girl, lest they be suspected of grooming the young for nefarious purposes.

He liked one professor at college quite a bit, mostly because the guy was so bitter he was honest about what a racket academia was, which gave Devon the boost he needed to drop out before his debt was too deep to touch bottom. After that, people started looking to *him* for fatherly guidance, because there was something about being tall and deep-voiced and bearded and employed that drew a ridiculous amount of deference.

Devon turned around in his late twenties and realized he'd have to become the man he was seeking if he ever wanted to find the dude, and that's what he'd been trying to do ever since. His efforts showed in: the paternal fondness and tolerance he had for his sister; the helping hand he had for a shell-shocked Wayne David; the take-your-licks attitude he enforced in himself when it came to getting romantically shot down and dismissed by some women, paired with the mutual respect for other women who saw him as a colleague, brother, or friend. All of this, if Devon was being as fatalistic as a Taylor Swift song, made him the exact kind of man he needed to be if he wanted to be attractive, useful, and receptive to someone like Garrett. Maybe it all worked out for the best?

They arrived back at Devon's place in the twilight, and though it was their own little love-nest and Oskar the cat was happy to see them returned to freshen up his food bowl, it seemed less lovely after their magical oasis in the woods. Before Devon's feelings could crash in on him though (he could feel the altitude lowering and knew to stop the decline before his mood took a dive), he had a suggestion.

"Hey, how about we move this place around, me and you," Devon said. "I pretty much just put everything wherever it first landed, we could get a whole new space out of it, if you want."

Garrett looked around, doing geometry in his head, imagining this thing there, that thing here, etc. He turned to Devon like they were about to run the mother of all heists and said, "I'm in."

It made sense that the bed stayed on the far side of the room and the sitting area in front of the door and next to the kitchen, as these were the places where guests would naturally stop to eat, socialize. But after that, Garrett had a lot of ideas on how to improve the flow.

"Right now when people sit, the focal points are the door and this dresser, we really don't need this dresser here. If you can handle it, how about we put the back of the dresser against the bed, like a little dividing wall?"

"Tell me where to move stuff and I'll move it, consider me Lurch," he said, trusting that Garrett, with his ancient repertoire of references, would know the Addams family's manservant by name.

Garrett got out Devon's meager cleaning supplies to help beat back the dust bunnies that sprang forth when Devon started moving things around. In the end, the bed became a private little bordello, with the dresser blocking the view of the pillows from those who sat on the couch, and the nightstand moved to the other side to create a slim walkway since two people were using the bed now. No more accidental tea-bagging when crawling over one another to leave the sheets; intentional tea-bagging only from hence forth.

Garrett gave the sleeping area a little roof with a shawl that he had by tacking two corners to the wall and the other two corners to the back of the dresser. He repurposed Devon's LED lights to festoon them over this new tent, concentrated all the weapons in one hidden spot behind the couch, and in the rest of the room he grew the seating area so that the desk was involved in the flow of it all, and the desk chair in easy range of turning to join the living room party. The kid also moved the tiny kitchen table out into the living room to fill the space left void by the dresser, and by the time he was done shifting appliances hither and thither in the kitchen, Devon was done mopping the newly exposed floor, a task which he usually only did about once a year. After they showered, the place felt brand new, and Devon felt much better.

"I like this," he told Garrett, brushing the kid's hair like a doll because Garrett said he could, and looking out from the bathroom at their fresh new expanse.

"It's our place now, isn't it, dear?" Garrett asked archly, playacting a little heteronormativity as if he suspected that was Devon's own thought, and he was right.

"Yes, darling," Devon said, with a quick squeeze of his new bride. "You make my house a home."

# 31.

With summer in full riot (literally "riot time" was a synonym for summer, though it was an antiquated phrase referencing wanton merrymaking and revelry, not authoritarian beatdowns), the political tides were starting to turn. After the casual, daylight murder of George Floyd, a certain amount of room was made for outrage. Like loosening a pressure valve, the powers that be knew people had to blow off a little steam when their own abuse was shoved right in their faces like that. Politicians and police took their knees, and said they understood the shock, the anger, the sadness, but like … a whole month? The ghouls at the top were starting to decide that the rest of the country had had enough upset. Let's get back to that pandemic, huh? Let's focus on how we can save the precious economy from all these inconvenient, gasping deaths?

Once the National Guard was on the streets and the people were breaking into the halls of power, it was a lubed chute into martial law. From sea to shining D.C., tactical teams started ramping up their storm-trooping, and finally just started black-bagging folks like they always wanted to. Unmarked vans, unmarked uniforms, no reason for detainment, no official arrest: in LAX, in DTX, in NYC, suddenly people were getting grabbed, blindfolded, and taken to windowless undisclosed locations for indefinite periods of time for the purposes of illegal search and interrogations. All of a sudden if any American still felt free, it was because they weren't paying attention.

Devon tried to feel fine about it. Not *fine*, exactly, but he tried to stay unruffled. He knew his country was capable of this, had done it before and the only difference this time was the citizenry had pocket cameras, but … perhaps Devon overestimated the amount of Mr.-Smith-Goes-to-Washington naïveté in himself. Perhaps all the lies laid deep in his head about "remember the Alamo" and "shining city on a hill" and "that banner yet waved" still caused him to believe he would never see such Gestapo shit in his own neighborhood, or that if he did, the country would care, would revolt, would smack back that kind of thuggishness like only Americans could: big and loud and proud. But … they didn't.

Devon wasn't the only one feeling sick to see supposed freedom lovers back the fash so fast. Wayne David got what he called "the heebie-jeebies" about it, too. He called Devon — actually called him on the ye olde fashioned telephone line — and they talked it over in hushed disgust a couple of days after Garrett and Devon's forest retreat was over.

Devon took the call in the bathroom, in the dark, so that his summer child could stay in the light and warmth of the kitchen making some vegan lasagna recipe he found online and humming peacefully along to whatever alterna-folk song was playing through his earbuds. Devon didn't want his dread to spread.

"Are you seeing this shit, too?" Wayne David asked. "I'm not having crazy flashbacks or hallucinations or nothing, right? There's secret police disappearing people in plain sight?"

"If you're crazy then we've both been smoking the same dope," Devon assured him. "Where the fuck are those militia assholes now, when we could actually use them? This is the tyranny they said they were training for, where the hell are they?"

"They're inside the vans, under the helmets," Wayne David said with a sigh.

"Are you okay, brother?" Devon didn't like the sound of that sigh, there was too much quit in it.

"I've been better, but I've also been worse."

The worst things Wayne David had seen and done during his service included accidentally killing a man with a ricochet round, a whole different hell than killing a man on purpose. Knowing that, Devon wanted to watch out that he didn't lose his pal to suicide. Wayne David felt the same way about Devon, because he knew about Devon's worst day in a war zone, too. It happened when an IED exploded the vehicle in front of Devon's to bits, and a soldier's lower leg blew back and nearly landed in his lap. Maybe Devon was the one with the foot fixation and not Garrett, some morbid coping mechanism from the trauma of nudging someone else's separated-but-still-stepping foot with his own, and dissociating from his body so hard he was still not sure he came all the way back in.

"I hear that," Devon said, and shook his head to try and clear the slate. "Hey, alright, the fall of democracy aside, what's something nice in your day? Or what's something you're looking forward to soon?"

"I am marinating the shit out of some ribs, doing a test drive on a new flavor ratio," Wayne David said. "If it's good, I'm making 'em again next week for my mom's Fourth of July party."

"Fourth of July, fuck."

"Right? Seems like they should cancel it this year, all things considered, but you know nobody will, or nobody but you liberals."

"Hey, liberals celebrate Independence Day, too. We just do it ironically like a Krampus Christmas. Upside-down flags, upside-down crosses, ritual butt stuff, you know the drill."

"I know where you stick that drill," Wayne David said. "Right in the ol' kit and caboodle."

Devon snorted, and then heard pans slam off of the stove.

"I've got to go, I think dinner's ready," he told Wayne David.

"Aw, that's so sweet, the little woman's cooking dinner for you? Or you know what I mean, not trying to be sexist and homophobic at the same time."

"I know what you mean, and Garrett's nonbinary, so you're not even in trouble. I tell you what," Devon said, his own accent getting stronger (as it always did) the longer he talked to Wayne David, "I love him so much I might beat him to death and eat him for dinner so he can never leave me."

"Ah, that's the Jeffrey Dahmer blue-plate special, is it not?"

"It is!" Devon said. "I'm kidding, I think, but if the news shows up at your door one day asking for your thoughts on your old friend, the Antifa Man-Eater, you'll know who they mean."

"And I will politely correct their pronouns or whatever to 'people-eater,' out of respect."

Devon laughed so hard he nearly fell off the toilet seat.

# 32.

## *The Militarization of American Police: How'd That Happen?*

### *From Watt to SWAT*

What weapons of war do U.S. "peace" officers have and why? Great question. The answer starts with SWAT (Special Weapons And Tactics) teams and ends with the military-industrial complex. During the riotous 1960s, Los Angeles decided they needed an elite squad of city soldiers to help control the unrest. The entity formed and refined between the Watts Riots of August 1965 (when two Black men were pulled over by white police in the Watts neighborhood of L.A. and the incident escalated to a five-day racially-charged melee between cops and the community that took 34 lives) and 1971 when SWAT personnel were given a full-time presence in the Metropolitan Division of the LAPD. This idea spread during the swinging seventies, so that in addition to regular police in cities, there also sprang up tactical units for Nixon's never-ending war on drugs (and Blacks and commies and hippies — you don't get the one without the others). In 1984, around 26% of towns with populations between 25,000 and 50,000 had SWAT teams, and by 2005, it was about 80% and rising.

*

## *The Infantry-to-Inner-City Pipeline*

From patrol officers in battle-dress uniforms (BDUs, the prettiest outfits for our thugs) to Air Force drones over protests (fun fact: the drones are learning to rain down tear gas from above!) to assault rifles, armored vehicles, grenade launchers, and bayonets (of all goddamn things), one may have noticed that their community cops are more *Operation: Combat* than Officer Krupke. This is due in large part to the Pentagon's 1033 program (previously the 1208 program), a hand-me-down operation to offload excess military equipment into municipalities for free so long as city budgets were willing to pay for shipping and maintenance. This program was renamed and enhanced by the 1997 National Defense Authorization Act, and gave preference to counter-drug and counter-terrorism requests for equipment. The act was signed by President Clinton in September of 1996, a few months before the February 1997 North Hollywood Shootout, which was the attempted robbery of a Bank of America branch by two men wearing body armor and wielding AK-47s. During the attempted robbery, the culprits sprayed over 2,000 rounds of gunfire, injured 20 people (officers and civilians), and damaged quite a bit of property. Though the robbers were killed by gunfire (from police and self-inflicted), the LAPD officers on the scene were so out-gunned they had to buy extra rifles at nearby gun stores during the standoff. After a scare like that, they said, "Never again," and since 1997 there's been a direct flow of military-grade weaponry for domestic use.

## *Why So Much Surplus?*

The reason the military has so much surplus paraphernalia is perhaps because Boomers were once sold on a war economy being a good economy. While Americans are told that guaranteed healthcare is unaffordable, and tuition-free public colleges (though once a reality in the U.S.) are impossible, and a universal basic income is the silliest of airy-fairy-unicorns-and-pixie-dust daydreams, the Pentagon's budget is consistently bloated, wasteful, and comically outspends the next top ten countries combined. In 2020, the U.S. spent $732 billion on "defense" while China, India, Russia, Saudi Arabia, France, Germany, the United Kingdom, Japan, South Korea, and Brazil collectively spent $726 billion. What are the chances that those ten countries are going to join together to take down America, huh? What enemy does America think she's preparing for? With money to burn, the United States goes through war toys like free Kleenex, disappears money by creating pie-in-the-sky prototypes they don't ever use (F-22 Raptors), and resupplies of shit the army doesn't even want (Abrams tanks). The result is an outlet mall's worth of war machines, and that stuff has gotta go somewhere, right? Surely it wasn't all made to simply spend money Brewster's Millions-style in some plutocratic (government of, by, and for the wealthy) nightmare while average Americans die of preventable conditions due to nutritional food deserts and lack of healthcare? Right?

## *The Convenient Changeover From Mayberry to Military*

It's always a big to-do when the president orders the military to work domestically, and it's mostly done for racial reasons throughout America's short history: to enforce integration, quell race revolts, preempt looting in majority Black and brown areas after hurricanes like Hugo and Katrina, or to break labor strikes. But if the cops are already standing by as a Junior Army, there's no need to bother! That being said, the answer to whether or not the police are militarized is both yes and no. Yes, in that they have the gear for fear, but no, in the sense that they aren't as well-trained to use their death machines as military personnel. They also don't have the same rules of engagement or swift consequences for bad actions as soldiers do. American police are bringing bazookas to break up barfights, turning ballfields into battlefields, and are at war with the very population they're hired to protect. Does that sound like an over-exaggeration? You must have missed the seminar.

## *Killology and Counterpoint*

You've got the reasons why the police force in America is militarized, now for the how, and the after-the-fact justifications. Surprise: it's another money-and-power grift! Specifically, seminars sold for $90 a ticket that feature a retired Lieutenant Colonel (Lt. C.) and his thoughts about killing. According to Lt. C., killology is "the scholarly study of the destructive act, just as sexology is the scholarly study of the procreative act. In particular, killology focuses on the reactions of healthy people [debatable] in killing circumstances (such as police and military in combat) and the factors that enable and restrain killing in these situations." It's this man who theorizes that there are three kinds of people: sheep, sheepdogs, and wolves. "If you have no capacity for violence then you are a healthy productive citizen: a sheep. If you have a capacity for violence and no empathy for your fellow citizens, then you have defined an aggressive sociopath — a wolf. But what if you have a capacity for violence, and a deep love for your fellow citizens? Then you are a sheepdog, a warrior, someone who is walking the hero's path." It's not an accident that Lt. C. compares killology to sexology, as he appears to find sexual pleasure in violence, and tells other supposedly useful sociopaths (specifically the police departments that American taxpayer money funds these talks and seminars for) that they can enjoy the same virility from violence. From a viral video of one of Lt. C.'s talks: "Cops say, 'Gunfight, bad guys down. I'm alive.' Finally get home at the end of the incident, and they all say, 'The best sex I've had in months.' Both partners are very invested in some very intense sex. There's not a whole lot of perks that come with this job. You find one, relax and enjoy it." You thought it was just sexually deviant serial killers who got hard with harm? No, no, apparently perfectly healthy semi-socio sheepdogs can, too. Lt. C. even has a marriage guidebook that his website describes as "a 90-day devotional that applies biblical principles to support and strengthen the marriages of military members, law enforcement officers, and first responders. Each day includes a Bible verse, an inspirational reading, quick tips, action steps for both husband and wife, and a prayer." Because Jesus Christ, the Prince of Peace who said, "Resist not evil: but whosoever shall smite thee on thy right cheek, turn to him the other also," who martyred himself for the sake of forgiveness for all the sins of humanity, that guy would approve of bloodlust in the marital bed. Totally checks out. A possible counterpoint theory on whether people can kill healthily comes from S.L.A. Marshall

(Brigadier General Samuel Lyman Atwood Marshall, also known as "Slam" because who could resist?), a veteran of WWI, reporter, author, and historian. Marshall also ran a bit of a grift based on his presumed combat expertise, claiming in his 1947 book *Men Against Fire: The Problem of Battle Command* that 75% of WWII soldiers who engaged in combat never fired at the enemy with intent to kill, even when they were under direct threat. He based that assertion on information gathered using novel group-interview techniques, and found it complicated years later when he visited Vietnam to conduct similar studies and noted that the hesitation to kill was all cured up. There's a chance he may have bullshitted his ratio-of-fire numbers as much as Lt. C. staked false authority on anecdotal police boners, but it's a relatively nice thought.

### *Do All Slain Dogs Go to Heaven?*

Here is some hard data on the loss of life that may finally wake up the humanity in us all. Ready? According to the Puppycide Database Project, the militarization of police in America has led to a massive uptick in murders of family dogs. A federal court in 2016 ruled that a police officer may shoot a dog if it barks or even moves whenever they enter a home for whatever flimsy reason they want. So: if you're not already afraid of the erosion of civil rights in a militarized police state, or of the way the "war on drugs" gives these municipal militias nearly *carte blanche* to bust into homes with no-knock warrants while the innocent sleep, lob flash grenades that have landed in cribs and exploded on babies, and confiscate any of your property or money for their own enrichment until you can prove you got it legitimately (civil asset forfeiture, aka the opposite of "innocent until proven guilty"), then … what about the doggies? Think of every cute puppy, loyal doggo, and protective pooch you've ever met or heard about, and get angry already.

# 33.

It was inevitable that the *V for Vendetta*-style black-bagging would come to their city too, and not long after it did, Garrett witnessed it firsthand, and got it on film, and went viral.

They were walking home from the action one night, the streets freakishly quiet, the streetlights unnaturally white and bright. He and Tula and Devon were silent, tired from hours of standing, walking, running, jumping, breathing tear gas, and getting jostled. Cortisol was gumming up their veins, and all Garrett wanted was to be home already, no more miles to walk. Was there anything more delightful than clean, bare feet between cool sheets? Even in hiking boots, after spending all day and half the night moving around, his feet felt hammered, and every step was another blow. Then an unmarked van rolled up.

Out came three figures in camo fatigues, matching neck gaiters (cute), body armor, helmets, and sunglasses at night. They had no names on their uniforms, only the word POLICE, and no identifiable features except that one of the soldiers was female, or at least had breasts.

"What are you doing?" Tula asked as the goons walked calmly to the group in front of them, surrounded one person who put her hands up, and walked her back to the van without a word. "Use your words, what are you doing? Where are you taking her, why is this person being detained?"

"Is this person under arrest?" Devon asked, and when the thugs said nothing, he spoke to the person being nabbed. "What's your name? Is it safe to tweet your name? We'll look for you, we won't forget about you."

"Samantha Rivera," she told him. "You can tweet. Am I under arrest?" Still no answer.

"Where are you taking her? What right have you to detain this person?" Tula asked. "What are your names, officers? If you don't identify yourselves, how do we know you're real cops and not random kidnappers?"

"They're both," Devon grumbled, as the door to the van shut and Samantha was disappeared.

"Is she your friend?" Tula asked the group that Samantha had been traveling with.

"Not really, I mean we only met her about an hour ago, just walking in the same direction," said a guy whose girlfriend was holding onto him quite tightly, looking around at every shadow on the street as if she might be next.

"Can they do that?" she asked. "I mean, was that even legal, just taking her without telling her anything?"

"Probably not legal," Garrett said, putting his camera away again. "Not that it matters."

They went home feeling a little sicker after that, and while tweeting out Samantha's name with the video of her capture. By the time Garrett was passing out from exhaustion, his video was being furiously shared. By the time he woke up the next day, he had dozens of requests to license his footage and interview him personally. He and Devon selected their favorite mainstream reporter of the bunch, and he put on a beanie to hide his easily identified locks, a local woman named Zoe Kapadia, who met him in a public park so they could have a socially distanced chat. Zoe was wearing a tasteful suit, looking like a television lawyer, whereas Garrett and Devon and the cameraman were decked out in schlub sacks of hoodies and cargo pants.

"The footage you captured was incredibly compelling," Zoe said, speaking into a field mic the size of a 1980s cellular phone, almost too big for one hand. "Care to comment on what that moment was like?"

"I mean, it was both surprising and not at all surprising," Garrett said. "We'd heard about people getting grabbed in Portland, saying they were searched without being questioned, never officially arrested, just … stolen, in a sense. They were snatched off the street, contained for a few hours, everything on their person was searched without their consent, and then they were out again. Some kind of nightmare catch-and-release to intimidate people, perform illegal searches of their phones, identify and round up others."

"Officials tell us these officers are a mix of National Guard soldiers and Border Patrol agents," Zoe said.

"That would explain why they're using war-like tactical teams to pick up American citizens," Garrett said, nodding. "We're nowhere near any border, and these protesters aren't hiding from anyone. In fact they're out here to speak, to be seen, to stand up for their brothers and sisters who are being casually brutalized and murdered by police. The punishment for exercising their rights? Getting snatched up in the night for no stated reason." Garrett shrugged. "We have these rights in theory, but when you use them, you realize you're not actually that free in practice."

That was the line that got clipped out and went double viral after the interview concluded and was uploaded to the local news and the internet. Garrett had a few more things to say about the ugliness he was seeing: people getting shoved around by the right-wing counterprotesters in full view of cops who lazily watched the bullying and did nothing, or went so far as to nod or wink; petty hurts like arresting people and making sure their cuffs were too tight, their position painful; hitting citizens with pepper spray when they couldn't wipe it away out of spite. It all added up to a grinding away of any *bonhomie* for humanity one had left.

When the interview was over, Garrett and Devon didn't leave the park. They instead found a grassy slope to lay out on and eat some sandwiches they packed at home, listen to music through shared earbuds. Garrett suspected that Devon needed this respite far more than he did, that he needed way more zen moments than he was getting, but didn't know how to say so, really. Their relationship was still in its infancy. Despite having ample opportunities to get a lot of living and sharing done in a very small window, Garrett and Devon still had gaps and silences between them, histories unknown. A crash course of character-revealing moments couldn't make up for the short amount of time they'd known each other, and Garrett often wasn't sure if he should say something, do something, and if yes, what would that something be? Garrett largely defaulted to keeping his mouth shut and letting his body do the talking.

Garrett reached over to take Devon's hand. Despite being different heights, their hands were about the same size, perhaps because Devon's were slightly smaller and Garrett's slightly bigger than average. Garrett started cleaning beneath Devon's fingernails with his own. Apparently his "love language" (something Garrett's aunt liked to talk about) was physical touch. There was an undeniable thrill to being allowed to touch someone and knowing they wouldn't mind it, that they'd in fact welcome it. Holding Devon's hand, or even just one of his fingers, was a comfort to Garrett. It wasn't unlike the way Devon kept playing with his hair. They were just a couple of grooming monkeys in love, and it was wonderful in its purity and simplicity.

"I wish there were clouds today, we could guess their shapes," Devon said, staring up at the sky that Garrett still felt was staring back at him after their mushroom trip. It wasn't a scary feeling, but it was intense, overwhelming.

Garrett brought Devon's hand down over his heart and forced himself to look at the sky. It was lighter blue at the edges, deeper blue at the center — a reminder that it was still all darkness and stars out beyond their atmosphere.

"I can still see shapes," Garrett confessed. He wondered if that was a normal side effect of doing drugs, or if maybe he'd irrevocably altered his brainwaves with just one dose. "If I stare far enough out and let them come, I can see the fish, swimming upstream." He put his other hand in the air to illustrate: waves, undulating waves.

"Lucky," Devon said. "You got to keep your friends."

Garrett squeezed Devon's hand in response.

# 34.

"This couldn't have come at a worse time, but I can't leave my cousin in the lurch," Tula said the evening after Garrett's park interview, while surveying her apartment for any last items she needed to pack.

Tula's cousin was getting surgery to fix a blown eardrum after what may or may not have been a case of COVID-19 in March (testing was still stupidly, infuriatingly limited, and had been non-existent in March), and needed Tula's help to watch her kids, who were home all day learning lessons online. There was a husband around, but he was a long-haul truck driver and only home sporadically. The family was holding on by a frayed thread, and Tula was the only one who could reasonably come help, because the other cousins had kids of their own or jobs that weren't as flexible as freelance reporter. Garrett was commissioned to water Tula's plants, bring in her mail, keep an eye on the place, etc.

"My sister had her eardrum burst a few times when we were kids." Garrett's eyes roved over Tula's place with a lot more wonder post-mushrooms. "She said it felt like the wind was touching her brain."

"Yeah, sucks," Tula said. "They hoped a surgery wouldn't be necessary, but it is, so I go." Tula finished inspecting her desk and moved to the kitchen. "If that means I'm missing my window of seduction with Hazel, oh well. Maybe I can keep her engaged via text and video chat until I get back. I finally got her to laugh at one of my jokes last week, she seemed so grateful. I think her job is really running her ragged and she's still volunteering at protests on top, it's too much."

"Sounds like you've got to get her in for one of your girly nights."

"If only everyone were as easy as you," Tula said, turning to Garrett with a comically overblown smirk-face before pouring out the last of a jug of dairy-based liquid from her fridge. "Really though, you and Devon make it look easy, just falling together like two edges of the same wound."

Garrett snorted. "That's a nice way to put it. I sure hope we don't fester."

"If my opinion means anything, I think you'll be alright. You're no Delilah, that's for sure." Tula came back through the living room on her way to double-check the bathroom for toiletry necessities.

Garrett grimaced to himself, wondering if what he was about to do was a good or even fair idea. He let his question fly anyway. "What's the story with Delilah? What was she like, what were they like together?"

Tula's rummaging sounds stopped, and she leaned in the bathroom door, hands in pockets, to give Garrett a hard look. "You're sure you want to know what I thought of Devon and Delilah?"

*Devon and Delilah*, that sounded too perfect, and Garrett badly wanted to know how perfect it wasn't. Devon talked about her like she might walk in the door at any minute, and Garrett didn't want that to happen, or if it did, he wanted to know that she wasn't welcome anymore.

"I'd ask Devon, but I don't want to reopen an old wound," Garrett pleaded.

"Nice, full circle callback," Tula said.

"But I would like to know, I guess, if they were good together? I get the impression it ended badly, but was it bad for both of them, or just Devon, and were they always going to end badly, or did it go wrong somewhere? And if it went wrong ..."

"How do you avoid it happening again?" Tula suggested. "Alright, take a seat."

Garrett sat down fast, and Tula cast one last glance at the bathroom before joining him in the living room, checking her phone for the time, and placing an order for a rideshare pickup.

"We've got about eleven minutes until my driver arrives, so here's what's up," Tula said, perched on the edge of her seat, ready to go at a moment's notice, but staring straight through Garrett with seemingly all of her focus. "I like Delilah, as a person. We actually have at least one hook-up in common since she swings every which way. She's super adventurous and optimistic in a lot of ways, and we're still friends on Facebook, for whatever that's worth. That being said, I did not like Delilah for Devon, and I did not like them together."

Garrett opened his mouth to ask the obvious question, *What about me?* Tula waved it away.

"I like you, too, you're a real sweetheart. You feel like one of my own little nephews. And I think you're a lot better for Devon, might even be great for him, though I'm not sure he's great for you."

"Devon says stuff like that all the time, like he's waiting for me to realize he's some piece of trash I'll want nothing to do with. It's like he's trying to incept the notion into my mind, is that something he does? Did he push Delilah away, is he doing it again? Or is that kind of self-doubt something she just couldn't take anymore, and he created a self-fulfilling prophecy? Or was the breakup not about him at all and he's just internalized a lot of garbage about it that can't help but project out?"

The faucet on Garrett's feelings and fears was open now, and they were pouring out. Tula checked her phone for the time they had left, and sighed.

"I can only tell you my opinions, it doesn't mean they're the truth. I think Delilah was just having fun with Devon, and he certainly had fun with her, it's hard not to. She wanted to find him another hot girlfriend, he was all about that. She wanted all of them to go party in South America for spring break, and they did — it looked like a fabulous fucking time. I think she had her fun and left to get serious with Calista, to do her growing up with someone else. Devon probably thought he was the one she'd choose for that, and he wasn't, and it surprised him."

"Ouch," Garrett said.

"Yeah," Tula nodded. "He's been missing her for way too long, but now he has you, and I think he's just about done missing her, because he's head-over-heels for you. So if he's worried that you're going to leave him, I would agree that the fallout from Delilah is the reason why, but I also think he's probably right about you, and smart to be cautious."

Garrett frowned, unsure if he should be offended. Again, Tula answered him before he could ask for clarification.

"It's just because you're so young, okay? You're an emotional newb and you really can't promise him any sort of commitment if you're being honest with yourself, right? You don't know how you're gonna feel, what you're gonna want, in five, ten, fifteen years, and he knows that about you, too, and it's breaking his heart."

"Oh," Garrett said.

Tula's phone pinged, and she stood up. "Come here, hug your auntie Tula," she said. "You look like a sad puppy, don't let me walk out on that note, give us a smile."

Garrett gave her the hug, attempted the smile, and Tula only shook her head.

"That's the best you've got?" She put on her purse and backpack, grabbed up her suitcase, and put a hand on Garrett's shoulder. "You've got my key?"

Garrett held up the key. "Got it."

"You'll remember which plants to mist and which to water right? You'll remember to lock my door every time you leave?"

"I swear it," Garrett said.

"You're a good egg," she said, watching Garrett lock up after them as they left the apartment together. "If you want my advice, just enjoy what you've got with Devon while you've got it. It's a good thing, I'm jealous as hell every time you assholes make googly eyes and hold hands and blow kisses and shit, you ain't subtle."

"Really? I thought we were trying to be discreet."

Tula laughed in his face from behind her mask, so it wasn't quite so invasive. "Fucking try harder. And don't worry that you'll probably leave him before he leaves you, that's no guarantee, right? Stranger things happen every day than you two dingdongs staying together forever."

Garrett couldn't argue with that.

# 35.

Another day, another protest, but this time a quiet one. Garrett was filming casually, just panning around at the beautiful people who showed up for solidarity. He was feeling alive, invincible, still enjoying the afterglow of the previous night's erotic encounter, which greatly calmed his anxieties regarding any exes Devon had in his past, that they could share something so … unique.

Last night Devon surprised Garrett with some absolutely thrilling new kinks. In the previous few weeks, all their sex had been normal, so vanilla it was practically wholesome. Then yesterday evening, Devon brought out a gift, a glittery shoebox that he had stashed behind the couch. He set it on the chest that was his coffee table and said, "So I have a proposition for you."

"Go on."

"These are what folks colloquially call 'fuck me pumps,'" Devon said, lifting the lid to reveal a pair of sparkly, rose-gold, three-inch heels. "And I would like to fuck you in them."

"Intriguing," Garrett said, smiling, and not exactly against the idea.

"If you're willing, I also have a little outfit that goes along with these shoes."

"Yeah?" Garrett asked, picking up one of the shoes. It smelled great, like a department store in the mall.

"Yeah. A pleated skirt, and a lace top," Devon said.

"Well … let's see if they fit."

Garrett stood up and stripped, got turned on just from being nude and looked at, so much so that by the time Devon wrapped the skirt around his waist and fastened it, his dick tented the pleats. The top was a button-up lacy white overshirt, and the final touch was a pearl necklace, a short choker that sat atop Garrett's Adam's apple. Devon got on his knees to help Garrett into the heels, and sat back when the outfit was complete.

"Give us a twirl," he said, and Garrett did, spinning fast enough for the skirt to lift and then flutter back into place. He almost overbalanced, but Devon caught him in a hug, and spoke against Garrett's midriff. "Last ask," he said, tipping his head to gaze up at Garrett. "How do you feel about dirty talk?"

Garrett thought he was fine with it, until he heard the filthy things Devon had to say, and realized that he absolutely loved it.

"Look at what a little slut you are," Devon said as he entered Garrett. "Standing here with no panties on, waiting for someone to penetrate your pink little boypussy." Garrett gasped, and his body flushed. "Oh, you can still blush, you dirty skank? You let me slide my slimy fucking penis in and out of you with no problem, but you hear a bad word and you blush? You've got to get a good look at yourself. Walk to the bathroom, slowly, so that my dick doesn't fall out of its cock holster."

"Okay," Garrett uttered, before shuffling with Devon into the bathroom.

"No speaking," Devon said, grabbing a fistful of Garrett's hair. "If you say one more word I'll shove my fingers down your throat. I might do it anyway because the sound of you gagging like a little bitch makes me hard."

"Jesus," Garrett said. He hadn't meant to speak, but it slipped out of him.

On entering the bathroom, Devon shoved Garrett against the sink and turned on the light. "What the fuck did I just say?" he asked. "You must want to suck on Daddy's fingers, huh?" Devon put the middle and ring fingers of his left hand in Garrett's mouth, across his tongue. "How dare you speak the name of Jesus while someone has sex with your anal cavity, that's disgusting. Look at yourself in the mirror."

Garrett did so, and it gave him such a thrill that a blush rolled through him again.

Devon undid the one button of the lace top he'd fastened in the living room, and started tweaking Garrett's nipples. "Look at you with your tits hanging out, and fuck juice running down your thighs towards those hooker shoes you're wearing." Garrett moaned against Devon's fingers. "Only sluts actually like getting fucked, so I guess we know what you are," Devon said, his breath against Garrett's ear. "Look at your big clit just oozing goo because you like getting ass-fucked so much."

Garrett reached for his dick, but Devon moved his nipple-tweaking hand, with its still-taped broken finger, down to block him. "Don't touch that, you little faggot. If you're gonna cum, it'll be because I'm jabbing your prostate with my cock so goddamn good that you can't help it." Garrett moaned again, a whimper. He started to sweat. "Mmm, Daddy likes to hear that, those helpless, mewling little noises you make. If you can't cum like this, maybe I'll higher some professional dick to come split you in half while I watch and fuck your face."

The fingers in Garrett's mouth started going in and out.

"I don't mean just getting my dick sucked," Devon clarified. "I mean I'll grab hold of your skull and violate the back of your throat until you swallow my load."

Garrett's dick was hanging engorged in the cool, ceramic sink, smearing that bright, white surface with pre-cum.

"How does that sound, hmm?" Devon's slid the palm of his left hand over Garrett's lower belly. "I can feel my dick defiling your nasty guts right now. How would you like having two cocks up there, hmm? Writhing against each other like snakes while you realize what a slut you truly are, to let two men fill your shithole with their fuckmeat at the same time."

Garrett's eyes rolled back. He was so close to orgasm, and Devon was about to prod him off the ledge.

"You'd do it, wouldn't you? Let some stranger inseminate you up the ass? No condom, just raw anal sex until he decides to breed your butt, and then you'd let me suck it out of there, huh? My tongue so far up your anus it tickles the back of your throat."

That was the line that finally put Garrett over the edge. As his balls started pumping out semen unaided, Devon took his fingers out of Garrett's mouth and stuck his tongue in there instead. He started to cum, too. He murmured, "Thank me for fucking you," into Garrett's mouth.

"Thank you," Garrett whispered, his hearing dulled with the pounding of blood. "Thank you, thank you." As his orgasm pulsed out of him, Garrett nudged the light switch off, and in the dark he turned around to hug the hell out of Devon. "Thank you, thank you," he repeated as Devon kissed his neck, his face, his lips, his ears, his eyelids.

Standing at the protest, dreamy-eyed over his sexy memories from the night before, Garrett hardly noticed that the cops had made a decision that today's protest was over until the pepper balls started flying, and struck someone standing less than ten feet from him. Garrett saw the guy drop, but didn't register the horror of what had happened until the guy — youngish, sandy-blond hair, tall and thin — screamed in pain. From somewhere in the crowd, Hazel and Lena rushed forward to assess the damage. Blood was pouring down his face from under the hand that covered his injury. When Lena pulled his hand away so they could help him, Garrett snapped a picture reflexively of the hole where this man's left eye used to be.

"How bad is it? Am I blind?" he asked, his voice shaking.

Someone closer to the carnage than Garrett was so sickened by the sight, she threw up. Hazel put her hand on the man's shoulder, looked him calmly in his remaining eye, and shook her head.

"I'm sorry," she said. "Your eye is gone."

The guy looked like he wanted to cry, but wasn't sure if he could anymore.

# VI. AUTONOMOUS

# 36.

"Finally something good comes out of this shit year," Devon said that weekend, when he heard his dreams had come true. "Present company excluded, of course." Garrett was laying on the couch, his head in Devon's lap. He looked up to see the phone screen Devon faced down to show him. The news said an autonomous zone had come to town.

"What does an autonomous zone mean?" Garrett asked.

It meant something different, something unique, to every community that had one. Seattle had their Capitol Hill Autonomous Zone (CHAZ), also known as the Capital Hill Occupied Protest (CHOP), where nearly everything was free and there were no uniformed police allowed to enter. Teenagers drank in public, those with weapons carried them openly in defiance of Seattle law, and food was available for whatever you could exchange for it. They knew the police would ultimately come to reclaim the Capitol Hill territory, but until they did, the freedom was a respite, a relief. Minneapolis had George Floyd Square, again a cop-free place on the very ground where George Floyd's life was taken from him by a cop. It began with a safe place for George Floyd's memorial, where people could contribute flowers or other remembrances, stand and grieve, hug and comfort one another without being hassled by police to move it along. Portland had the Red House eviction defense, an outcropping of militant housing activism on Mississippi Avenue to stand in the gap between the Afro-Indigenous Kinney family and cops who were there to illegally and heartlessly evict them during a pandemic. Devon couldn't wait to see what his city did with the autonomous template.

"I believe in this shit," Devon said. "When I went to Rojava, I was just so goddamn proud of humanity, that out of pain and oppression, freedom rises like a phoenix."

"Rojava?"

Devon grinned, reached for his laptop, and pulled up the series he wrote on the place. "It's a stateless democracy grounded in anarcho-communist principles and I'm jealous as fuck that we don't have one just like it in North America, like … why are we sleeping on the job here? What the fuck?"

He set his laptop on Garrett's chest, and the kid sat up to receive it, to read up on the Autonomous Administration of North and East Syria, aka Rojava.

"Long story short, it's feminist as fuck. In a sea of gender-based oppression with ISIS whipping people to ribbons left and right for the smallest infractions they can think of like belting a burka, women took up arms and carved out a safe space for themselves that's sustainable and fair to all. Community conflict resolution without cops, women soldiers strapped more for defense than offense, humane treatment of their captured enemies. It's a beautiful thing and I hope it flourishes."

"More evidence that women are the superior version of human being," Garrett said, shaking his head, impressed. "It's like when they do those micro-loans in Africa, you give a woman a dollar and she'll find a way to make it support the next three generations, give it to a man he'll probably eat it or blow it up, light it on fire. Just useless."

"It's sad but it's true," Devon said. "I fucking love setting money on fire."

The first order of business for Devon that day and every day going forward for as long as possible was to get into that autonomous zone and revel in it. For as touch-and-go as his emotional state had been all year, Devon felt that the air in a space where cops were not welcome would feel lighter, taste better, and he had to find out.

Since this autonomous zone originated out of the taking of the City Hall Plaza, it was named the Plaza Land Autonomous Zone of America, so that when shortened it would still be known as PLAZA. That was just objectively precious, and Devon's first mission was to find and interview whoever was responsible for that name so he could shake his or her or their hand. Garrett was prepared to go with him on this trip to their city's tiny freedom fiefdom, but he wasn't anywhere near as exhilarated at the prospect as Devon.

"You look like Christmas came early," Garrett said as they waited for the subway and Devon bounced on the balls of his feet.

"I'm a kid in a commie store," Devon said, stepping onto the train and hoping that by the time he stepped off, he'd be looking at the off-the-grid carnival of his dreams.

The PLAZA blocks did not disappoint.

Even Garrett was engaged and fascinated as they walked up to a cluster of concrete security barriers and orange traffic cones borrowed from a nearby construction site and clustered into the middle of the street so cars could not enter the Zone. Devon's first question was whether they had a plan to let ambulances through, a main entrance or a way to move this shit rapidly. People in suburbs often thought they wanted speed bumps to protect the tranquility of their neighborhood, without thinking that those things didn't lay down for rescue vehicles, slowing down the emergency response to one's capitalism-caused heart attack. This place could fall victim to a similar flaw; the guards accepted Devon's notes, said they'd take them under advisement.

The people milling around the autonomous zone were Devon's kind of people: men building tables and barriers out of trash, women organizing food and crafts, teenagers delighted to be un-minded among rule-breaking adults, everyone watching everyone else with eyes that said, *You cool? Can you believe we're really doing this? Don't you love to see it?* Devon absolutely loved to see it.

He and Garrett were allowed in as journalists, but they didn't do any investigating at first, just took in the sights, and the smells.

"Is that barbecue?" Garrett asked, smelling the breeze like a bunny rabbit.

"Yeah, you hungry?" Devon asked.

"I wasn't a minute ago, but now ..."

They continued down the street, closer to the plaza that had been boarded up and abandoned by officials until all this unrest calmed down. What with the pandemic and all, the people who worked at City Hall shouldn't have been in there anyway, as most bureaucratic business could be easily done over Zoom. It was in the shadow of this government building that someone had set up some grills and was turning meat on one and veggies on the other. When Devon and Garrett approached, they were each given their choice of snack free of charge (Devon a handful of ribs in a paper towel, Garrett a shish kabob of Brussels sprouts covered in the same sweet sauce as the meat), and they walked away to see more sights with sticky lips. There was a man handing out gas masks and rainbow flags from the back of his van — he told each person who approached, "Pride was a riot, never forget." A collection of knitters and crocheters in camp chairs next to a radio bopped their heads as they wove their yarns. Folks wandered about amiably drinking beer in the quiet streets.

Devon wouldn't have been surprised to find a petting zoo and a cotton candy machine, it felt like a county fair in a downtown street, and it was glorious. It would be so pretty to see every street overtaken with pedestrians, every office closed and quiet, every concrete jungle overgrown with vines and yarn after a bloodless overthrow of useless commerce. Wouldn't that be a wonderful world?

Devon and Garrett found a hose set up as a washing station where they cleaned their hands and faces after their unexpected brunch (not before Devon threatened to lick Garrett's face clean right out in the open; Garrett only rolled his eyes). They started introducing themselves to people, asking them if they felt like answering questions, would they consent to being filmed for an interview? Everyone was in a charming mood, even when their answer was "no comment," almost like a blissful cloud had surrounded them, like the opposite of tear gas. Devon noticed, however, that even among the people who did want to answer questions, no one wanted to talk about what happened after this Zone collapsed.

"How long do you think the cops and the city will let people have this space?" Devon asked. "What happens after? How does this end?"

"I don't know?" answered one woman with a curious inflection and a shrug. "I think my hope is that the officials see this and take us seriously, that they understand we don't need them as much as they need us, the people, and that if we can govern ourselves with peace and kindness and charity, why can't they?"

# 37.

Police and city officials had a lot of sour shit to say about the PLAZA as the day wore on.

"People need to get back into their businesses and offices without being confronted by these blockades," said the Mayor.

"What's been happening on these streets for the past week has been brutal and lawless, and at the end of the day, completely unacceptable," said the Chief of Police about the citizens and not her cops.

"We support *peaceful* demonstrations, but ..." said the State Governor, clearly eying a run for higher office.

Devon laughed at every equivocating pronouncement that lit up his phone. He'd never felt safer on these downtown streets than he did knowing there were no cops or bosses or property owners around to hassle him. It's one of those weights you don't feel until it's lifted, like the trips Devon has made to countries without a glut of guns among the population. It's not that he wanted to give up his own arsenal, it's just that it was damn nice to take a break from being on edge all the time, from looking over his shoulder and staying peripherally aware of what was behind his back.

Someone had come along to crowbar off the spike plates that were riveted in place to make sure homeless people couldn't sit down, one of the more insulting uses of public money he'd ever seen. No money to house the unhoused, but to keep them uncomfortable? Blank check, baby. Devon laid atop one of these liberated spots and put his earbuds in, closed his eyes, and tucked his hands behind his head. He was comfortable and trusting, knew that no one would fuck with him because the vibe was too chill. No one would tell him he couldn't rest here, no one was going to try to steal the phone off his chest (or if they did they wouldn't get far) because this bubble of peace and quiet was too precious to them all after weeks of being shoved, trapped, gassed, and assaulted by state thugs.

Garrett was off doing photography for art's sake more than articles, an aspect of him that Devon wasn't fully cognizant of until Garrett returned to him and showed what he'd found: a graffiti rose with a ribbon around the stem that read "Rest in Power" in cursive; neat rows of homemade face masks as mesmerizing as a quilt; a collection of protest signs tucked into some leftover portable fencing, making those hideous barriers a lot less ugly.

Devon and Garrett's heads were close together as they leaned in to share these images, and it occurred to Devon that they were missing something. Because Devon had a vision of his own, of a home he and Garrett would one day share, where these pictures would be framed on their wall, but where was the focal piece? What image should that be?

"Hey," he said, tilting his face toward his riot son. "We haven't taken any couple photos."

Garrett thought back quickly to their few short weeks of infatuation, and confirmed. "No, we haven't."

Devon wondered, "The moment is now?"

"Now or never, right?" Garrett lifted up his camera with one hand, and put the other arm around Devon's shoulders. He twisted his wrist, watched the camera lens adjust itself, and turned to kiss Devon on the cheek just in time for the volley of snaps. Devon got to thinking about how they didn't kiss in public much either, not after that first night on Tula's roof, and he wondered how many more wonderful firsts they had to look forward to as Garrett reviewed the shots acquired for the best capture.

"You know," Devon said, "no matter which way you count it, this week is the one-month anniversary of the day we met."

"Shouldn't we count it by month?" Garrett asked, not looking up from his task.

The light in the sky was ripening to late afternoon, and Devon clarified. "If a month is exactly four weeks, our month is tomorrow, if it's first-to-first, second-to-second regardless of irregular monthly lengths, it's the day after the day after tomorrow."

Garrett smiled, maybe at Devon's accounting, or maybe because he found what he was looking for. "There she is," Garrett said, and handed his camera to Devon for his approval.

There they were: masks down, eyes lowered, a subtle smile perking up Devon's cheek just above his beard, at the very moment that Garrett's lips touched down upon his skin. Not only that, a long stretch of autonomous zone could be seen just over Devon's shoulder, and the color of Garrett's hair had the same highlights as the bricks in the wall behind him. A boy could win an award over something like that, but Devon would have bet the world that this picture would stay personal and private, just between them.

However, what Devon said was, "Well, we've got our Christmas card right here."

Garrett snorted, took back his camera, and sighed. "How much longer do you want to stay in this place?"

"Forever," Devon said.

"Right? No, but really."

Devon had meant forever, really, but he also knew what Garrett was talking about. "I was thinking I'd stay the night, meet the midnight crowd, volunteer for a little guard duty, get a little drunk."

"Oh, you mean to participate?" Garrett asked, because one month in, he just didn't know Devon that well yet.

"I think I stopped being an observer as soon as I stepped onto this hallowed ground," Devon said. "I mean, officially I'm only here doing anything as an embedded reporter, but unofficially I want to help out. I've been in besieged encampments like this before, I might be able to supply some tactical and practical advice if anyone's willing to take it."

"Hmm," Garrett said.

"You're thinking I shouldn't?"

Garrett set his hand briefly on Devon's neck, then said, "No, I'm thinking I shouldn't, I'm more of an inside cat, but you can have your fun." He began putting his camera away. "I'm thinking I should stop by Tula's to check on her plants, eat dinner that isn't street meat, get a little work done, watch something funny like a little stand-up maybe, and end my night in bed with Oskar the cat."

"That's a good plan, too. I'll bring you breakfast in the morning, how does that sound?"

"It sounds like breakfast in bed for our anniversary," Garrett said, raising his mask and standing to go. "See you then."

So a month to them was four weeks on the dot. Devon noted that decision as he waved goodbye.

# 38.

As the afternoon faded, the PLAZA people changed. Day-trippers went home, and the nightlife awoke. Devon first exchanged a three-hour guard shift for some booze, the kind of barter system he could really get behind, and by the time the sun was fully down, he was dancing around a trashcan fire to live music. It wasn't just one band either, it was a real showcase of musicians who weren't allowed into their usual venues during the pandemic, just coming out to share the love. Devon was buzzed enough to dance and weave to every offering, from a baby folk trio to a solo rap artist to an old-school folk duo to a rhythmic poet to one sweet, sage soul (a white-looking woman who could have been a hard-living forty-five or a well-maintained sixty) who brought out a motherfucking triangle and asked for a sing-along. Devon was skeptical that such a diverse crowd would know all the words to the same song, but this woman had an idea.

"If you matter and you know it, clap your hands," she sang, and dinged her triangle twice. "If you matter and you know it, clap your hands." Two more dings, claps occurred, and voices started amplifying her. "If you matter and you know it and you really want to show it, if you matter and you know it, clap your hands."

A hush fell over the fireside crew, and people farther out started to shift nearer.

"If you matter and you know it, stomp your feet," began round two, and this time people were into it. "If you matter and you know it, stomp your feet." The stomps shook the street. "If you matter and you know it and you really want to show it, if you matter and you know it, stomp your feet."

The rule of three said she had one more round for them, but this one changed the mood profoundly. "If you matter and you know it, can you breathe?" No chime this time, but people gasped. "If you matter and you know it, can you breathe?" No one sang with her, but though her voice quivered, this woman finished her song. "If you matter and you know it but you're not sure you can show it, if you matter and you know it, can you breathe?"

She started to cry, and a lot of other people did, too. Devon saw one Black man cross himself and heard a brown-skinned woman say, "God bless you."

Devon's tears were sitting on his eyelashes like dew on blades of grass. When the woman turned towards him, he couldn't help but open his arms, and she walked right into them like they'd known each other all their lives.

She sobbed against his chest. Devon blinked, and his tears fell into her hair, which was like soft, spun steel. He laughed because sometimes his emotions crisscrossed like that, and he said, "Damn, girl, you can really rain out a parade."

Her next sob hiccuped with a surprised laugh, and the spell on everyone else broke. There was a sigh of relief, the street started mingling again, and Devon and this woman, Brenna, became best friends for the rest of the night.

Why was Brenna out here wrecking feelings tonight? Because her ex-boyfriend was Black, and her daughter had also been Black, which is why when the daughter went to a hospital complaining of agonizing pain in her swollen leg, the hospital staff thought she was exaggerating, or drug-seeking, or overreacting. They said that at twenty-two, she was too young to be in any serious condition, that she should go home, and if her leg still hurt in a few days, skip the hospital and see her in-network doctor instead. Brenna's daughter Amelia died about two weeks later after flying home. She died in her mother's arms.

"She'd hurt her knee playing volleyball earlier that year," Brenna said, sitting on the asphalt with her knees tucked under her sweater because it was chilly just a few feet away from the fire. Devon wanted to cradle her, she was a little woman and he was a hot mess of a drinker, just radiating warmth, but he couldn't hold her while she was telling the story of cradling her daughter into the grave. "It was obviously deep vein thrombosis. I mean, I didn't know that, but it's textbook symptoms. She was at college, the doctors said she should wait to see if her ACL healed on its own before surgery. I talked to her on the phone, I thought it couldn't be that bad if she went to the ER and they took an x-ray and said it wasn't a big deal. But after her injury she drove 12 hours to where her boyfriend lived, and she told that ER she wasn't insured, so they didn't listen to her at all after that, and then she flew home to me and her father, and two days later the clot hit her heart, and she was gone."

"That's horrible," Devon told her. He was leaking tears again but wicking them away as they came. He was also drinking slowly and steadily, rapt with attention and devotion to his new safe-space buddy.

Brenna smiled softly, sadly. "You want to know the worst part?"

"No, but yes," Devon said.

Her smile lengthened; Devon had endeared himself to her. "She actually was insured at that time, she just didn't know it. I found out a week later when I got a letter telling her she'd been automatically enrolled in COBRA after she graduated and left her work-study job. But she told them she wasn't insured, and so she's gone now."

Devon had followed the story intently, and even in a boozy haze knew that there were a dozen ways it could have been different. If Amelia hadn't needed to play volleyball to keep her scholarship, if she hadn't gotten hurt, if she'd been given surgery right away, if she hadn't driven so far, if she hadn't run into this shitstain hospital, if she hadn't gone there at the exact moment her insurance was in flux, if she hadn't then flown home because she was in so much pain that all she wanted was her mommy.

Devon swallowed a lot of salty swear words and instead said, "I guess you were a Bernie Bro for this last election, weren't you?"

Brenna nodded over her sweater tent. "You could say that, yeah. I didn't vote for Hillary, that's for sure."

"That's so weird, because feminist icon Gloria Steinem said younger women were only interested in Bernie because they were interested in boys and the boys were with Bernie. And former secretary of state Madeleine Albright said there was a special place in hell for women who don't help each other, so ..."

"Sounds like Gloria was a slut and Madeleine is a cunt?"

Devon laughed so loud he startled nearby birds pecking at the food dropping on the street. He loved this lady.

"No, I don't care about those women," Brenna said, waving away her strong words, but coming out from under her sweater. "But they don't care about me either, or my daughter. Anyone who is against single-payer healthcare even though Canada has it right above us thinks it's okay that my daughter died, at twenty-two years old, from something incredibly treatable if you catch it soon enough. What's feminist about that?"

"Not a goddamn thing, Brenna."

Their conversation didn't end there, they stayed up all night having the kind of deep therapy that Devon once found in Tula. Sometimes you met somebody and barfed out your soul to them, and they to you, and even if you never met again, it was the most deep and beautiful and human connection in the world.

Brenna said, "You know I loved my daughter so much, I feel like I'm less of a person without her, but I don't think I was a good mother. I made some mistakes, I had some issues with drugs when she was little, I wasn't there for her. I mean, her father was worse, he didn't even try that hard, or care, when she was a baby. But then I was so messy by the time she could remember, she thought I was the bad parent. Maybe I was, maybe we both were."

"Hey," Devon told her, "it's anecdotal and all, but my mom wasn't perfect either, right? She used to lock me in a dark closet to punish me and sometimes she forgot. She used to crank up her music in the car when my sister and I were being too loud in the back because she was sick of the sound of our voices — that shit hurt our ears. I have it on good authority from my sister that she thinks I'm a slut, and she's right, but she says it in a mean way when there's nothing wrong with me, but you know what? She's also the mom who took me to the emergency room when I had a fever even though she was bone tired and I was probably fine, because she just wouldn't risk losing me like that." Brenna put her hand over her heart and nodded, because she knew that feeling. "My dad wouldn't have done it, and there's no replacing love like that, and there's no forgetting it. Who was holding your daughter when she died? Her mother. Who did George Floyd call to when he died?"

The tears fell out of Brenna's face like twin waterfalls. "His mother!"

Devon was crying again, and they were hugging again. They had to after a revelation like that.

"You hadn't put that together before?" Devon asked Brenna, hugging her as firmly as he hugged his own mom as a kid when she wanted him to help crack her back. Brenna's heaving sobs were a clear answer to his question. "I don't care what you did or didn't do," he told her, "everyone wants their mother in the end."

When they sniffled away from each other and started laughing again (so they would not weep anymore), Devon noticed the sunrise was near.

Good morning, America.

# 39.

## *When Does Autonomy Work?*

### **Defund the Police?**

When people hear a phrase like "defund the police" or "abolish the police" they might think, "Oh yeah? Well, who are you gonna call when you're robbed or raped, huh? What if some methed-up criminal breaks into your house at night, you want a social worker to get back to you in two to three days?" Two problems with that so-called logic: one, cops don't prevent crimes from happening, and they don't solve that many of them either, and certainly not in a timely fashion; two, your neighbors aren't always out to get you. In fact, when the government fails, neighbors often step up to save themselves and each other. They do it because of ... what's that faggotty cuck libtard thing? Ah, empathy.

### **Citizen, Save Thyself**

Maybe you've gotten into a spat with a petty neighbor about them not picking up their dog's turds from your lawn. Maybe you've had issues with porch piracy or heard stories about malicious mailbox damage and you think everyone is truly trash except for maybe half of the people who go to your church. But just as there are many examples of casual discourtesies from the dentist's office to the DMV, when life is on the line, there are a lot of people who become the heroes they want to see in the world. For example:

- **Hot Car Experiments:** These results won't sit right at first, because experiments in which people leave a realistic-looking baby doll in a hot, locked car to see who will stop to help provide a lot of mixed data. First, many people do not notice a quiet child in the back of a car. Second, even when experimenters add wailing sounds, people don't hear it over their earbuds or don't look around to see why there's crying. However, the people who do ultimately stop to help are people with that Ron Ridenhour gold in their souls: they either know how quickly a car can bake an infant's brains (people who work with kids, rescue workers, and yes even select cops), or they've had or known a baby at some point and think, "If this was my child I'd want someone to get involved," so they get involved. It should be noted however that more people react stronger and faster to a dog in a trapped car, so review the previous section on the problems with SWAT in our police forces and do better, folks.

- **Natural Disasters:** From fires to earthquakes to hurricanes, while the news still goes with "if it bleeds, it leads" and especially loves to show supposed looters (quick cheat code for the game at home: white people "find" and "rescue" food and shopping items, people of color "loot" and "steal"), it's also true that neighbors come out to aid strangers long before the National Guard shows up to police the populace so they don't turn native and savage (which they won't — it's not Mad Max out here just because the power lines are down). From Florida to New Orleans to Texas, those with working boats will go out to save any living soul stranded on the island of their roof after a hurricane (and sometimes name themselves cute shit like the "Cajun Navy"); after earthquakes in California, volunteers search and dig for survivors, just as New Yorkers did after the Twin Towers collapsed on 9/11 (before getting robbed of first-responder funds meant to help them with their medical needs afterward, but it's congresspeople who do that, not fellow humans apparently); during the ever-increasing nightmare wildfires in the western U.S. from Oregon to the Tijuana border, people will not only help evacuate each other, but also each other's pets and livestock animals (and even the unowned creatures of the forests).

- **Unnatural Disasters:** It's often a bittersweet thing to know that humanity shows up after what insurance companies call "acts of God" (so they don't have to pay out) but are far more likely to be climate change i.e. man-made catastrophes. It's an entirely different feeling when good people have to fight against bad to save a life. Prime example: the Ycuá Bolaños supermarket fire in Paraguay in 2004. Much like the Triangle Shirtwaist Factory fire of 1911, what happened was that management wanted to maximize profit. Those fire safety protocols? Meh, those cost money, and a fire may never start. Not locking people inside the building? Eh, but then they could steal stuff, the dirty thieves. How about at least unlocking the doors when the fireball begins? Again, no. The incomprehensible tragedy of 146 deaths in the Shirtwaist Factory can't hold a candle to what happened in Ycuá Bolaños, because the Shirtwaist employees were at least allowed to try and escape any way they could (some burned, suffocated, fell and were impaled, or jumped rather than stay to be roasted to death once the pain from the flames became unbearable). But in Paraguay in 2004, the doors were locked *after* the fire began, ostensibly because the owners were worried that customers would leave without paying. Over 300 bodies of men, women, and children were pulled out afterward, and over 400 people would eventually die due to their injuries. The owner of the store who built the death trap ultimately got a 12-year prison sentence for this carnage; his son who managed the store and gave the order to lock the doors got 10 years; the guard who was "just following orders" in locking those doors got 5 years. This was only after a retrial, because at first in 2006 the courts said "involuntary manslaughter" (wrong on the "involuntary" part) which maxed the sentences at 5 years for each. On further consideration after violent demonstrations from the survivors and families, the 2008 verdict came back as "negligent homicide." Again, that word "negligent" doesn't seem to fit, but at least they went to prison for a little bit longer until of course they were released early for good behavior (they seem like nice chaps). If you're wondering why this miserable story is in this inherent humanity section, here is why: when the fires started, decent people did everything they could to break the thick glass windows of the store when they couldn't open the doors. They did their best to bust through brick walls to save even one life if they could, and one woman named Liliana Hernandez who lived next door to this massive supermarket let firefighters chop holes through her walls looking for weak spots to the inferno fortress. There was still humanity on display, just not enough.

It's not all bastards out there, but it is a battle of numbers.

## *The Root of All Evil*

Long story short, average people can do heroic things when they see a situation and say, "There but for the vagaries of fate go I." Sometimes being brave and kind and doing for others is so natural it's instinctive, imperative, and there are only a few things that can ruin that beauty where it goes. Theoretical physicist Steven Weinberg had a hot take in a *New York Times* interview from 1999: "With or without religion, you would have good people doing good things and evil people doing evil things. But for good people to do evil things, that takes religion." True, but money can do it, too. Would more people notice a distressed child in a hot car if they weren't caught up in the capitalist rat race? Would we have fewer and less severe "natural disasters" without the environmental holocaust perpetrated by large corporations? Would anyone lock hundreds of people in ovens without first believing that they were coming for his own "hard-earned" money? When people say we need less or zero brutal policing, it isn't because crime is so fun and we all love criminals (although considering the legends that grow up around bank robbers … one could make that argument). It's just that perhaps without scalding the humanity out of people for the pursuit of money, we wouldn't need to employ cops to protect property and order. Why steal if you can have, you know? And people will work for the good of one another, even without being paid, it happens after every disaster and tragedy. One last thought to send you on your way: gardeners sometimes refer to the flowers and plants that show up in their gardens with no effort or intention on their parts as bonus plants (if they're welcome; noxious opportunistic plants are known as weeds). Birds drop and winds blow seeds into these little Edens, and if they stand up on their own to be counted, there's a term for them: volunteers. Volunteer plants, volunteer flowers, or volunteer blooms: they grow and flourish and contribute without anyone making them do it. People can be like that, too, sometimes, if you leave them alone.

# 40.

Garrett had never lived alone. While Devon was spending the night in an autonomous zone full of people, happy to be at the center of a hive, Garrett relished a night during which he was truly on his own … except for Oskar the cat.

"Hey boy," Garrett said when he arrived home, all his chores for the day complete, and dinner already half-prepared in the back of his mind — some simple ramen with vegan fake-beef crumbles and tofu mush to dress it up. Speaking of dressing up, that was also Garrett's plan for the evening.

The outfit Devon gave him, he wanted to revisit that on his own. He took a very bubbly shower. He let his hair air-dry as he ate dinner and watched makeup tutorials so that his curls would be at full-bodied bounce. Then he opened the bottle of sparkling pink wine he bought on the way home, mostly because it would match his new shoes while getting him tipsy. He put his face on first.

It was nothing too dramatic, as Garrett only had a basic set of makeup that he rarely used, but he did put on foundation that disappeared his freckles, tinted his lips a seashell blush, and did a little shading to give himself the appearance of womanly contours: a more feminine hairline, higher cheekbones, and a light V on his chest to mimic cleavage. Then it was time for the clothes.

Garrett put on a white tank top he had with a heart-shaped ruche at the collar designed to complement a breasted body, added Devon's lace top over it, and put on underwear this time before adding the skirt so he could tuck himself out of sight. Lastly, he stepped into the shoes.

Garrett was not very well-practiced at walking or even standing in high heels, because had he been seen in such a state growing up, there would have been an aggressive reeducation process to promote his "natural" masculinity. However, just having the shoes on made him feel nice — this was gender euphoria, the opposite of gender dysphoria. He was so much taller in the heels as he put his hair in a half-ponytail and spun around for Oskar the cat this time, who watched Garrett do this unusual dance with dilated pupils. In a human being, large pupils meant love, lust, or a recent trip to the optometrist. In a cat it probably meant alarm or discomfort, but so long as Garrett left Oskar unmolested on top of the dresser, surveying his domain, it was allowed.

Garrett decided the purpose of his night was to practice his runway walk. He put in earbuds and turned on some music, started prancing, dancing, and twirling around, careful not to be too rambunctious lest he twist an ankle or disturb the downstairs neighbors.

When Garrett got too drunk to keep his footing, he switched to taking selfies under various different lights and with a range of facial expressions (allure, surprise, cute cheer). He took several with Oskar the cat as well until Oskar got sick of the attention and moved to his customary spot on the couch. Then Garrett sat down in Devon's big chair, crossed his legs like a lady, and with a swirling mind, reviewed the fruit of his photoshoot.

It wasn't until Garrett had selected the best pictures that it occurred to him: he had no one to share them with. Suddenly, on what had been a charmingly playful and carefree night, Garrett was slowly gutted. He turned off his music and let himself cry.

Garrett's friends from childhood, if that's truly what they were, had nothing to do with him now. His parents and siblings and even his aunt would not accept pictures like this; they would see them as the symptoms of mental illness and block his number forever. His editor liked Garrett but only professionally. Tula liked Garrett, he was her so-called riot son, too, but she was Devon's friend first, and always would be. Devon would welcome the photos, but Devon was only one man, and a lover was not the same as a friend. If these pictures showed up on Devon's phone they'd likely be seen as a flirtation, and that was fine, but Garrett didn't take them for that reason, and he had no one who would see them the way that Garrett saw them. It made him sad for a few minutes.

Oskar jumped into his lap, perhaps drawn to comfort this new energy, or because he was bored, or because he liked the taste of tears, nice and salty. When Oskar started licking Garrett's face, he laughed and wiped his eyes.

"Thank you for these kissies," he said to Oskar, and gave the cat a hug before getting up, stepping out of his heels, and opening a new can of wet food to treat the cat. "Kissies from kitties," he chanted a few times, before saying, "Maybe I'm getting my period, I hear they always show up on the day you put on a skirt, hmm?" Oskar was unresponsive to the joke once he had some food to focus on, and Garrett turned down the lights and washed his face, an attempt to reset the mood. Before he took off the outfit though, he had one more treat for himself.

Garrett let his hair loose so it would pillow around him when he lay down on the bed. He slid his underwear off so he could masturbate freely, remembering the way Devon manhandled him, whispered degeneracies against his ear, and the way he felt under Garrett, over him, surrounding him when he picked him up in those big bear hugs. Garrett caught his discharge in a sock, and in the mild bliss that followed, he thought about how much he missed Devon after only a few hours of solitude. Maybe it was unhealthy to be so emotionally dependent on someone else so soon, or maybe this riot son had just caught a bad case of the love bug from Devon, and it would pass in due time. Or maybe Garrett just wouldn't like living alone if this was the kind of hyper-introspective bullshit one had to deal with when not distracted by another person's breathing, moving, being.

Garrett got into his pajamas, took the rest of his wine bottle to bed with him, and couldn't wait to be asleep already, as solitude had become dull. He fell asleep scrolling through pictures hashtag'd #transwoman, #transgirl, #transisbeautiful, and woke up when the nearly empty wine bottle he clutched like a stuffed animal was plucked from his arms by Devon the next morning.

Garrett smiled before he opened his eyes. When he did peek he saw Devon holding a bag of food and swigging the last dregs of that warm, sweet, flat wine.

"Hey, party people," Devon said. "Sit up if you want breakfast in bed."

Garrett shifted upright and made room to pull Devon into the sheets. Grimy though he was from a night on the street, Garrett wrapped both his arms and legs around his guy and took in a big whiff of him.

"You smell like smoke," he said. "And that food smells awesome, what is it?"

"Breakfast burritos, yours don't have meat," Devon said as Garrett kissed him all over his neck and shoulders. "Miss me much?"

"Yes, but don't get a complex," Garrett said, making Devon laugh, which banished the last of Garrett's sad ghosts from the night before.

They made a mess in bed feeding each other fries and dropped pieces of egg, talking as they chewed like the savages they were.

"My night was wild," Devon said. "I met this wonderful woman, she told me about the day her daughter died. We wept and hugged, I love her so much."

Garrett loved that about Devon, how he prat-fell into love like Sideshow Bob walking into rakes. How was this guy so worried about losing Garrett when he plucked people's hearts out all the time like ripe berries? His family loved him, Tula loved him, Michelle loved him, Wayne David would die for him, and *Devon* was worried about being left alone? Garrett wondered if he truly knew the meaning of the word.

When he finished his food, Devon set the wrappers on the floor and laid back rubbing his belly mound. Garrett rubbed it, too, as one might rub a Buddha statue's tummy for luck, and then retrieved his phone from under the pillow.

When Devon opened his arms in invitation, Garrett snuggled close. "I had a little photoshoot last night. What do you think?" He selected one picture of himself kissing a tolerant Oskar on the head like one might bend down to smell a rose, and showed it to Devon.

"Hey who's this babe, you got her number?" Devon asked, taking the phone so he could examine the picture close to his eyes. "Think she'd want to be my wife? She's cute."

"You're being silly," Garrett said, tugging his phone back.

"I'm only silly if you're silly, honey. Are you sure you're not trans? If it's process-ongoing I won't bug you about it, but it won't change how I feel about you, just know that."

"I don't know," Garrett said. "I like being pretty and I like my penis, and that's about all I'm sure of right now."

Devon reached over to swipe his finger across Garrett's phone screen so they could look at more pictures together. When he reached the end, he kissed Garrett's forehead, and Garrett turned over to lay atop Devon and make out with him. The taste of sour wine and salty breakfast was no impediment. At one point he kissed down Devon's cheek to whisper in his ear, "I love you, too." Devon said it first a month before, and though one month sounded like hardly any time at all, it felt like an eternity had happened since then, and like this return of affection had been a long time coming.

Devon put his hands around Garrett's face and turned it so he could kiss back to Garrett's lips. He kept going, making a journey of his own to the other side of Garrett's head. Once there, he whispered back, saying, "Happy anniversary, my love."

# 41.

In an effort to reconnect with other people who surely loved him, Garrett reached out to his Aunt Lilith later that day. He wanted to say hi, to hear about the house-mouse projects she had going on, to tell her about his new acquaintances and adventures, and to get her blessing for it all. He asked her if she had time for a video call, and they were off to the races immediately with chatter.

"You remember how this place looked when you dropped me off?" Garrett said. "I've improved it." He showed her the friendly parts of the living room and kitchen (skipped the gun zone), and then brought the phone to the fairy-light structure over the bed.

"Ooh, that's super cute. I bet that's fun at night, you've got little stars above you as a nightlight."

"Yeah, that was my thinking," Garrett said, sitting down on the bed so those lights would be his backdrop. "How are you doing?"

"I've made some improvements around here, too." Aunt Lilith took him through the new hacks she'd learned on the internet for tidying up a kitchen pantry, showed him some new throw pillows she'd sewn out of old blouses and filled with old pillow fluff, then sat down on the futon in the den that used to be Garrett's room for a while and said, "It's awfully quiet around here without you, but I'm glad you're happy."

"I am happy," he told her, and then took a deep breath before saying, "I think I'm in love."

He couldn't just say, "I am in love," full-stop, because it felt too presumptuous. First of all, Garrett was now and had long been keenly aware of how young he was, and how much even the smartest young person couldn't know such a thing for sure. People told him as much, just like they told the girl in *Fahrenheit 451*: "I'm seventeen and I'm crazy. My uncle says the two always go together. When people ask your age, he said, always say seventeen and insane." But people frequently said it about their past selves, as if the older they got the more they were amazed they'd been able to find a door to get out of the house every morning when they were teenagers. Some things people only learned the long way, like what love is and what it isn't. Also, after so many years on the compound making up stories about which girls Garrett was supposed to think were datable, just saying "I'm in love" didn't mean much in itself — it was being honest about it that mattered the most.

"You know what? That is so great," Aunt Lilith said. "And you know what else it is? It's brave, thank you so much for telling me that."

Garrett felt the gorge in his throat rise and grinned to try and hide it. "I hoped you would think so, Aunt Lilith. You've always been so good to me."

"Well, that's because I've loved you since you were just a little tadpole in your mummy's tummy," she said, nudging the corners of her eyes, which had gone misty with emotion. "I loved you way before old what's his name, this guy you're seeing. What's his name again?"

"Devon," Garrett said, and it felt so nice he said it twice. "Devon Amis."

"That's it," she said, as if it had been on the tip of her tongue (it hadn't). "When can we meet him?"

It took a few rounds of "really?" before Garrett believed she actually wanted to meet Devon, and that Uncle Wes would be okay with it, too. After that, Garrett had to wonder … did he truly want his worlds to join like that? He thought he did, but what with being eighteen and insane, he doubted himself. He asked Devon about it, but Devon had no reservations whatsoever.

"Sorry, if they want to feed us for free, what's the problem?" he asked when they were brushing their teeth together that night. "If you're worried about me, don't be, I can be on good behavior." Brush, brush, spit. "I've talked myself out of at least three knifings in my life, I can get people on my side." Rinse, gargle, spit. "I won't embarrass you."

"What if they embarrass me, though," Garrett said. "I mean, I love them, I would have been really screwed without their help, but they've got some nasty opinions, and Uncle Wes in particular might unload them at dinner."

"We'll work out a series of signals," Devon said, dropping his toothbrush in its cup. "Tug your left ear if you want me to kick his ass, tweak your nose if you want me to let him think he's kicking my ass, cross your eyes if it's time to go."

Garrett spit his last mouthful of toothpaste in the sink and rinsed the water around so the scum wouldn't stick to the side of the bowl. He still couldn't look at the sink for long without remembering being pressed against it, but the memory didn't distract him as much as it used to. In one way, that was useful, because he didn't have time to get hard whenever he saw porcelain. But in another way it was sad that everything faded away like that eventually, everything.

"He won't want to fight, Uncle Wes has never hit anyone and he's very proud of it," Garrett said. "Not man, nor woman, nor child, nor dog, he believes in that part of Jesus's teachings, the pacifism part. That doesn't mean he isn't racist sometimes and ornery about supposed welfare queens."

"That's what you get with men of a certain age," Devon said. "I don't have to say a word back to him about any of it if you don't want me to."

Garrett followed Devon around the room as they picked up in preparation for bed: dishes in the sink, cat bowls full, clothes off the floor, lights out. When they crawled into bed, it was with their phones in hand to review the day side by side. All was normal for the first few minutes: more videos of people being bashed and blamed for getting bashed by the police; the death toll of COVID-19 hit a few new and impressive watermarks; there was an explosion in Tehran killing mostly women, ho-hum. All was par for the course until Devon stiffened, and enlarged the words on his phone to read them again.

"What's wrong?" Garrett asked, and then waited, patient but pensive, until Devon was ready to say.

"It's an email from Fiona," Devon said, frowning at his screen still. "Our mom got some blood results back that don't look good.

She had cervical cancer a few years ago, and this says the numbers are in a bad direction this time. Fi says she'll let me know what the next appointment says."

"Should you call your mom? What time is it in Texas?"

"It's too late to call, and Fi wasn't supposed to tell me anything yet, so I can't call without upsetting her." Devon sighed, clicked his phone off, and dropped it on his chest.

"Are you okay?" Garrett asked.

"Yes and no, you know? This could be nothing, which means there's no need to worry, or it could be something, which means there's still no need to worry because worrying doesn't do shit but make you more vulnerable to inflammation and opportunistic infections." Devon rolled his eyes back, then closed the lids on them. "I'm sorry, I don't mean to burden you with this."

"Hey," Garrett said, setting down his own phone and lifting up on one elbow. "Eyes on me."

Devon cocked his head towards Garrett, then opened his eyes. "Hmm?"

"When I feel overburdened, I'll tug on my right ear," Garrett said, except he reached over to tug on Devon's right ear. "If I think you're pressuring me too much, and not being respectful of the power differential in our age disparity or whatever you worry about all the time, I'll lick down my left eyebrow." Garrett brought his hand back to lick his thumb, but then rubbed the spit on Devon's brow. That got a tiny laugh out of him. "If I think you should stop treating me like I'm still undecided about you, I'll pinch my chin." This time Garrett pinched his own chin, and Devon understood the difference.

Devon waved Garrett down for a minty-fresh kiss, the universal signal for *us*.

# 42.

The date was set for the next afternoon. Wednesdays were stasis days for just about everyone, even protesters, so Garrett and Devon could absolutely clear the day for a late family lunch. They woke up to fool around, got up to shower and stretch, perked up to buy a bottle of wine and some fancy cookies for dessert, and took a train until they reached the end of the line, where Aunt Lilith was waiting to pick them up.

"Hi boys!" She waved when she spotted them, and Garrett led the charge in trotting towards her. "I would hug the crap out of you but, you know, the pandemic. You don't mind sitting all the way in the back of the van, right? And keeping your masks on the whole time?"

"Of course, Aunt Lilith," Garrett said. "This is Devon."

"Howdy," Devon said, smiling under his happiest mask, which had cartoons of gamboling kitties playing with yarn. "I'd shake your hand but I'm holding these primo cookies, also 'cuz of the pandemic."

"He gets it," Aunt Lilith said with a nod at Garrett. "Get in and we'll get going. Wes has set up our yard so we can socially distance ourselves like we're at an outdoor café, I think this will be fun."

Garrett thought so, too. Even with the masks and distance, it felt so wholesome and normal to bring his boyfriend home to share a meal with the fam. Who does that? Only people on TV; it had never been Garrett's life before that day. In the midst of the weirdest year anyone could remember, it was like an oasis in the desert, an autonomous zone in a police state, a port in the storm.

Garrett and Devon were asked to bypass the inside of the home and head straight to the backyard. "You're always welcome in our house, of course, but I know you've been out in all those crowds, and we just want to keep it as quarantined as possible," Aunt Lilith said. "Except for the guest bathroom, we're not pooping in the yard quite yet. We'll just sterilize it after you go, no offense."

"It's not the first time folks have had to hazmat a bathroom I've been in," Devon said. "COVID is just a polite excuse for what was going to happen anyway."

"You're funny!" Aunt Lilith said, opening the lock on her fence and ushering them through. "He's funny," she told Garrett. Garrett nodded at her.

Uncle Wes was happy to see them as well, standing in a mask over his grill, tending the fire.

"Hey there, Gare bear," he said.

"Hey Uncle Wes, this is Devon," Garrett said, setting the wine bottle in a cooler of beers and sodas sitting in the shade. Devon deposited the bakery cookies on a card table set up for food. The food table served as a barrier between the patio chairs and table that were always in the backyard, and a set of camping chairs with a pop-up table for the honored guests.

Devon hit it off with Uncle Wes right away by asking him what he was cooking on, and telling him about the creative ways he'd seen cooking fires started abroad: gunpowder fires, dung fires, snack chips, and different ways to build kindling to guard against the wind. Garrett and Aunt Lilith sat separated by six feet (she had measured out the distances beforehand and marked them with popsicle sticks), and smiled at their guys bonding over manly topics.

For two hours everyone found light subjects to talk about in the midst of a garbage year. Wasn't it sweet that whales were singing louder because there were fewer planes in the sky and ships in the sea? That's because the low- and mid-frequency sounds those transports used to communicate irritated some whales with constant ambient pollution, but with so much commercial travel halted, the whales were having a nice time. Did you hear that traffic smog was clearing out of cities in China, cities like San Francisco? That the water in the canals of Venice were clear again like they haven't been in years? Maybe a silver lining from the pandemic was that people might realize how wonderful a healthy planet could be. That $600 boost to unemployment was actually helping some people get out of debt after years of working dead-end minimum wage jobs, and wasn't it nice when the government actually supported people instead of criminalizing them?

Everyone agreed that it was good people weren't left to starve after their jobs were forced to close, but somehow the tone of the talk wavered on the phrase "through no fault of their own." Uncle Wes used it, and though Garrett and Devon said nothing, they stiffened, and it was noticed.

"The government can't just pay people to not work forever," he said, looking to Aunt Lilith for support. "Hopefully people are using this time to get some new skills so they get better jobs once this is over, let it light a fire under their butts, so to speak."

"Well, and I'm sure you'd agree, Wes, that people with children could use extra support," Aunt Lilith said, trying to bridge the gap. "Until the kids can go back to school, you've got to prioritize the kids."

"That makes sense," Uncle Wes said, "but some people had more kids than they could afford before all this. You can't charge responsible people who are raising their kids on their own to support people who couldn't control themselves."

Devon glanced at Garrett, maybe looking for one of their signals, but Garrett couldn't remember which were which, he just wanted this landslide to stop. Devon seemed to notice that, and he tried.

"Higher wages for all would be great," Devon said, skipping his true philosophy which held that no one should have to work to live. The half-measure didn't work.

"Well, but low wages keep an opening in the market for low-level education and first-time employees," Uncle Wes said. "Bosses and owners shouldn't have to pay a lot of money without knowing folks can do the job, right? Which means they'd only hire people who already had all the … what do they call it? Privileges. With no experience or education, people need a chance to start somewhere, that's why low-wage jobs are important."

"What about high-level education people who are in those jobs and can't afford to pay back their student loans?" Devon asked. "I know Ph.D. baristas, Masters degrees with three jobs and no health insurance, what about them?"

"Why are all your friends with such fabulous educations working for such low wages?" Uncle Wes asked. "Why don't they teach?"

"Those three jobs are teaching jobs." Devon's eyes darted an apology at Garrett, who mostly just felt hot with shame. Shame for his family, shame that he couldn't make Devon lie to appease them, shame for himself that he thought this meet-and-greet would work.

"What did they get, a degree in philosophy or something?" Aunt Lilith asked. "I mean, I'm sure it's interesting, but those kinds of classes should be a hobby, not a job."

"A double major in History and Education, actually, but I've also known a war veteran living in his stepmom's basement, it's just not a meritocracy out there. I'm a college drop-out, and I make more than four times the minimum wage because I lucked my way up the ladder."

"You say 'luck' but I bet you made your own luck," Uncle Wes said. "You've got a good attitude, you learn new skills, gain experience. If everyone were like you we wouldn't have an issue. But they're not, and you've got to make sure they don't take advantage."

"If everyone were like me, we'd be in a Mad Max hellscape," Devon said. Garrett forced himself to laugh, so that it would sound like a joke. The tension dissipated, but didn't fully disappear.

Lunch was done. Garrett and Devon helped break down their station and followed Aunt Lilith back to the car. The return to the train station was totally silent until it was time to say goodbye.

"It was nice meeting you," Aunt Lilith said to Devon, but it was clear she didn't mean it.

"Lunch was great, thank you so much for having me." Devon stepped away to make room for a private farewell.

In her aside to Garrett, Aunt Lilith told the truth. "You know, I am so proud of you," she said. "I'm so glad you're making friends and you like your job and you're taking care of yourself. It's everything I wanted for you when we took you in."

"But there's a but?" Garrett asked, pressing his tongue to the roof of his mouth to keep from crying.

"Not a but, more like a … well, a pause maybe," Aunt Lilith said. "Maybe it's time for you to just be on your own."

"Socially distant?" Garrett suggested, trying to smile.

"Yeah! It's a good thing. You don't need us anymore, that was always the plan, right?"

"Right. You gave me everything I needed to be independent."

"I'm so glad you think so," Aunt Lilith said. She was a sweet woman, with hair like Garrett's but a face like his mother's, the mother he may never see again because she didn't think he lived a godly life. "We'll always be here if you really need us, but I think you've got this."

"Thanks, Aunt Lilith."

Again, they couldn't hug goodbye, but they could mime blowing kisses over their masks. Aunt Lilith got back in her car, and Garrett waved at her until her van was out of sight. He rejoined Devon on the train platform, and they stood in silence looking at the long, empty tracks until Garrett sniffed, and Devon turned to see a tear fall down one cheek.

Devon lowered his mask, leaned down, and quickly kissed the tear off Garrett's face before anyone could notice and scold them for mask frippery.

"Don't read too much into that kiss, I've just got an electrolyte deficiency," Devon said. "I lick everyone's tears, it's not personal."

Garrett laughed. How did he do that? How could Devon turn a bad mood good like flipping a dime?

"Are you okay?" Devon asked.

"She sort of broke up with me, but I don't know what else I was expecting." Garrett sniffed up his feelings, and looked forward to the air conditioning on the train that was chugging towards them. "They're okay with me having a boyfriend, but they can't handle the rest of me."

"Shyeah, they'd have to fight me for that job," Devon said, putting an arm over Garrett's shoulder. "But are you okay?"

"I am," Garrett said, and was relieved to find it was true. He was disappointed but okay, sad but okay, on his own and okay.

"Of course you are, my son," Devon said, gesturing to let Garrett step through the train's opening doors first. "You are riot-forged."

# VII. IMPACT

# 43.

With July upon them, folks were gearing up for Independence Day. It meant an uneasy shiftiness among the regulars at the protests mid-week, and a redoubling of participants on Friday. Devon and Garrett did some stretching before they went out on Independence Eve, and Devon had some beautiful luck tripping a couple of pro-fascist, waddling man-brats as they rushed past him to yell sexist racial slurs at girls they clearly thought were pretty. He laughed, he ate a hot dog from a food truck, and he got a flurry of messages in the afternoon saying the fuckwad who broke his hand a few weeks ago was finally arrested.

"Took 'em long enough," he said to himself, scrolling through the news stories until he found the footage.

Tyler Travis was back home in his own state of Indiana and still assaulting people, this time a woman that he and his ilk chased across a street telling her she "smelled like Antifa" until he hit her with a stream of bear mace and pursued her through a park for a while. There were uniformed cops following slowly after the whole affair like they were chaperoning kids on a field trip, but they didn't stop anyone, didn't arrest or assist, didn't say a word. Devon wondered if the woman was okay. He would be able to ask her himself later that afternoon.

Wayne David had reached out to her when he realized it was the same guy who'd messed up Devon's hand, and offered to interview them both for his YouTube channel. She agreed, so Devon turned in early-ish to make that appointment. He couldn't spot Garrett in the crowd, but texted him the plan: *I'm heading home to talk shit online*

*about the proud chauvinist pig who broke my finger, see you for dinner.*
He logged on just in time to see that Mr. Travis was already out on bail.

"Why wouldn't he be out on bail?" asked the woman going by her online handle, RoeDoe, and wearing a mask for the interview to stay as anonymous as possible considering the torrents of sexism already raining down on her for having the nerve to take her opinions outside. "I mean, he's already assaulted at least two people on camera, I'm sure he's learned his lesson."

"Indeed," Devon said. "Whatever could go wrong?"

"Well, so," said Wayne David, taking control of the show. "Devon let's start with your incident. What happened when you met this accused piece of shit?"

RoeDoe laughed, and Devon checked his calendar. "So on June fourth, almost exactly one month ago, Tyler Travis attacked me with an ASP baton. I'm a reporter, I was there filming, and he went to knock the camera out of my hand and, in doing so, broke my finger. For the record, I was clearly identified as press with a press badge and the word PRESS written on me in at least five spots, including my backpack, helmet, and mask."

"Yeah, but can he read?" Wayne David interjected. "Have you considered constantly bleating the words 'I'm press' so that the literacy-challenged can understand why you think you're allowed to be outside when they're outside?"

RoeDoe laughed again and shook her head. "This guy already can't remember that you're not supposed to hit anyone. I doubt he's distinguishing between occupations. You're either on his side, or you're the enemy."

"So, Devon, you reported this assault on your hand, and nothing happened, right?" Wayne David asked.

"I talked to my lawyer and we reported it to the police. My publisher did the work to identify this guy using the tattoos you can see in the footage, and they either failed to arrest and charge him or they haven't even tried."

"Well, they're also busy beating press asses," Wayne David said, "and he left town, so that's super hard. They'd have to call other police to go get him, and that's a whole thing, ain't it?"

"It's a whole damn thing," Devon agreed.

"So Tyler Travis heads back to Indiana and assaults RoeDoe next," Wayne David said. "Today is July third, so what happened this time?"

"Right, so I'm in Indianapolis for the Fourth of July weekend. Not to party, of course — hello, it's still a pandemic — but to stand up to whatever the racists are planning to do at the capitol. So far, it's looking like a weekend of protest-hopping, tomorrow we're heading to Brazil to protest for Black Lives Matter and for immigrant rights ..."

"That's Brazil, Indiana?" Wayne David asked.

"Oh, yeah, not like actual Brazil," RoeDoe said, "though I wish I was having that kind of Fourth of July, traveling to a beach vacation? Yes. But no, more like the Clay County Courthouse. And on Sunday, I think there are plans to protest some Catholic bishop who said BLM are wolves in wolves' clothing, thieves and bandits, trying to devour the poor and make money off of fear. They're maggots and parasites, blah blah blah, so ... yeah, fuck that guy. We're gonna go make some noise about that in Carmel. Again, not the Mount Carmel in Israel, the other one, in Indiana."

Devon and Wayne David laughed now, with Devon chiming in to say, "That's too bad, though. He could have given his own Sermon on the Mount. Jesus said a bunch of crap about justice and caring for the needy ..."

"Love and selflessness and all that jazz," Wayne David added.

"... but this guy can update that for everyone, ranting like a drill sergeant and calling us all maggots, sounds beautiful, sounds like God's love," Devon finished saying, just as Garrett returned home.

"What sounds like God's love?" he asked, and then realized that Devon was on live internet and put his finger over his lips, shushing himself.

Devon thought quickly that the answer to "what sounds like God's love?" was the sound of Garrett coming home, but there was no opportunity to say it before the moment passed.

"Right, anyway," RoeDoe went on. "Those are still our plans for the weekend despite what happened today near the capitol. Maybe you saw the video, I didn't see it until way after because I had goddamn bear spray in my eyes, but I got too far from my group and too close to the Nazis and Klan members and Proud Boys and whatever they call themselves. They kind of swarmed around me, calling me a twat, telling me I smelled, to get out of the country if I didn't like racism, fuck Antifa over and over again. The cops were with them, on their side of the street, and only followed them as they followed me. They didn't do anything to stop all this, just let it play out and only arrested him later when I filed a report. I guess I'll try to press charges against him, just to put it on the record of this dude so that whenever he tries to or actually manages to kill someone, they can't pretend it was an isolated incident, but …" RoeDoe shrugged.

"It's always worth speaking out," Devon said.

"I think so," Wayne David told her. "So thank you for talking to us, and thanks for showing up in the first place."

RoeDoe nodded and said, "It's an honor."

# 44.

It was the Fourth of July, and Tula had returned. *Boom, boom, boom* on Devon's door when the daylight was still in its dawn phase, and Garrett and Devon still casual in kimonos. They looked at each other, wondering if this was their unlucky day, until they heard Tula's voice.

"Your best friend's outside your door, let her in," she said.

Devon grinned and got up to do as he was told, while Garrett rushed to the bathroom to comb his hair and get presentable.

When Tula walked in, she carried a six-pack of beer and a plastic grocery bag of other goodies, including treats for Oskar the cat, who received her first hug.

"Who's my favorite neutered man?" she asked Oskar. The cat sniffed aggressively at her bag and got a handful of chewy treats scattered on the floor for him to find.

Devon got the second hug. "I'm gone for a week, and I forget how tall you are," she told him. "Too bad you need athletic aptitude to play basketball, am I right?"

"Yeah, tragedy of my life," Devon said before they both turned to see Garrett emerge from the bathroom, dressed and tucking his freshly-combed curls behind his ears.

"Kiddo, c'mere," Tula said, giving Garrett yet another squishy hug. "You know I came home to two new blooms, and one of my most stubborn air plants has produced a pup? You took such good care of them, this is for you." Out of her bag, she produced a small cardboard box. Garrett opened it, peeled back some tissue paper, and there were three tiny plants inside: one was dark green and wrapped tight in its own leaves like a cigar; another was light green and looked like a starburst; the third was more blue-green and had Medusa-like tentacles.

"Aww," Garrett said. "They're so little!"

"Air plants, friend to all us self-centered generations," Tula said. "Leave them near a window and spritz 'em with water sometimes. There's your starter kit."

Garrett took them to the window straight away to assemble them in the sunlight, and Tula turned to Devon so they could both smile over their son for a moment. Such a sweet, nurturing boy; how lucky could two riot parents get?

"Gonna offer me a drink?" Tula asked, pointing to the beers she had brought. "Hazel hasn't forgotten me since I've been gone; she's gonna come out and protest with us tonight."

"Oh, so we're celebrating? Then let's get this party started," Devon said, twisting off a couple of caps so they could cheers. "Happy birthday, U.S.A."

They had lunch. Tula had brought potato salad and veggie dogs, Devon cooked up some broccoli mac and cheese, and Garrett made them red-white-and-blue smoothies (strawberry, vanilla, and blueberry stacked in each cup, photos taken for social media bragging purposes). They split the six-pack as they ate, but not evenly (Devon had three beers, Tula two, and Garrett just one). They researched where the action was in their city as they digested their patriotic feast, and they quickly turned sour on the America they had to deal with each day. It wasn't all sparklers and freedom all the time, not even close.

They caught the news as it rolled in.

Garrett said, "Fifty-five arrested in Nashville for trespassing. The protest was started by teens at Bicentennial State Park, and ended at Legislative Plaza with a moment of silence for two Black men killed by Metro Police officers, Jocques Clemmons and Daniel Hambrick. Their mothers were there and hugged."

"Sounds unruly," Tula said.

"Tennessee Highway Patrol says they moved barriers after being told the grounds were closed, so the whole group's gotta go to jail,"

Garrett said, then scoffed. "They called this 'incident' after the peaceful, well-organized demonstration a 'clear provocation by those looking to instigate trouble.' Very doubtful."

"Well, cops would know a provocation when they see one," Devon said. "It's their specialty."

Tula had another story. "Schenectady's got a Black Lives Matter and Gay Pride combo rally for their Fourth of July. That's how it's done, New York, big liberation party for everybody. Hundreds marched from Gateway Park to City Hall, and meanwhile dozens held a pro-cop rally outside the police department," Tula snorted, "hosted by the Upstate Conservative Coalition. One of the organizers said, 'The Thin Blue Line doesn't see color, it doesn't see socio-economic status, it doesn't see sexual orientation. It's only trying to help people.' This guy!"

Devon and Garrett laughed and laughed along with Tula.

"And they say conservatives aren't funny," Garrett said, "but just listen to that deadpan delivery."

"Oh, here's a doozy," Devon said, sitting up. He would have to get dressed and ready to hit the streets again soon; this story could provide the energy. "A woman cop in Springfield, Massachusetts, Hispanic mother of three. She's a rookie police officer, still in her one-year probation period. She was fired last week because she liked and shared, oh wow, hold onto your fucking hats … a picture of her own niece."

"That bitch," Tula said.

"Yeah, well, here's the twist: her niece was at a BLM protest in Atlanta and was holding a sign that said 'shoot the fuck back' next to a fellow hero in some kind of Halloween mask with a sign asking, 'Who do we call when the murderer wears the badge?' Fellow cops complained, and the Police Commissioner called her up. One of her coworkers told her, 'You have a lot of haters, you're going to get in trouble.' Another one told her she was 'either too dangerous or too stupid to safely associate with' and to please stay as far away as she could."

"That's good advice for her," Garrett said. "We should all stay far away from cops, I hope she sees this as a blessing."

"Nah, she wants her job back," Devon said, closing down his phone and standing up to stretch, to get his shit together to head out. "She was in the Special Victims Unit, maybe she actually gave a damn, but that's what that probationary period is for, to sniff out the good cops and get them the fuck outta the ranks."

"I hope she reforms her ways, but I don't trust cops who are fired or forced to resign," Tula said, getting up to shuffle their leftovers around while Devon located his going-outside pants. "Good cops quit."

"Ooh," Garrett said, grabbing the beer bottles to rinse them for recycling. "I'd like that stitched on a pillow."

Devon smirked at himself in the mirror and thought, *Christmas present.* That pillow was going to look great on their couch someday.

# 45.

The crowds were jumpy when Devon, Garrett, and Tula finally joined the fray. Some people were furious, some people were singing, and some people were drinking not-so-discreetly, but the cops weren't hassling them about it … yet.

Not for the first time, Devon felt a kinship with a character from the 1995 movie Stonewall: Matty Dean, the main white dude with his flyover state accent who arrived in the colorful and diverse New York City just in time to fall in love with a crossdresser and stand for a riot against the police. When Matty realized the action was kicking up — like the can-can legs of the drag dancers who lip-synced between scenes like a Greek chorus — the guy gleefully exclaimed, "It's the Fourth of fucking July!" Similarly, no matter how far across the world he traveled, or how many cities he lived in, Devon still had that same core center of Johnny-Come-Lately from the Heartland about him. Today, on the real fourth of July, in this summer of riots, the memory of that cinematic moment was more on-the-nose than it had ever been before. The day felt both dangerous and exciting to Devon, like the smell of gunpowder in the air.

Devon watched as two protests came up against each other, once again from opposites sides of a street. His side was full of wild hair, colorful plumage (clothes), and the diversity of your average college pamphlet (though rarely the diversity of the average college class). On the other side were white men of all kinds of girth but only a few significant uniforms: the black-and-camouflage soldier LARPers (Live

Action Role Play), the khakis and polo shirts of the Identity Evropa and Vanguard America types (your prep school Nazis), and a newer battalion of Hawaiian shirts that came about due to some sad online word association (from referring to the second coming Civil War they wanted after the movie Breakin' 2: Electric Boogaloo, to calling the event "Big Igloo" because to them it sounded like "Boogaloo," to then changing it once more to "Big Luau," and wearing their bright Parrothead-looking shirts under the insect-black of open-carry weapons).

Garrett hustled back to Devon's side after getting some pictures of a shoving match between different kinds of alt-righters (they weren't the type to say, "Oh, excuse me, sorry if I stepped on your toes," were they?) and sighed as he re-did his ponytail, combing out the sweat. It was going to be a hot one.

"What are you thinking about?" Garrett asked.

"Fascist fashion," Devon said. "The right has always been full of such thieving trash. Mussolini stole the fasces, Hitler stole the svastika, which was a symbol of light and luck until he shit all over it, and now these jerks are stealing Hawaiian shirts with absolutely zero spirit of *aloha* in their bodies. They look like they'd join in with a boozy sing-along to 'Margaritaville,' but no, false advertising, they think if there's a second Civil War, they can win this time, or at least enjoy some murdering."

Devon came out of his short trance of a rant to see Garrett smiling at him, his mouth an affectionate smirk and his eyes alight with liking what they saw. Devon smiled back, but looked away quickly because sometimes eye contact that strong and pure was like staring into the sun, bad for the corneas.

Devon was formulating an idea, about to say something along the lines of, "Perhaps I'll write a satirical article like a fashion show critique, from Hugo Boss OG Nazis to these Abercrombie twerps," when a car at the corner turned the wrong way, towards the protest. It reversed as if it could have been a mistake and the driver was trying to turn around, but the reverse was too fast, and then the car came speeding forward into the crowd, the leftist side.

From Devon's vantage point, he and his camera could see the throng shift like a school of fish, in rippling waves, with people realizing what was coming and turning away or trying to jump to the side. But not everyone could make it in time. The car smashed into flesh, with a couple of people flying over the hood from the impact. Several rows of bodies compressed against each other, against parked cars, bikes, and metal barriers. Folks fell and some were trampled.

The car reversed again, and was able to flee unimpeded because everyone was leaping out of its way. After a few seconds of chaos and crash, there was an even briefer moment of inhale before the screaming started, and people swarmed back in to try and help those who were hurt.

Devon and Garrett stayed out of that fray since they had no real medical skills to contribute. If Hazel or Lena were nearby, they were probably in there, but the cops were already quickly yelling at everyone to get the fuck out and go home. The tone was not in the interest of safety, but in the manner of, "Look at this mess we've gotta clean up now! This is why we think your freedom of speech rights should shut the hell up."

More officers dedicated themselves to driving people back than to stooping to help. They weren't going to reach Devon and Garrett too quickly, so each of them kept recording what they could while never straying far from one another. When it was time to flee, they'd leave together.

When people started hustling past them to get away from the cops and the mayhem, Devon and Garrett started closing up shop to turn and join them. One Black guy, maybe in his forties with a fresh injury to his leg, limped towards them. Devon reached out to support the man to a nearby tree he could lean on.

"Is your leg okay? Want me to find you a medic?" Garrett asked.

"It's fine … not broken," he said, out of breath, hand over his heart. Devon pulled out a bottle of water and offered it over. Garrett took a Manila folder from his backpack full of whatever documents he carried to fan the guy, who looked like he'd been through a wringer.

"You got hit by the car?" Devon asked.

"Nah," the man said, before chugging some water. "Kicked, I think. I'm blessed, though. Some lady died down there."

"Someone died? You saw this?" Garrett asked. He had to ask if this was eyewitness testimony, because if so, maybe their cameras needed to come back out, or it was time to hit the record buttons on their phones, something.

"I heard someone say it," the man said. "They said, 'I can't find a pulse. She's gone.'"

Goosebumps rippled over Devon's arms, and the hair on his head prickled up. He and Garrett wouldn't know that they knew the dead woman until hours later, all Devon knew in the moment was a deep, selfish gratitude. If somebody had to die today, he was so damn happy that it wasn't his love, his found treasure, his riot son.

# 46.

## *All Lives Splatter:*
## *Car-Ramming Attacks Against Activists*

### Stochastic Terrorism and Vehicle-Ramming

"All Lives Splatter," isn't that cute? Just a fun, widely-circulated joke about intentional vehicular homicide being shared by police officers, bosses, and racially-stoked citizens. That is about what "stochastic terrorism" means: "the public demonization of a person or group resulting in the incitement of a violent act," aka terrorism, which is described as "the unlawful use of violence and intimidation, especially against civilians, in the pursuit of political aims." For example, right-wing publication The Daily Caller posted a minute-and-a-half long video with the headline, "Here's A Reel Of Cars Plowing Through Protesters Trying To Block The Road," that is playfully set to a cover of Ludacris's "Move Bitch" (with aggressive lyrics beginning, "Move bitch, get out the way"). This post was picked up and disseminated by an echo chamber of other websites, including Fox Nation, "an entertainment streaming service brought to you by FOX News," they proudly proclaim. The posts went around in January of 2017 and were taken down in August, after Heather Heyer was murdered. Who is Heather Heyer? Tragically, one of many. On September 11 of that same year, the Chelan County Sheriff's Department in Washington state posted a meme from a group called "Libtards; ya gotta love 'em!" that said "ALL LIVES SPLATTER, nobody cares about your protest, keep your ass out of the road." The image included a drawing of a vehicle with a mangled body behind it, a fleeing person in front of it, and another body about to be impacted by the hood of the car. That body had a bow on its head, presumably marking it as female. Similar memes with identical language were still being used by officials in 2020: a West Virginia Fire Chief had it on a T-shirt in June, and a Seattle detective posted the meme online just hours after the vehicular homicide of local protester Summer Taylor in July. Who is Summer Taylor? Again, another one of many. Let's say their names.

### *Crowd-Ramming Intimidations, Injuries, and Deaths*

Here are just a few examples of protesters being assaulted or killed by vehicles ramming through crowds or targeting them directly in the years preceding 2020.

- **November 25, 2015 — Minneapolis, MN: Unidentified Juvenile.** A sixteen-year-old girl at a Black Lives Matter protest outside of Minneapolis Police's 3rd Precinct (prompted by the failure to indict the Ferguson, MO police officer who killed Michael Brown) was injured when a forty-year-old man ran his honking vehicle through the crowd. The driver was originally listed as a "victim" because according to the police report his "vehicle was damaged by a large group of people" and while "attempting to flee from the mob, he struck a pedestrian." After a review of video evidence, the driver was later changed to "suspect" and the injured pedestrian child was recognized as the victimized party. The driver later pleaded guilty to failure to yield to a pedestrian, a misdemeanor with no jail time, plus a $575 fine.

- **August 9, 2016 — Ferguson, MO: Unidentified Man.** At a peaceful vigil on the second anniversary of Michael Brown's death at the hands of police, a car sped through a crowd of roughly 75 people and struck a man so forcefully that he flew through the air. Shots were fired at the fleeing car in response. Again there was video of this pedestrian being run down on a well-lighted street, but the police said the act was unintentional, that the woman driving the car was "very, very cooperative." No one in the vehicle was injured, but police issued a plea to the public to help identify those who shot at the car. The protester was badly injured and taken in a private vehicle for medical help. No arrests were made.

- **August 12, 2017 — Charlottesville, VA: Heather Heyer.** In response to the white supremacist Unite the Right rally regarding the removal of a Confederate statue of Robert E. Lee, thirty-two-year-old Heather Heyer and other counter-protesters were attacked when a twenty-one-year-old Nazi enthusiast rammed his car deliberately into the crowd. Again this was caught on video, showing the preemptive reversal of the car so it would have room to speed up before crashing into a crowd of human beings. Again the driver argued that, while safely seated in a Dodge Challenger, he "feared for his safety." In addition to Heather's death, 19 other protesters were injured, including a woman who suffered a broken pelvis and other long-lasting injuries, and another individual who required multiple surgeries on her right leg after the attack, as well as continued use of a wheelchair and cane. The 45th President of the U.S., upon hearing about this event days later said, "I think there's blame on both sides." The driver was found guilty of first-degree murder, five counts of aggravated malicious wounding, 29 counts of committing federal hate crimes, as well as a hit-and-run charge. He was sentenced to life in prison twice, by federal and state courts, along with other penalties.

- **April 1, 2018 — Sacramento, CA: Wanda Cleveland.** While demonstrating against the police killing of Stephon Clark, who was killed unarmed in his grandmother's backyard, sixty-two-year-old Wanda Cleveland was struck by a Sheriff's Department vehicle, the officer-driver of which did not stop to render aid. During the incident, which was filmed, two Sheriff's Department vehicles were stopped among protesters. The lead car crept slowly forward as a megaphoned voice became increasingly irritated at having to repeat, "Back away from my vehicle." When the lead car moved up, the second vehicle rushed forward in an unnecessary and possibly malicious burst of speed, knocking Wanda to the ground. "He never even stopped," Wanda said. "It was a hit-and-run. If I did that I'd be charged." She was taken to the hospital with minor injuries to her head and arms that nevertheless cost over $43,000 to treat. In October later that year, California Highway Patrol deemed Wanda was at fault for being in front of the public service vehicle that hit her and failed to stop and render aid. She filed a lawsuit in 2019 seeking damages for her injuries.

- **August 14, 2019 — Central Falls, RI: ICE Detention Protesters.** In solidarity with the Black Lives Matter movement, protests were also held against ICE (Immigration and Customs Enforcement) detainment and imprisonment of Latine asylum-seekers, immigrants, and children. Outside of the Wyatt Detention Center in Rhode Island, peaceful demonstrators, including the Jewish activists who organized similar nationwide protests to try and see these facilities (likened to concentration camps) shut down, were terrorized when a corrections guard rammed his vehicle through sitting demonstrators, breaking the leg of a sixty-year-old man. Law enforcement then swarmed in, not to detain the driver, but to pepper spray the protesters. One of them was a woman in her seventies who went to the hospital due to being maced. The officer who drove the vehicle ultimately resigned.

- **July 4, 2020 — Seattle, WA: Summer Taylor.** During a closed highway demonstration, twenty-four-year-old Summer Taylor and another thirty-two-year-old protester were rammed by a twenty-seven-year-old in a Jaguar XJL. He drove the wrong way up an Interstate exit ramp and maneuvered around a three-vehicle barricade to hit both women. The one who survived suffered multiple fractures and internal injuries that required several days in intensive care at the hospital. Summer Taylor died due to her injuries. Again, this murder was filmed, again the perpetrator claimed this was an accident and pleaded "not guilty."

Videos posted online of these incidents never fail to call forth a wave of racist comments, violent vitriol, and talk of human beings as "speed bumps."

### *It's Not Terrorism if It's Legal*

Under the law, it's somewhat difficult to pretend that gunning a vehicle through a crowd of people is accidental. Fortunately for psychos, some lawmakers want to make vehicular attacks and homicides a little more legal if they're against the right kind of protesters. Here is some of the language put forth in state House and Senate Bills (HB and SB) between the deaths of Heather and Summer:

- **Florida's SB 1096 and HB 1419:** SB 1096 prohibits a person from interfering with or obstructing traffic during certain demonstrations or protests, provides criminal penalties if they do; exempts a driver from liability for injury or death to any person who does bother traffic under those circumstances. HB 1419 does the same as above, but specifies burden of proof.

- **Kentucky's HB 53:** An act to make wearing a face-concealing mask or hood while engaging in a public protest a Class A misdemeanor; make obstruction of traffic a Class A misdemeanor; prohibit any person (including a public servant) from preventing official police duties during a protest; abolish all criminal or civil liability for a motor vehicle driver who accidentally causes injury or death to a person obstructing the flow of traffic during a public demonstration that has no permit (exemption for intentional infliction of injury or death).

**North Carolina's HB 330:** Provides immunity from civil liability to drivers who, "while exercising due care," injure anyone blocking traffic in a public right-of-way during a protest. Drivers should not be immune from "willful or wanton conduct."

- **North Dakota's HB 1203:** "Notwithstanding any other provision of law, a driver of a motor vehicle who negligently causes injury or death to an individual obstructing vehicular traffic on a public road, street, or highway may not be held liable for any damages," and "a driver of a motor vehicle who unintentionally causes injury or death to an individual obstructing vehicular traffic on a public road, street, or highway is not guilty of an offense."

- **Rhode Island's HB 5690:** A driver who is "exercising due care and injures another person who is participating in a protest or demonstration and is blocking traffic in a public right-of-way shall be immune from civil liability for such injury."

- **Tennessee's SB 944 and HB 668:** SB 944 "provides civil immunity for the driver of an automobile who injures a protester who is blocking traffic in a public right-of-way if the driver was exercising due care." HB 668 is identical to the above.

- **Texas's HB 250:** An act that says, "A person operating a motor vehicle who injures another person with the motor vehicle is not liable for the injury if, at the time of the injury: (1) the person operating the motor vehicle was exercising due care; and (2) the person injured was blocking traffic in a public right-of-way while participating in a protest or demonstration." Exemption is made for "injury caused by grossly negligent conduct."

These bills help to make extremists feel safer when terrorizing those exercising their constitutional rights to speak and to petition the government for a redress of grievances.

# 47.

Hazel was gone. Blunt force trauma to her torso. Possibly a hate crime since the car was driven by an avowed white supremacist and neo-Nazi.

He was twenty years old, barely. His mother was calling into Fox News saying he was her very sweet baby, he wasn't racist he was just proud of being white and that's okay, also he was only afraid of the crowd and the crash was an accident caused by fair and understandable panic. He was called "cherub-faced," "clean-cut," and "shy and unassuming" by news outlets. The cops he was allowed to turn himself into said he was calm, not angry when he talked to them, and that he seemed to show remorse. He already had a crowdsourced account online stacking hundreds of thousands of dollars for his defense.

Hazel was misidentified several times as Chinese, not Vietnamese. They said she hailed from both San Jose and Ho Chi Minh. Many outlets decided to just say Asian and call it a day, while totting her up as a victim of the president's insistence on saying "kung flu" regarding COVID-19. They said she was a nurse and a medic interchangeably, because she worked as a paramedic but at some point in her life also studied to be a nurse. She was thirty-nine years old, and her parents couldn't be understood for comment because their English was only so-so. Her partner medic had relatively nice things to say about her, but it was like he was giving a performance review, not an obituary soundbite. "Hazel was a hard worker, and she was really good with female patients because of her empathy. She taught me so much, and we're all going to miss her." Lena had posted an editorial about her dead friend, but it was less about Hazel herself — her habits, her life — and more about her death, the unfairness, these goddamn Nazis infesting America in political offices, police departments, and school boards. A fair point, but not so fair to Hazel.

Garrett took a quiet back seat to all of this for the first twenty-four hours. He watched Devon worry about Tula, watched Tula vacillate between numb, sorrowful, and poisonously unsurprised. She wouldn't meet Garrett's gaze for the rest of the day, even though they took her all the way home on the fourth and stayed the night again. They heard her crying under the fireworks and/or explosions of the night, but left her alone.

It was Devon who knew why she couldn't look at Garrett for a little while, and he explained when Garrett whispered over the side of the couch, "She can't possibly blame me, right?"

Devon sat up and put his lips right against Garrett's ear, so he wouldn't be overheard.

"She might be blaming herself a little, since she's the one who invited Hazel out on the Fourth," Devon said. "She was also hoping Hazel would be for her what you are to me, and right now part of her is furious that her riot treasure is gone, and mine isn't. She loves you though, she knows that and I know that and I hope you do, too."

"Of course I do," Garrett whispered back. "She trusted me with her plants and she gave me some, what else is that if not love?"

Devon smiled. Even in the dark, Garrett knew the sound of it.

"If Tula looked at you too soon, and you saw her thinking, 'Why not you instead of her?' she couldn't stand it. She wouldn't mean it, not like that, but she's hurt, and part of her wants everyone else to hurt just as bad."

"Oh," Garrett said. He wouldn't want to see that in Tula's eyes; he might never forget it if he did.

"It'll pass, we've just gotta be patient with her."

The very next day, there was a vigil.

Some local representatives were there, but nobody who was nationally recognizable. The captain or chief of the EMS department read a statement, Garrett didn't know what their top brass was called.

Clergy came out from several different faiths — Christian, Jewish, Muslim, and Buddhist. They said a few words that all who were gathered could agree on: this shouldn't have happened, hate is ugly, and Hazel was a healer and a hero who deserved better. Everyone said her name, wrote her notes, lit candles, and left flowers and trinkets at the tree near the place she was killed.

Hazel's father was there, too. He accepted handshakes and condolences, but no one Garrett knew spoke to him. All he had to say was, "Thank everyone for coming. My wife is grateful that you are here for our daughter because she's too sad to be here today. I thank you, Hazel thanks you, she was everything to us."

Michelle and Jarvis were in attendance as well, each of them stony with control of their sorrow. Michelle hugged Tula when that short speech from Hazel's father made her cry, but Tula pulled herself together in under a minute. She crossed her arms, sniffed up her tears, and started cracking jokes about nothing towards Devon. Michelle and Devon traded places like electrons, and when Michelle came to stand beside Garrett she asked him, "Would you like to pray with me?"

Garrett hadn't expected anyone to ask, and it nearly startled him. He figured he was among friendly atheists to a one, but when it was offered, he realized that he would indeed like to pray, very much. He hadn't done it in years, not since his parents kicked him out, made him feel as if their God didn't want anything to do with him anymore, and since that was the only God whom Garrett had ever known, he stayed away.

"You wouldn't mind?" Garrett asked.

Michelle put out both of her hands, palms up, and Garrett placed his hands into hers.

She went with an oldie and a goldie, the King James Version of the 23rd psalm.

"The Lord is my shepherd; I shall not want. He maketh me to lie down in green pastures: he leadeth me beside the still waters. He restoreth my soul: he leadeth me in the paths of righteousness for his name's sake. Yea, though I walk through the valley of the shadow of death, I will fear no evil: for thou art with me; thy rod and thy staff they comfort me. Thou preparest a table before me in the presence of mine enemies: thou anointest my head with oil; my cup runneth over. Surely goodness and mercy shall follow me all the days of my life: and I will dwell in the house of the Lord forever."

Garrett mouthed the words along with her, but didn't speak lest he start crying, too. Something about Michelle made it seem like you could fall apart because she wouldn't, at least not today.

"Thank you," he told her, swallowing hard so his voice wouldn't waver. "That was very nice." The prayer was very nice, the gesture and offer even more so.

Tula went home with Michelle and Jarvis so she wouldn't be alone that night either. Devon and Garrett went home to Oskar the cat, and Garrett thought that the roughest part of the day was over, but there was one more blow.

After some tender kissing in the shower and eating only the barest amount of chips and trail mix for dinner (they had no stomachs or enthusiasm for anything else), Devon checked a message on his phone and blanched.

"What happened?" Garrett asked. They were lounging on their different devices in the sitting area, their legs woven together, and Garrett felt Devon tense and look like he was about to be sick.

"I ... uh," Devon sighed hard and grabbed the top of his head, yanking his hair. "It might be bad news for my mom, but I can't deal with this tonight."

Devon tossed his phone aside, and Garrett reached for it.

"Do you want me to ...?"

"Don't fucking touch that," Devon said, his tone too harsh.

Garrett pulled back like he'd been stung, and Devon immediately apologized.

"I'm sorry, hey, I'm sorry." Devon slid from the couch so he could crawl on his knees the few feet to where Garrett sat. He put his head in Garrett's lap. "I don't talk to you like that, I'm sorry."

"I know you don't talk to me like that," Garrett said, which is why it had shocked them both so much. He petted Devon's hair, still damp from the shower, and combed his fingers from temple to chin through Devon's beard, nearly the same way he scritched the cat. "Is it that bad?"

"When I say I can't deal with it tonight, I mean it," Devon said, picking up Garrett's hands so that they rested in his palms, almost like the prayer with Michelle. Devon kissed Garrett's knuckles. "It's Schrödinger's news right now. It could be the worst, or it could be Fiona overreacting, and I just can't know until tomorrow, and you can't either, so please don't ask me about it."

"Ask you about what?" Garrett said.

Devon's grateful smile was all Garrett needed to know about for the rest of the night.

*

# 48.

It was Monday morning, and Garrett waited to see when Devon would check the email or whatever about his mom, but Devon only looked to see if his phone was charged as far as Garrett saw. He left it on the dresser when he went to the bathroom. He checked his computer to see where today's action was. He and Garrett went out after noon to stand with those who weren't ready to sit back down again.

There was an earlier curfew tonight, and lockdowns were tighter. Because of the pandemic, because of the heat, because of the death that drew national attention that week. Rather than extra compassion, understanding, and respect, the government authorities were getting more frustrated, embarrassed, and pissed off that these protests were still happening.

They got about three solid hours of protest, saw signs about Hazel, and located Tula as she was volunteering at the medic station with Lena in grim silence. Then it was half an hour of soft hassle from the cops, and then the tear gas canisters were launching again.

"For your own safety, leave the street. For your own safety, return home," droned a bullhorn voice. Translation: "If you don't want to be blamed for what we're about to do to you, or what we'll allow your enemies to do to you, get out of our way."

Then it was another half hour or so of running from arrest, a flight that, for Garrett, Devon, and Tula, ended when some citizen saw what was happening from their front porch, and walked out to open the gate to their yard.

"Thanks for coming my invited guests," announced a brown man over and over, a man who would later explain to the folks he harbored and the reporters among them that he was ethnically Indian, and for that reason deeply hated white imperialism.

"I haven't gone to any protests," he said, an apologetic note in his voice. "It's just I have to work, and I don't have anyone nearby who would feed my birds if I was arrested." He had two parakeets in an upstairs room, and while he let people into his house to cool down, use the bathroom, tend their wounds in the kitchen, and rest on the couch, he requested that no one go upstairs as it would disturb them.

Two punk-looking youths stood guard at his stairs to enforce that request, and one woman suggested he put a fitted sheet over his couch and take up any rugs he didn't want street shoes on. "We don't want to thank you for your kindness by staining your fabrics," she said, which got a chuckle from all who were close enough to hear it.

"You're doing your part now, sir, and we thank you," said a man who came to shake hands with their savior. "What's your name, by the way?"

"Veer," he said.

"Well, that suits," said the handshaker. "You're letting people 'veer' into your life."

"It means 'brave,'" Veer said, and smiled like this might be one of those moments where he felt that his deeds lived up to his name.

Garrett, Devon, and Tula found a corner in this man's house where they could sit on the floor and keep out of the way. The cops were right outside Veer's gate and kept trying to step into the yard and drag people out for arrest, despite being told loudly that they had no goddamn right. But they knew they had no right to the house, so everyone crammed in tight and hunkered down to wait until morning when the curfew was lifted. There were discussions nearby about what pure Gestapo shit this was, how the American police were an occupying force, how they were all prisoners in their own neighborhood tonight because of the so-called "protect and serve" set out there. Some people took naps.

That was when Devon finally checked his phone.

Garrett sat squished between him and Tula, unsure about how exactly he stood with Tula, though she was the one who shoved him through the gate when she heard Veer welcoming protesters. He watched Devon's face go from stony to sickened to sorrowful in the space of about a minute as he read the message from his sister. Devon put his head between his knees and started breathing deeply, the kind of breathing you do to keep from screaming. That's when Tula noticed what was happening.

"Devon, is something wrong? Are you hurt? Panic attack?" she asked.

"All of the above," Devon said.

"Is it about your mom?" Garrett asked.

"It is."

Garrett put one hand on Devon's shoulder. Tula reached out to touch his knee, and they waited for what was clearly bad news.

Soon Devon looked up at Veer's ceiling, blinking back tears, and said, "My mom is dying, and I'm gonna have to go home for as long as it takes."

"The cancer?" Tula asked quietly. She knew about the cancer; she had known Devon for years, and may have even met his mother for all Garrett knew.

"It's in her lungs this time, it's not worth fighting, and she says she doesn't have any more fight in her anyway."

Devon wiped at one eye, then looked at Tula, then at Garrett. Tula looked at Garrett, too, for the first time since the loss of Hazel, and her face was a mien of pity.

"I'm so sorry, kid," she said. "Turns out he's leaving you first."

And then, even though this was Devon's tragedy — his mom dying, his responsibility to go take care of her and witness it all and comfort his sister and plan the funeral and close out the estate — for some reason, Devon and Tula were comforting Garrett. Hugs and kisses and coos, and for what? He would soon find out for what.

Devon leaving for an indefinite period of time meant he had to figure out what to do about his apartment. Did Garrett want to sublet it? Would he adopt Oskar the cat for the duration? If that was too much responsibility, Oskar would go to Tula, and Garrett would have to find some way to be on his own again, because he wasn't exactly welcome back with Aunt Lilith, was he? He had grown so comfortable in the span of just six weeks with Devon that he couldn't believe it was really ending, but Devon and Tula believed it. They both knew, as parents sometimes did, just what their son was in for long before the child realized it himself: *You won't like the doctor's office. You can't have that thing your heart is set on. You don't know how ugly the divorce will get, but we do, oh honey, we do.*

When dawn came to Veer's house, Garrett had agreed to sublet with Oskar. They would work out a rent/storage fee arrangement on paper because, as distasteful as it was to draw up a contract between lovers, all agreed it was the smart thing to do. So what if it took six months, a year? Garrett would wait in their love nest, pining and patient, until Devon returned to him. Devon might come back diminished, saddened, changed, but everyone had to change sometime, didn't they? Garrett would grow while he was gone but they'd still be in love just the same, right?

Neither Devon nor Tula was willing to confirm that before they shambled back onto the street under the sleepy rising sun.

# 49.

Devon had little to pack. Garrett watched him gather pants and paperwork into one small suitcase in a matter of minutes, though his flight back to Texas wasn't until the end of the week. They spent those last few days making love, making out, making meals, making jokes, making light of what they couldn't control as if it was no big deal. But when the day finally came to say goodbye, it was an enormous deal.

Devon said he couldn't do this goodbye at the airport, that he wanted his last vision of Garrett to be at ease, in the exact place he would hopefully come back to someday.

"You make it sound like you're the one who's dying," Garrett whispered when they discussed this detail under the fairy lights before bed, afraid it was too insensitive. But Devon never flinched from frankness.

"A part of me might die, though," Devon told him. "And you might be flourishing by the time I come back broken, and you might meet someone in the meantime who starts as a friend but then fits you so much better than I do, and we'll both agree that it's no one's fault, but it'll be over all the same."

"Why do you have to paint a sad picture of stuff that might never happen?" Garrett asked. "Why not imagine that when you come back, we're exactly what we need from each other? What if it feels more right than ever, like regrowing a limb you thought was permanently severed, but it's real? What if by this time next year we're getting engaged and shit?"

"Would you want to get married?" Devon asked with a smirk from beneath him, as Garrett leaned over him, and traced patterns over his chest with a long fingernail.

"Why not?" Garrett asked, suddenly shy.

"It's just so heteronormative." Devon started a small tickle fight after that, a game they both won. Their prizes were sweet gasps for breath and the echo of laughter.

Devon's flight home was early on Saturday, July 11. Garrett looked it up, wondering if there was any extra special significance to the day, and discovered it was something called "Cheer Up the Lonely Day," which damn near offended him with how fitting it was.

Devon ordered a car to take him to the airport, and put his pack across his back, and looked at Garrett like he was leaving his best girl and heading off to war, but he wasn't exactly sad. Garrett had been expecting anguish, tears, but Devon only leaned on the door, took in the room, and then settled his gaze on Garrett.

"We may never be here again," Devon said.

They didn't know then that for the rest of the year, the country was going to get drastically worse. By January 6 of 2021, senators would be sent scrambling from an armed insurrection of lunatics and white supremacists storming the capitol; Wayne David would witness and report on it firsthand. By February of 2021, the week of Valentine's Day, Devon and Garrett wouldn't even be able to speak to each other because the power grid of Texas would be offline due to a freezing winter storm; a taste of climate change that would kill hundreds across the state via freezing temperatures, loss of power, and carbon monoxide poisoning from trying to use their cars to stay warm. By April of 2021, Devon's mother would be gone (just two weeks before the murderer of George Floyd would be convicted on April 20); it would take him several more months to close out her life and set up his sister. Only then could Devon try to find his way back to his boy, who would be his own man by then, potentially engaging with someone else; or perhaps Garrett would be that mythical Lone Star lover who found their one-and-only and never strayed. It would be longer still before Hazel's killer was convicted; only then would Tula begin letting go of what they could've been.

But first: the goodbye.

"You know that no one ever forgets their first love, and that's who you are to me, right?" Garrett said, stepping up to Devon for their last embrace for a while. He was dreading the alert on Devon's phone that would whisk him away, but also anxious to rip the Band-Aid off to find out how much life in this apartment was going to ache without him.

"That's right," Devon said as he put his arms around Garrett. His eyes were wistful; his N-95 mask and plastic face shield were ready to go beside his phone, necessary to block him from the COVID-19 virus during his trip home, but not yet, not before one last kiss. "And there's no one else like you for me, no one else like you at all." Devon shook his head as he started kissing Garrett's hair, his face, his lips — there was a taste of cleansing sorrow in his mouth, like rain. "My riot son."

# About the Author

L.A. Fields is a two-time Lambda Award finalist and author of literary, historical, and LGBT fiction. Works include the young adult *Disorder Series,* a modern retelling of the Leopold and Loeb crime titled *Homo Superiors,* and the Sherlock Holmes pastiches *My Dear Watson* and *Mrs. Watson: Untold Stories.* Fields has an MFA, a day job, and a calico cat named Kobb.